DEATH
ON
CALL

DEATH
ON
CALL

Sandra Wilkinson

DODD, MEAD & COMPANY
New York

Published by Dodd, Mead & Company, Inc.
79 Madison Avenue, New York, N.Y. 10016
Distributed in Canada by
McClelland and Stewart Limited, Toronto
Manufactured in the United States of America
First Edition

Library of Congress Cataloging in Publication Data

Wilkinson, Sandra.
Death on call.

I. Title.
PS3573.I44255D4 1984   813'.54   83-20839
ISBN 0-396-08334-X

For Rob . . .
my husband, my best friend, my love

1

TUESDAY MORNING

January 18

Rosemary Cleaveland nodded hello to the hospital employees and physicians who got off the elevator. As she stepped aboard, an obese Portuguese housekeeper bumped her aside, shuffled to the rear of the cab, and tried to tuck herself into a corner. The woman's eyes were large with fright. "Four!" she said, trying to catch her breath.

Rosemary's frown changed to a look of compassion. She knew Maria Silva. After pressing the elevator button for the fourth floor, then the one for the second floor where her office was located, she asked gently, "Is something the matter?"

The housekeeper's eyes focused and she apparently recognized Rosemary as the hospital's assistant administrator for she relaxed and said, "Yes, I . . . "

A hand passed through the space between the closing doors, triggering the electric eye. The doors reopened and Steve Hammond, the head of purchasing, jumped aboard. He pointed an accusatory finger at the housekeeper and then turned to Rosemary. "This woman is a thief! I caught her stealing syringes from the trash truck."

Perspiration had beaded on the dark hairs of the Portuguese woman's upper lip. "See supervisor," she spouted in broken English. She reached into her bulging uniform pocket and pulled out a used intramuscular syringe. Holding it up and looking toward Rosemary, she whispered, "See him and tell."

Rosemary noticed the long needle still intact on the syringe. "Good idea. Your supervisor should be told. It's okay, Steve. The nurses on one of the units aren't breaking needles off the used syringes. This woman probably noticed a needle poking through a plastic bag on the trash truck. All employees are afraid of getting hepatitis, V.D., or AIDS from these things." She turned to the woman. "Did you get stabbed?"

"No unnerstan."

"Of course she doesn't," Steve said. "She's a thief."

The woman was pulling other syringes from her pocket when the door opened onto the second floor. Several employees stepped aboard.

"Show that syringe to your supervisor," Rosemary instructed, and held out her hand for the others. "I'll talk to the director of nursing about this." Steve followed Rosemary off the elevator.

"See supervisor, see him and tell," the woman whispered as the door closed.

The second floor of the hospital's Main building was devoted to administrative departments and as Rosemary and Steve walked down the long corridor, they passed offices for nursing, business, and computer operations.

"Why would she take syringes out?" Steve asked. "She could just have told her supervisor, George Jones. And furthermore, why would she run when I caught her?"

"Maria Silva has worked here for years. I doubt if she's turned junkie."

"Maybe a friend of hers is hooked. But I'll tell you this,

I'm keeping an eye on those trucks from now on."

Rosemary stopped in front of her office door and un-locked it. "I'll talk with her after I see Jayne McCarthy. The nurses aren't destroying syringes as they should and we've got only two weeks before the inspection."

Steve shrugged and continued on toward fiscal services. He was a tall, handsome man with dark hair and eyes and a keen sense of humor which he seemed to have lost this morning. Rosemary watched him for a moment, then went in and closed the door.

Located on Memorial Drive in Cambridge, Riverside Hospital overlooked the Charles River and, beyond, Kenmore Square and the skyline of Boston. From her office window, Rosemary saw lights twinkle in the dark morning as the city's pace began to quicken. After hanging her coat in the closet, she glanced at the mirror behind the door and ran a hand through her deep auburn hair, trying to fluff the natural curls into place. She was thirty-four, a petite woman with fine features and expressive hazel eyes. Of her many attributes, patience was not one, and she moved with the restless urgency of a miner after gold nuggets.

At her desk, she opened the middle drawer and threw in the syringes. "Damn it," she said aloud, irritated with Jayne McCarthy for failing to keep on top of nursing procedures. For the past few weeks, Rosemary had con-centrated on preparing the hospital and its large staff for an inspection by the survey team from the Joint Com-mission on Accreditation of Hospitals. She had been arriv-ing at seven o'clock each morning and staying late, and although she didn't expect the same long hours from de-partment heads, she did expect them to comply with Joint Commission standards.

Jayne was not expected on duty until eight o'clock, and

several bulging manila folders containing mail and business papers needed Rosemary's attention. She opened the first folder and began reading.

Jake Mason opened the terminal laundry chute door and stood aside while linens, soaked with urine, feces, and blood, fell slowly onto the tiled floor. During his thirty-five years at Riverside, he had watched the laundry chute pass thousands of tons of soiled laundry, hundreds of misplaced dentures, safety pins, hearing aids, pencils, eyeglasses, even an occasional amputated hand, finger, or leg.

The snowy January morning had activated his emphysema and he coughed violently, the hacking noise reverberating through the terminal laundry chute room. He clutched at his heart as if to protect it from another myocardial infarction.

He spat into his handkerchief then looked at his watch. Jake liked to get the laundry out of the chute, bagged, and onto the loading dock by seven-fifteen each morning. He was running late.

Stooping over, he opened a white cotton bag and began shoving mounds of dirty laundry deep inside. The accreditation inspection started in two weeks and soon administration would remind the head nurses to bag their linens before throwing them down the chute. Jake chuckled to himself as he remembered the State licensure inspection last year. An inspector found loose linens in the chute room and reprimanded administration. Instantly, sure as you please, the linen started coming down in bags. Through the shit chute, he thought, and chuckled again.

He liked his job. Men from maintenance down the hall always stopped by to say hello. And over the years, he had accumulated many hospital friends, a blessing because he lived alone in Cambridge.

He picked up a handful of bloody towels and shoved them into a bag. The chute was a timetable of nightly events. At three o'clock each afternoon, just before he went home, Jake closed the laundry chute door and from that moment, the laundry fell in departmental layers, starting with the evening shift and continuing through the night. The blue towels were from labor and delivery. Must have had a newborn baby soon after I left yesterday, he thought. Next, a load of green drapes from the operating room, then heavy sheets soaked with urine from one of the medical-surgical units, followed by physical therapy's pink towels.

Patients on the Gold Coast, the thirty exclusive private rooms on the top floor of the Main building, had pale blue sheets dotted with pink rosebuds and striped with green ivy. Census must be low up there, he thought, only six sets of linens. He shoved them into a bag.

With head bent, working as quickly as his sixty-two-year-old bones would move, he noticed something fall into the middle of the pile. He reached over and grabbed at the denture plate.

Suddenly, a thundering rumbled above him and before he could straighten up, the chute exploded laundry, flattening him inside the pile. Panic shot through him as a crushing weight fell on top of the heap with such force that it pushed the air from his lungs, causing a moan to escape from his lips.

He thrashed violently, trying to break through the soiled sheets. He pushed, inching his way out of the pile like an insect breaking through the earth. The weight on his back shifted, rolled off, and landed in front of his face.

He saw the dead woman. Two cold, staring eyes bulged out of her purple face. Between two pale lips hung a beefy red tongue.

"My God . . . my God . . ." Jake gasped and fought to get untangled. His thrashing caused her hideously contorted face to fall closer. Her dry tongue licked his cheek.

"Oh, God . . . help me . . . oh, my G . . ." His heart stopped beating. All movement in the room stopped. The two corpses lay together as the laundry continued to fall through the chute like dirty snow, gently covering their bodies.

"Mrs. Cleaveland, I'm here," Peggy said, poking her head through the door that connected their offices.

"You're early," Rosemary said to her secretary. "Good. When Jayne McCarthy arrives, tell her I want to see her immediately."

"Will do."

With deep concern, Rosemary reread the letter in front of her from the Joint Commission on Accreditation of Hospitals. The president informed her that the Commission had received a request for a public information interview from a member of the laboratory staff. He requested that Rosemary arrange a time and place for the interview during the morning of the first survey day, and that she inform the lab technician.

"Inform her," Rosemary said aloud. "What the hell is the interview for?"

As required by the Joint Commission, Rosemary had posted a notice of the survey dates as well as the procedure for requesting an interview with the team. Penny Abbott had obviously read the notice, although it was inconceivable to Rosemary that Penny's supervisor had not resolved her problem. Rosemary decided to visit Tony Carasino right after the nine o'clock department head meeting. She worked steadily through the remaining papers, forcing herself to concentrate. She had been the assistant administrator of Riverside for a year and during that time, her boss, Felix Monroe, had gradually delegated most of his responsibilities to her. He trusted her judgment and, while she ran the hospital, he began to enjoy long lunches with friends and associates. She didn't mind his absences, in fact, she preferred making independent decisions. Felix only interfered when a medical staff problem arose for he was a product of the sixties when physicians ran hospitals while chief executive officers carried out expensive modernization programs. But time changes roles and rules and, by the seventies, government cost reimbursement regulations had curbed expansion programs, although Felix still believed that every concession should be made to keep doctors happy.

Rosemary disagreed fervently with Felix, knowing that others suffered at the expense of certain physicians' micromoments of happiness. She felt that her patience was constantly tested during cumbersome arguments with Felix. The primal deceit was having to show outward respect for Felix's inequitable decisions.

The intercom on her desk buzzed. "Yes?"

"Mrs. McCarthy came in early today, but her secretary can't locate her. She'll keep trying."

"Has Betty McCloud dropped off the updated personnel job description book?"

"Not yet. Wait a minute, the telephone's ringing."

Peggy came back on the line. "It's Charlie Donovan from maintenance, line ten fifty. He sounds kind of desperate."

Rosemary pressed a button. "What can I do for you, Charlie?"

"Come quick," he panted, "down to the terminal laundry chute room."

"What's the matter?"

"Can't tell you on the phone, just hurry, please."

Rosemary grabbed the letter from the Joint Commission and hurried into Peggy's adjoining office. She had gotten to know Charlie during her year at Riverside; he would never summon her without a critical reason. "Cancel Jayne and when Mr. Monroe gets in, tell him I'm in maintenance and will catch him at the meeting."

Peggy stopped typing. "His secretary says he's in a foul mood this morning, even yelled at her for putting sugar in his coffee when he drinks it with sugar all the time."

"Maybe he's sweet enough." As she left the office, she caught a smirk on Peggy's face.

"You'll grow a beard before the elevator arrives."

Rosemary turned and saw Ted Fielding and Steve Hammond walking toward her. As hospital controller and head of all fiscal matters, Ted was a serious man. She knew that he and Steve had coffee together every morning and were considered to be good friends although their personalities differed greatly. Steve teased the nurses and caused stampedes for his attention. The grapevine often carried rumors of nurses who had fallen in love with him and others with broken hearts. No one was quite sure of his marital status although the grapevine said he was separated. Ted, on the other hand, was entrenched at home with a wife, four children, two dogs, two cats, and a large basket of bills to pay.

"Want to join us for breakfast before the meeting?" Ted asked.

Rosemary smiled at his invitation. "Wish I could but I haven't time. Thanks anyway." The lights above the elevators indicated that they were all ascending and she decided to take the stairs down to the basement.

As she rounded the last turn and stopped to open the basement door, she noticed that the wall fire extinguisher was missing a December inspection sticker. Come on,

Charlie, she thought, what are your men doing? With or without the accreditation survey, the maintenance men were supposed to be taking care of these minor details.

She walked swiftly toward Charlie's office. He was sitting at his desk with his hands folded in front of him.

"Charlie?"

"Have a seat," he whispered.

"What's the matter?"

His short, stocky body sagged and his face drooped as if he were about to weep. "Jake Mason is dead."

"What?"

"And Maria Silva."

"What are you saying? Where are they?"

"When I got here this morning, Tom O'Leary asked me to check out those sprayers in dietary. After that, I came back down to organize my men and I saw the laundry carts still in the hall. Jake always had them on the dock by seven-fifteen, so I . . ." Charlie swallowed hard. ". . . I looked inside the laundry chute room. The light was on but the bodies were completely covered with laundry. . . . I didn't know until . . . The chute door was open and when I went to latch it, I tripped over . . . a leg."

Rosemary looked directly at him, trying to absorb his words. "I saw Maria a short while ago. She was going up to housekeeping to see George Jones." She paused. "Does anyone else know about this?"

"No, I sent my men on their preventive maintenance rounds."

"Did you see anyone unusual around this area?"

"No."

"Let's go look."

"You don't want to do that. Take my word for it; the sight is . . . terrible."

"I'll go by myself." She stood and Charlie reluctantly rose

from his chair. They walked down the corridor together, neither speaking a word. Charlie found a key on his large ring and unlocked the door. The smell of dried blood and human excrement filled Rosemary's nose as the door swung open, and she fought a wave of nausea.

A single neon tube bathed the small room with cold, gray light. At her feet was a large pile of soiled laundry, and on top, the two corpses. Rosemary sucked in her breath at the sight. A piece of cording was tight around Maria's neck. Her face was purple and dark patches of pooled blood had settled around her hairline. The beefy tongue hanging from her mouth was maroon and dry, and her popped eyes were rolled up in her head. Next to Maria lay Jake Mason, a look of terror frozen on his face.

Rosemary shut her eyes, then looked again. "Let's go."

She watched Charlie close and lock the door. "Don't let anyone in here," she said. "I'll call the police; be sure to let me know when they arrive."

2

Department heads drifted into the conference room, poured coffee from an urn, and sat down at the long table. Conversations were pinched and nervous and centered on the inspection. They knew that Rosemary would not tolerate criticism from the Joint Commission surveyors for mismanaged departments or careless neglect of details. When she first arrived at Riverside she had given the supervisors full responsibility for their departments. She expected high quality performance and got it, sometimes at the expense of a department head. But they liked her, because she stood on principle and showed no favoritism.

Steve Hammond lit a cigarette, leaned back, and blew a fast series of smoke rings into the air, then flicked an ash toward an ashtray and missed.

"Steve, where are your manners?" snapped Mabel Goldstein, the medical records administrator. She brushed the ash onto the floor, let out a long sigh, and began twisting her thin hands. Mabel worried about everything, but today she was especially worried about the inspection, her department, the physicians, administration, medical audits, and incomplete records.

"Calm down, Mabel," Steve said with a smile. "You'll worry the last fifty pounds off your bony frame."

Mabel's arms fluttered in the air. "You should have my problems. Only two weeks left and I have over five hundred incomplete medical records. Those doctors won't even sign their charts, much less write a history and physical. What am I to do?" She turned to John Kelley, the chief pharmacist, who was sitting on her other side. "John, if you see any physicians floating around, tell them to see me, would you?"

John Kelley's freckled face broke into a smile. "In my department, all I see are bottles and jars. Want me to slip your physicians some speed?" He paused when he noticed her serious face. "We're all behind, but we'll make it." He patted her hand, then leaned forward. "Hey, Steve, could you tell me who orders ether around here? I've got to get rid of any partially used cans."

"Sure," Steve said. "I'll find out for you." He looked at Mabel. "You don't drink it, do you, honey? For your nerves?"

She shot him a poisonous glance.

Rosemary sat down next to Jayne McCarthy, the director of nursing, who was still smiling at Steve's comment. Dressed in a white uniform and a white frilly cap that looked like a cupcake wrapper, Jayne was tall, thin, starched and pressed. Fourteen years at Riverside had drained most of her creative vitality, and although still quick-witted, she relied on her supervisors to handle nursing service while she labored tediously over unnecessary paper work.

Jayne glanced at Rosemary and whispered, "You look terrible. Do you feel okay?"

"Yes. Where have you been all morning?"

"Putting out small fires, you know, the usual crap."

12

Rosemary was not in the mood for small talk. "Be in my office at ten-thirty."

"I have a meeting then."

"Cancel it."

"I can't. I'll call when I'm free, around eleven o'clock."

"Good morning!" Felix Monroe said cheerfully as he came through the door. He sat at the head of the table, legs crossed, and peered out at the assemblage over his glasses, his silver hair encircling a gleaming bald dome. Felix's list of credentials made him well qualified for his job as chief executive officer. He was wealthy and his knowledge of Cambridge and Boston dignitaries had gotten him trustee positions on several large company boards.

"Is everyone here?" he asked.

After leaving Charlie's office, Rosemary had called the police, and then looked for Felix, to no avail. Sitting forward, eager to speak, she said quickly, "Mr. Monroe, I have something vitally important to . . . "

"In a minute, Mrs. Cleaveland. Our upcoming accreditation survey is foremost on everyone's mind." He pulled a tiny piece of paper from his pocket. "I spoke to the chief executive officer at Mass. General, and he gave me some tips to pass along to you. They were surveyed a couple of weeks ago."

"Mr. Monroe," Rosemary insisted, "I must tell you what happened this morning."

"Not now, please. This inspection is important to us." He read from the paper. "The administrative member of the team wants to see the list of your employee educational programs. He's a stickler on fire, bomb, and disaster drills."

Drill bullshit, Rosemary thought. She leaned back and studied the bored faces around the table.

Felix droned on. "Be sure your personnel know the location of the fire alarm boxes, hoses, and standpipes. As the administrator goes around, he'll stop any employee, but especially nurses, and ask them to describe the patient evacuation procedures."

On Steve Hammond's left was Frank Grinnell, the head of central supply who wore a yellow jacket and yellow pants every day of the week. People called him "Jaundice" behind his back. Steve nudged him.

"Do you know how the nurses do the patient evacuation procedure?"

"Yes," Frank whispered back. "If there's a fire, the nurses take the patients outside, or to a safe area."

"No, no. It's when they line up the patients, bend them over, and shoot 'em up with ice water from the standpipe."

Frank was mortified. He turned away, trying to hide the deep red flush that crept over his sallow face.

Felix looked over his glasses, cleared his throat, and continued to read. "The physician member wants to see detailed evaluations of your department's standards. Unlike surveyors of the past, he goes over every inch of the hospital, the freezers in dietary, reagents in the laboratory, radioactivity in nuclear medicine. Be prepared."

"Is Felix a boy scout?" Jayne whispered to Betty McCloud, the personnel director on her right. Betty smiled.

"The nurse member of the team used to be a public health nurse so expect her to be conscious of infection control policies and procedures. Any questions?"

Rosemary and Mabel both said yes at the same time but Mabel blurted out, "What am I to do about my incomplete medical records? It's more than half our monthly discharge rate. We'll lose our accreditation for sure." Her face was contorted as if she was trying to hold back a flood of tears.

Felix tried to soothe her. "I have letters going out today. If physicians fail to complete their records by Friday, their privileges will be temporarily suspended."

"It won't work," Mabel babbled.

"It will," said Felix. "Furthermore, the chiefs of medicine and surgery are helping with this."

"Mr. Monroe," said Tom O'Leary, the new head of dietary, who was as wide as the deep fat fryer in the kitchen. "What happens if we don't pass the survey?"

"We will, Tom." Felix sat back, filled and lit his pipe.

"But what if we don't?"

"Hospitals that lose accreditation also lose Medicare reimbursement benefits; they might go bankrupt if that happened. We'll get our three years, Tom. Riverside is in good shape."

Rosemary looked at Felix, then at Tom. Don't worry, she thought. Don't worry about Jake and Maria lying dead just one floor below us. We'll just shove their bodies under the carpet until the surveyors leave.

The head of physical therapy, Sam Crowell, raised his hand. "Mr. Monroe, when are they going to finish installing that new computer? I can't plug in my hot packs and ultrasound machines."

Felix glanced down the table at Sam, a large man who ran a well-organized department. "I'm afraid you'll have to be patient with this project. By the end of the week, the biomedical engineers should be finished converting all the electrical outlets in the hospital. The computer components are due in over the weekend and, starting on Monday, each department will be connected. Soon you'll wonder how we ever got along without it."

15

The enormous computer system was Rosemary's pet project. It had taken her months to convince Felix and the board of management that Riverside was ready for MOM III. When installed, the computer would control every outlet and every electrical function at the hospital, from patient monitoring systems to the heating, ventilating, air conditioning, and lighting systems. Although very expensive, the computer would eventually pay for itself in efficiency and economy.

Many other department heads agreed with Sam. They were having trouble keeping the peace. Felix asked them to be patient, then turned to Rosemary. "Mrs. Cleaveland, do you have an announcement?"

"Yes, I do," she said, aggravated at having to wait through questions and answers which seemed totally insignificant. "This morning, two of our employees were found dead in the terminal laundry chute room . . . "

3

TUESDAY MORNING
January 18

Pediatrics was quiet. Two children watched television at one end of the unit. A nine-year-old boy with his leg suspended from a series of ropes, pulleys, and slings played games on his small calculator. Lucy Bonnet slept in a small, glass-enclosed room. On the wall above her crib, a decal cow jumped over a decal moon, and a pink hippopotamus smiled a toothless grin, its teeth pulled off by the many children who had occupied that crib.

A candy-striper sat at a table in the middle of the unit, sorting small, medium, and large pajamas from the cart of clean linen.

Dr. Iama Farrah entered the pediatric unit and approached the nurses' station. He spotted the head nurse at the desk. "Hello, I'm here on consult to see Lucy Bonnet. Do you have her chart?"

The nurse stopped writing, got up, and located the chart.

"What can you tell me about her?" he asked.

"Her parents took her to the family physician a couple of days ago. She had a middle ear infection and a headache and he put her on Erythromycin. Then yesterday morning, Lucy vomited, seemed listless, and they thought she might have a stiff neck. The parents called the doctor, who said to bring her to the emergency department." The nurse flipped the pages of the chart to the laboratory results and read, "The cerebrospinal fluid tap indicates her sugar is down slightly, protein up a little, a few white cells, but nothing more definitive. Gram stain negative. A culture was taken; let's see if the results are here." The nurse handed the chart to Dr. Farrah and rifled through the basket of incoming mail.

"Here it is, CSF negative." She handed the slip to the pediatrician.

"No growth? Interesting. Was a blood culture done?"

"Yes. That was negative too."

"How about a throat culture?"

"No."

"Let's go see her."

A staff nurse was sitting in the rocking chair, reading a true romance story when they walked into Lucy's little room. She quickly closed the magazine and sat on it.

Lucy woke up. She tried to raise her curly blond head off the pillow. Huge tears covered her wide blue eyes, then rolled down her cheeks.

"What's the matter, darling?" Dr. Farrah asked, lowering the side rail on the crib.

"I don't feel so good."

"What hurts?"

"My head and all over, everywhere."

Dr. Farrah felt her hot skin and asked the nurse for Lucy's vital signs. As the staff nurse rattled them off, he gently took Lucy's leg and flexed it up toward her chest, then pulled the leg straight. Lucy cried out in pain and grabbed her thigh.

The doctor frowned. "A positive Kernig's," he whispered. "Lie on your side, Lucy." He helped her turn as she whimpered. He put his hand on the back of her head and pushed forward. Her ankle, knee, and hip flexed and she screamed with pain.

"Sorry, Lucy, honey, be right back." He got up and put the side rail into place. "You," he said to the staff nurse, "watch her carefully. I want vital signs every five minutes."

"What do you think?" asked the head nurse, following behind him to the nurses' station.

"Positive Kernig's sign, positive Brudzinski, and all the right symptoms. The kid's got meningococcal meningitis, and we've got a problem. Get those children to their rooms," he yelled to the volunteer as he strode into the station and yanked off his jacket. "This whole unit is in isolation now. Damn negative culture. I don't understand it." He turned to the head nurse, who was standing with her mouth open. "Come on, come on, get an I.V. started, five percent dextrose in water. I want I.V. Penicillin G, one million units, and Chloramphenicol, eight hundred milligrams, I.V., now!"

While the head nurse set up the solution, Dr. Farrah sat at the desk, looked over Lucy's chart, then stared at the culture report. After several moments, he picked up the telephone and dialed bacteriology.

"Doctor, Doctor . . . " The nurse from Lucy's room ran into the station.

"What?" he snapped.

"She's stopped breathing."

He threw down the phone, jumped up, and ran to the room, followed by the two nurses. Yanking the side rail down, he jammed his stethoscope into his ears and listened for Lucy's heartbeat. "Shit. Get me a cardiac board," he yelled over his shoulder, then smashed a fist into Lucy's chest and listened again. Quickly, he pinched her nose with one hand, held her head back with the other, and started mouth-to-mouth resuscitation.

The head nurse ran to the nurses' station and dialed seven for *"Code Red, Pediatrics, Code Red, Pediatrics."* She grabbed the emergency cart and sped back.

The staff nurse pumped Lucy's chest with her palms, then Dr. Farrah, between breaths, shouted orders to the head nurse. "Give me four c.c.'s of adrenaline; cardiac needle." He breathed into Lucy's lungs. "Where the hell is anesthesia?" He breathed for Lucy again. "Get the I.V. started," breath, "with soda bicarb," breath. He stopped to let the staff nurse pump Lucy's chest.

Within seconds, the life support team arrived and began working on the child. The anesthesiologist inserted an endotracheal tube and pumped air into Lucy's lungs with an ambu bag; Dr. Farrah did a cut down for a C.V.P. line; the head nurse drew up Epinephrine, Mannitol, Hydrocortisone, and handed the syringes to the cardiologist; the staff nurse monitored the blood pressure while the intensive care unit nurse attached E.K.G. leads to Lucy's chest and watched the cardiac monitor screen; the nursing supervisor wrote everything down on the medical record.

"She's into ventricular tachycardia," cried the I.C.U. nurse.

The cardiologist grabbed the defibrillator paddles and held them on Lucy's chest. "Stand back." The nurse pressed the button and four hundred watts of electricity charged through Lucy's heart, making her body rise from the bed. They watched the monitor screen. "No good, let's hit her again."

After an hour of intensive emergency care, Dr. Farrah took Lucy's head in his palms. "Lucy," he whispered, "Lucy, talk to me, please." She lay still, her face peaceful. The blue eyes stared up at him, void of pain and sight.

4

TUESDAY MORNING
January 18

The elevator door slid open at the basement level. As Rosemary stepped out, a large, brass-buttoned officer held his palm in front of her face.

"Ya can't get off, sister; police business down here. Now be a good girl and ride back upstairs."

Never before had she been denied admittance to any area of the hospital. Shocked and angry, she glared at the burly policeman blocking her way.

"I'm Rosemary Cleaveland, the assistant administrator here."

"Sorry, can't let you off the elevator."

"Two of my employees are dead, officer. I demand to know what's going on. Who's in charge?"

"Detective Lieutenant Tanner."

Rosemary had known a Pete Tanner from her college days at Radcliffe and wondered if this was the same man. She and Bill Cleaveland, star football player for Harvard, had double dated with Pete and his girl. After both men graduated from Harvard, she and Bill had lost track of him.

"I'd like to speak with Lieutenant Tanner," she said.

"He's busy."

The policeman held the elevator door, not wanting it to close without a passenger aboard. Rosemary stepped toward him. "You will either get him for me or I'll find him myself."

"Sorry, sister, no one is allowed down here but if you give me your name again, I'll ask him to call when he's free."

Rosemary saw that the laundry chute room was cordoned off. Two small signs hung on the rope; one read *Murder Scene* and the other *No Smoking*. Policemen in blue uniforms intermingled with men wearing sports jackets and coats. One man dabbed at the wall with a brush while a photographer flashed his strobe light, making the area look like a lightning storm. A man with a stethoscope around his neck wrote on a clipboard and called out a garbled sentence. In answer, another man appeared from the laundry room, tall, wearing a navy suit, his face worried. Rosemary recognized Pete Tanner and felt a surge of relief that an old friend was in charge of the investigation. She saw that he was, in fact, quite busy.

"Okay," she said to the officer, and backed into the elevator. "I'm Rosemary Cleaveland, assistant administrator, extension ten fifty. Be sure to tell Lieutenant Tanner personally."

Alone in the elevator, she thought about Pete. Although a serious student, he had laughed easily and teased with delightful charm. She wondered if he had changed over the years. She had. Three years after she married Bill Cleaveland, he was killed in an automobile accident. Bill's death had made her turn inward, made her aware of the value of life and the brevity of existence. She still missed him.

The elevator arrived at the fourth floor. Rosemary got off and noticed a cord across the laundry room door and a sign, *No Trespassing.* She turned left and proceeded down the hall. The laboratory consisted of a myriad of inter-related departments. She passed the blood bank, hema-tology, bacteriology, nuclear medicine lab, pathology, looking for Tony Carasino.

She knew that Tony was devoted to his laboratories. He selected his personnel as carefully as he selected high quality materials and precision instruments. Aside from demanding excellent performance from staff and machin-ery, he demanded cleanliness and orderliness. Each of the laboratories was immaculate and all but one office gleamed from scrubbing. The bone of contention was Dr. Kreutzer's hurricane down the hall.

Rosemary had often heard Tony complain about Kreut-zer, especially when Kreutzer fired Maria Silva for snooping in his office. No one believed that she had snooped anywhere, for she could barely read English. Tony had appealed to Rosemary for a transfer and, within the day, Maria was moved to the first floor.

Rosemary found Tony in the chemistry lab where he looked more like a grocery clerk than a lab technologist. On the counter in front of him were three dozen eggs, dried milk, cornmeal, as well as assorted petri dishes, multicolored agars, solutions, pipettes, and flasks. She watched him dip several eggs into a solution.

"Hi, Tony."

He turned his head and looked at her with large brown eyes which bulged out from their sockets. "Oh, hi, Mrs. Cleaveland, be with you in a minute."

"Having breakfast?"

Tony smiled. "Not on your life. This is mercuric chlo-ride." He punctured the eggshells, aspirated the whites, then carefully aspirated the yolks, putting each in a flask, adding a solution of sodium chloride, and pouring small amounts of the mixture into several plates.

"I thought you bought commercial agar," she said.

"We usually do, but the automatic chemistry counter is broken and Doctor Kreutzer has us making up special media for his studies. Also, the students use this stuff."

"You have the time?"

"No, but we do it. That was terrible news about Jake and Maria. Everyone's beginning to suspect everyone else."

"What are they saying?"

"Some think Jake killed Maria, then took his own life. Others think she fell through the chute and landed on him. . . ."

His words took her by surprise. Rosemary hadn't considered Maria falling through the chute.

Tony continued. "There are a lot of stories buzzing around, like they were having a lovers quarrel, or maybe someone in the hospital killed them."

That was the last rumor Rosemary wanted spread around and she said abruptly, "No! I saw them, Tony, and I'm certain that whatever happened was strictly between Maria and Jake. We won't know until the police are finished with their investigation but please don't let your personnel speculate irrationally."

"I'll try."

"Did you know that your bacteriologist, Penny Abbott, requested a public information interview with the Joint Commission surveyors?"

Tony looked up sharply. "She did? What for?"

Rosemary pulled the letter from her pocket and gave it to him.

He read it quickly. "When are you going to schedule the interview?"

"I'm not, because we're going to resolve her problem. Why did she write to them?"

"I don't know."

"She hasn't told you?"

"About what?"

"Come on, Tony, how should I know if you don't? I want you to find out and tell me, then we'll talk to her together."

"Okay."

"Will you see her today?"

"If I have time."

"You will find time before the day is out," Rosemary said firmly. "Do you understand?"

"Sure, today. I'll see her today."

"Call me." Rosemary took the letter and left. Usually efficient, always eager for new problems, Tony's lackadaisical attitude surprised and angered her. On her way to housekeeping, she passed Dr. Kreutzer's office and saw him looking down a microscope. As the medical chief of the laboratory and the chief pathologist, he was supposed to manage the lab departments and provide medical guidance to Tony. Instead, and for the past few months, he had relied on Tony to handle the labs while he feverishly worked on two research grant proposals totaling a half million dollars.

Farther down the hall, she passed a scowling older man and then went in to see George Jones, the head of housekeeping.

"I'm popular today," George said, standing to greet her. "A detective and now the assistant administrator!"

"That was a detective?" she asked.

"Yeah, Dow was his name, the bastard."

"Why do you say that?"

"He has a way of making you feel like you just shot your mother."

George waited until Rosemary sat, then lowered his tall, slender frame into the desk chair. He constantly had volumes of problems and assorted woes which, in his estimation, were completely unsolvable.

Before he could elaborate, Rosemary asked, "Did you see Maria Silva this morning?"

"No."

Rosemary looked at him carefully. "She was headed up here to see you."

"Well, if she came by, I didn't see her. Like I told that detective, I had one of my employees in here for her yearly evaluation. The door was closed."

"She wanted to tell you about the disposal of used syringes."

"What about them?"

"You don't have her syringes?"

"I don't have *any* syringes. What's the problem?"

"Nurses are not breaking the needles off . . . "

"That again? Honestly, we go through that at least once a month. Did she get pricked? Well, I guess it doesn't matter. She won't be contracting hepatitis in heaven, God bless her soul." George crossed himself.

"It's the same old dead-tired problem, George, and I would hope that between your staff and Mrs. McCarthy's supervisors, we'll see broken syringes in tomorrow morning's trash." Rosemary glared at him. "Let's hope so."

She left him and as she went downstairs, her mind wandered back to Tony's comment about a fall through the laundry chute. It was just possible that someone on the fourth floor had strangled Maria, then pushed her down the chute. But Maria must have weighed over two hundred pounds.

Rosemary walked slowly down the second floor corridor. The chute doors were close to the ground. Someone would have to get Maria's upper torso through the door, then lift up her feet and shove. The mechanics of the death gave way to its realization and Rosemary shuddered at the memory of Maria's purple face.

5

TUESDAY MORNING
January 18

Felix's matronly secretary, Miss Truslow, was dabbing at her nose with an embroidered handkerchief when Rosemary entered. "Good morning, Mrs. Cleaveland, I've got a terrible cold; sorry." She blew her nose with vigor.

When the obstreperous honking ended, Rosemary asked, "Is Mr. Monroe in?"

"Yes. Let me tell him you're here." The secretary buzzed the intercom and announced Rosemary's presence. "Go on in."

"Thanks." She passed through a mahogany door and saw Felix standing at the large window, looking out at the Charles River.

She said softly, "Felix."

He turned, looked at her, then sat at his highly polished desk. "A detective named Dow just asked me about the death of our two employees, insinuating that I had something to do with it. He wins the pernicious bastard of the year award."

"Dow was here? Where is he now?"

"I don't know. He came to tell me that he and another detective have taken over Charlie Donovan's office in maintenance, and if we know or hear of any related detail, we are to call them."

"What have they found so far?"

"Not much. At least Dow wouldn't say. He's a sour man." Felix rubbed his brow with both hands.

"Do you feel all right?"

He sighed and lowered his head to his palms. His bald head looked like a face void of eyes, nose, and mouth. He rubbed his eyes and sat back. "Come sit down and I'll tell you." He put a hand on his chest. "My heart has been fibrillating recently, for probably no reason other than a touch of old age. I saw my doctor yesterday and he referred me to a cardiologist at Mass. General. I'm booked for admission tomorrow. I told him about the accreditation survey but he insisted that I go in for a few days and, frankly, I wouldn't mind the rest. It might make me live a little longer." He opened his desk drawer, extracted a bottle and shook out a pill. "For my heart," he explained.

Rosemary sank back into the plush leather chair and watched Felix swallow the pill with a glass of water.

"Don't look so sad," he said, "they haven't buried me yet, and won't for a while."

"I feel miserable for you and angry at myself for being too busy to notice that you weren't feeling well. What time will you be admitted?"

"Nine in the morning. Now tell me, what's going on around here?"

Rosemary told him about her meetings with Tony Carasino and George Jones. "Jayne McCarthy has been elusive today but I intend to have her work on the syringe problem. My biggest headaches are the rumors about Jake and Maria. I need some answers from the detectives." A depression had settled in and Rosemary's voice faded into a whisper. "Jake and Maria were two very nice people. Maybe they detested each other; maybe someone had a grudge against them, but why kill? I don't understand it."

"Death is no stranger to you," Felix said softly.

She knew he was referring to the accidental death of her husband. Shrugging, she said, "Familiarity with death doesn't create a friendship, especially when death robs me of people I love." She noticed that Felix was struggling to listen while his eyelids drooped from the medication. "So much for philosophy. I'll let you know how the investigation progresses."

"Cooperate with the detectives," he murmured. "Chances are they're five steps ahead of you."

"I will." She gently closed the door.

Down the second-floor corridor were the offices of the director of nursing. Rosemary stopped by and asked the secretary if Jayne was in, learned that she was working on an alternate laundry system with Charlie Donovan, and left word for her to stop by on her way to lunch. Irritated with Jayne, Rosemary went back down the hall toward her own pair of offices.

Peggy sat with dictaphone earplugs in her ears. She was a young, vivacious woman whose jaw was in constant motion from either talking or chewing gum.

"Plugged in, I see."

"What?" Peggy turned and noticed Rosemary.

"Deaf," said Rosemary, pointing to her ears.

Peggy took off the earphones and stopped the machine. "Did something weird happen around here this morning? This place is jumping with cops and everyone is talking behind their hands."

"Yes, something terrible happened. Jake, the laundry man, and Maria Silva, a housekeeping aide, were found dead this morning, in the terminal laundry chute room."

Peggy stared at her in disbelief. "Honest?"

"Honest."

"Do you think someone . . . you know . . . like murdered them?"

"No, I think Jake had it in for Maria." Although not certain what happened, she didn't want Peggy frightened by the thought of a murderer in the hospital.

"Why?"

"That I don't know, but every behavior is motivated, and motivation is what the police are investigating."

Peggy gulped and then reached for a stack of papers. "Steve Hammond sent these purchase orders for you to sign. Here's a list of medical audits you wanted. Murder at Riverside, huh? It'll hit the soaps. Here's a list of doctors who have not completed their medical records. Dr. Kreutzer in pathology is in a stew about something. I think he speaks German when he's angry 'cause I've no idea what his problem is." She flipped over a page in the notebook. "Bob Friend called and wants you to call him back after three o'clock. I don't know who elected J. B. Harris the chief of the surgical staff, but his ego has gone berserk. He came by to wink and tell me how cute I am and to ask if you would call him; something about not suspending the docs for their records. He'll be in his third-floor office for an hour or two. That's it." She closed the notebook. "Murder . . . phew!"

"Thanks, Peggy. I'll get to them when I can, but let me know when a Lieutenant Tanner calls. I'm on my way to personnel."

"Will do." Peggy shoved a stick of chewing gum into her mouth and picked up the earphones. "Mrs. Cleaveland?"

Rosemary turned at the door. "Yes?"

"This dictating machine is practically brand new but the bleeps and crackles send me off the chair. May I call Mabel Goldstein for a loaner until this one is fixed?"

"She may not have a spare one right now. Call Steve

Hammond and ask him to get you a rental."

Rosemary walked down the steps to the first floor. Riverside, a large community hospital, had one hundred and ninety medical-surgical beds plus a large intensive care unit and other specialized inpatient units for nephrology, neurology, psychiatry, obstetrics, pediatrics, and the exclusive Gold Coast, which was on the fifth floor of the Main building.

Almost engulfed by Massachusetts Institute of Technology, the Main building of the hospital was used at first only for MIT students. Over the years, the hospital had expanded with the Concord building on the west and then the Sinclair building on the east, both neatly attached floor by floor to the Main building. Although both wings had small elevators for patient transportation, the largest bank of elevators was in the Main building, which also housed the trash and laundry chutes.

Riverside's patient population had grown to include not only MIT students, but the young, the old, the citizens of Cambridge, and those from seventy-three other cities and towns. During any one day, Riverside cared for politicians, drunks, corporate business heads, welfare cases, pampered housewives, and abused children. But no matter what his or her background, no person was turned away. Rosemary made it her business to see that everyone received high-quality care by trying to bring in only those department heads who excelled in their own fields. She left the rest of the recruiting and hiring to Betty McCloud, the head of personnel.

"Hi, Betty," Rosemary said when she walked into the office.

Betty looked up from her records. She was a tiny woman with dark eyes that were red from crying. Her mouth was shaped like a raspberry Life Saver. "Oh,

Rosemary, it's awful, Jake strangling Maria like that, then keeling over." Betty was the center of the grapevine, the base station for directing and receiving news. Her office was across from the lobby and next to the elevators, in the midst of the traffic pattern, and people, while waiting for an elevator, stopped by to pick up or drop off the latest juicy gossip much like a swarm of bees on their honey route.

Rosemary sat in the chair opposite Betty's desk. "Is that what is circulating, that he killed her?" The detectives had to be spreading the word about strangulation for she had not told the department heads.

"Yes, poor devil. I've known him for sixteen, no seventeen years." She dabbed at her eyes with a tissue. "He was the type of man who wouldn't wring out his wet hat much less someone's neck. We're taking up a collection for her. Want to help out?"

"What about a collection for him?"

"Oh, no, Who would give a plugged cent for a murderer?"

"He may not have murdered her . . . "

"What? You mean she killed him . . . or someone killed them both?"

"No. I mean maybe it was entirely unconnected with the hospital." Rosemary bit her tongue, sorry she had spoken so quickly. Betty wouldn't listen to her now that she had proposed an alternative. In her experience with large groups of people, she knew that a small piece of inane news, when shot across the electric current of the grapevine, can finally emerge as an ugly rumor which, along the way, has destroyed several reputations. "I'm not implying anything. I just think you should hold off on your collection until we know more, that's all. And please, stay out of it; don't get involved. Without more information, you're only passing along conjectures."

"What if people ask? What do I tell them?"

"That you don't know anything. Tell them you have a source who will keep you informed but, for now, you haven't the vaguest idea what happened. Okay?"

"If you say so." Betty and Rosemary needed each other, and both were willing to make mutual pacts. Rosemary fed carefully thought-out administrative news to Betty's grapevine, the fastest way of informing employees. She had told Betty about the accreditation survey in advance of the departmental memorandum, making each employee feel more knowledgeable than the higher-ups. Betty told Rosemary all the latest items on the vine, bits of information that were an excellent gauge of employee morale and a fast way to nip ugly rumors.

"I came down to see Jakes and Maria's personnel records," Rosemary said. "Will you get them for me?"

"I can't, I mean they're gone. A rude police sergeant came to pick them up and ordered that all records be restricted. I can't even let you see your own."

"Well, I'll be damned!" Rosemary got up and headed for the door. "Let me know when the restriction is lifted." She left, feeling cheated and angry. If restrictions had been placed on the personnel records, she wondered about the computer printouts on payroll, time, and employee information. Not wanting to wait for the elevator, she rushed into the stairwell and took the stairs two at a time toward the second floor.

Ted Fielding didn't notice her standing in the doorway of his office. His left hand flew down a list of numbers while his right hand quickly pressed calculator keys. When he got to the end and tore off the tape, Rosemary cleared her throat.

"My love," he pointed to a chair next to his desk. "What

brings you to my mysterious world of digital readouts?"

"I need to see the December and January payroll runs."

"Over here." He led her to a table which held books of computer runs. He found January, opened it for her, then looked for December. "Did we overpay you," he asked, smiling, "or do you want to donate more tax dollars to the feds?"

"The government would like my entire paycheck." She found Jake Morgan's name and checked to see if he had missed any days of work. His salary was regular each week. She checked Maria Silva and went through the December book.

"Can I help with something?" Ted asked.

Rosemary was thoughtful for a moment. "Can you program that terminal to give me a list of everyone on duty last night and this morning, and everyone who was supposed to be on but called in sick?"

He jotted down what she wanted. "Anything else?"

"I don't think so."

"This is about the two deaths, isn't it?"

"Yes."

"Are you looking for something in particular?"

"Not really. Maybe a lead of some kind, something irregular."

"Speaking of irregular, why are we changing computer companies?"

"What do you mean?"

Ted went to his desk and sorted through several piles of paper. "We ordered MOM III's brain from IBM."

"That's right."

"Now we're getting the components and software from . . . let me see . . ." He looked at a few purchase orders and pulled one out. "Compulectrics."

Rosemary walked over and looked at the order.

"I asked Steve about this," Ted said. "He claims the hardware is identical; Compulectrics components will fit the IBM system, and they took a hundred thousand off the purchase price. Not bad."

Rosemary tightened. She didn't want another problem compounding those she had acquired already this morning. "Damn it, Ted, we're not switching companies. A change would mean more delays, changes in workmen, new programmers."

"I think Mr. Monroe approved."

"I don't care who approved. The answer is no."

"I've got another one for you." He handed her a second slip. "It's an approval for an electron microscope."

"Dr. Kreutzer?"

"Yup."

"I told him *no* a month ago. We can't order expensive equipment on everyone's whims and fancies. He'll have to put this in his next fiscal budget, or into his grant application."

"He says he can't wait."

"That's too bad. As of right now, I want you to freeze all new equipment orders. No one seems to realize or care how much equipment costs. I should tell Kreutzer to solicit money from the patients; they're the ones who eventually pay for all this."

"He'd do it."

Rosemary relaxed. "He would, if he had time. May I have those orders? And give me any new ones you receive."

"I will. I'll get you those computer runs as soon as possible."

In the payroll office, Rosemary asked the clerk for the December and January time cards. She went through the stacks, noting that both Jake and Maria punched in at seven o'clock each morning, and out at three-thirty. They were as regular as the tides.

"I'm back, Peggy," Rosemary said as she entered her office. "Where's Jayne?"

"She's going to meet you in the cafeteria in fifteen minutes."

Rosemary dropped the papers on her desk and stared out the window. An icy January wind raced up the Charles River from the east, smacked the hospital, and made the window shake. To her left, a bus stopped on Massachusetts Avenue, let off a passenger, then proceeded across the Harvard Bridge. Her eyes followed it and caught sight of a neon light, somewhere near Kenmore Square, flashing on and off, methodically stabbing at the gray-white storm front.

She shivered, pulled her suit jacket around her, and wondered what Pete Tanner was doing. She knew that a Sergeant Dow had seen Felix, George, and Betty, and probably many others. As she thought about the detectives, she grew impatient. Why hadn't they called her? They were investigating this case in aggravating secrecy.

With Felix away, she'd have to cope alone with the police, and suspicious, frightened employees. She hoped that Pete Tanner would understand her position, and help her. It was all coming too fast.

"I'm going to lunch," she said to Peggy on her way out of the door.

Peggy glanced up from her typing. "Phone okay now?"

"I guess so, why?"

"Telephone repair man said he had an order to fix it. He was here about a half hour ago."

Rosemary shrugged her shoulders. "It wasn't broken."

6

TUESDAY AFTERNOON
January 18

Rosemary paid for her lunch and looked for Jayne Mc-
Carthy amid the garden of colorful uniforms. At a table
near the long expanse of cafeteria windows, she spotted
Jayne's white frilly cap, then her waving hand. Through
the windows behind her, the raging snowstorm made
MIT's Kresge Auditorium flicker in and out of view. Two
bent figures hurried along Amherst Street toward Massachusetts Avenue while fierce wind gusts ballooned their
coats and threw wisps of snowflakes up in rising spirals. It
was a perfect backdrop for Jayne, who looked like a snow
queen in her white uniform. She reigned as cold and aloof
over her nursing units as she did now over her grilled
cheese sandwich, poking it unceremoniously as Rosemary
approached.

"Vermin," Jayne said.

Rosemary put down her tray and sat. "What do you
mean?" A long black hair protruded from the sandwich as
if a tiny mouse had forgotten to pull in its tail. "Don't be
silly. It's probably some sort of chemical additive to make
the cheese chewy."

"I'm going to give Tom O'Leary a piece of my mind."

"You have more important things to do."

"What do you mean?"

Rosemary pushed aside her wilted salad and leaned forward. "Mr. Monroe is being admitted to the Philips House at Mass. General tomorrow."

"What? Has our unflappable administrator finally flipped his fool cork?"

"No," Rosemary said evenly. She didn't agree with Jayne's unsympathetic attitude toward Felix. "He's been experiencing recurrent fibrillations."

"Poor dear." Jayne pressed a finger on the sandwich, leaving a round imprint. "What about the inspection? You'll have to handle it alone, I guess."

"No, I'll have your help."

"What do you want me to do?"

"Escort the physician member of the team."

"I usually get the nurse."

"I know, but this time, I want one of your supervisors with her. J. B. Harris will go with you and the physician."

"Oh, no. He'll make an ass of himself."

"The chief of staff must go along, you know that."

"Will you prime him, and me too? I don't know what the medical staff does."

"You should," Rosemary said. "You should also know that nurses are not breaking needles off syringes."

"How do you know?"

"I know because Maria Silva gave me several used, unbroken syringes this morning."

Jayne stared at Rosemary. "You saw her?"

"Yes."

"Where?"

"On the elevator. She was on her way to housekeeping to tell George Jones about the needles."

"Did she see him?"

"Apparently not."

Jayne sat back. "Turn my knobby knees into Jell-O. I wonder why she went to see Jake?"

"I don't know."

"What did you do with the syringes?" Jayne asked.

"They're in my desk drawer."

"Can I have them?"

"What for?"

"To show the nurses that I have evidence of their poor nursing practices."

"No, Jayne. I intend to give them to Lieutenant Tanner. By the way, I hear you got here before eight o'clock this morning."

"I did."

"What were you up to?"

"I saw the night supervisors before they left."

"And then?"

A sour look crossed Jayne's face as if to suggest that Rosemary should mind her own business. "Nothing else special."

Before either could say anything more, they heard Jayne's name on the paging system.

"Jayne McCarthy, call ten eleven. Jayne McCarthy, call ten eleven please."

"Damn." She got up. "That's pediatrics, I'll be right back."

As Rosemary watched her leave, she weighed the depth of their friendship. She wanted to be open but their relationship was superficial and one-sided. Jayne told her everything, but Jayne told everyone everything. Rosemary didn't trust her with personal confidences because she knew that in the course of a day every nursing employee would be discussing Rosemary's problems.

Rosemary looked around the cafeteria. Some candy-stripers were sitting at a table with several nurses' aides. Near them were maintenance men in brown uniforms sitting with delivery room nurses in blue lab coats. John Kelley, Steve Hammond, and Ted Fielding sat together, forks raising and lowering as they ate and talked. She watched people get up and others sit down. They came in and they went out. The endless flow and ebb of life, so beautifully illustrated in a hospital, she thought—her hospital. When she arrived a year ago, Riverside was floundering financially amidst luxurious trappings. Several strong physicians were building fiefdoms in their departments with overpaid secretaries, excessive numbers of employees, expensive technical equipment, and each vied for prestige, power, and money.

Through months of fortitude and cries of protest, she peeled away the fingers attached to the hospital's coffers and changed the power structure by requiring researchers to seek outside funding for pet projects, and by redirecting the flow of money to weaker departments.

Jayne returned to the table. "That was Dr. Farrah, yelling as if I was responsible for World War Three. A patient in pediatrics, Lucy Bonnet, died this morning and he wanted to know why the spinal culture came back negative, although every sign pointed to meningococcal meningitis. I asked him to call the lab and he said he did but the bacteriologist dissolved into tears. You know, that's the second time this week that a doctor has complained about no growth cultures."

"You could check with Dr. Kreutzer."

"The Kraut wouldn't know if his laboratory disappeared inside a test tube."

"What do you mean?"

"He's been too busy with his latest research studies, the meathead."

"He's our Nobel candidate," Rosemary said and smiled.

The two women deposited their trays on the conveyor belt and headed for their offices.

Peggy poked her head in the office door. "Okay for Lieutenant Tanner and Sergeant Dow?" Rosemary stood as the two men walked around Peggy to get in.

"Hello, Rosemary Winston Cleaveland, it's been a long time." Pete Tanner shook her hand. Aside from a few gray hairs at his temples, he hadn't changed over the years. He was tall, slender and, in his navy three-piece suit, he looked more like a banker than a detective lieutenant.

"I lost track of you and Bill after graduation," he said. "How are you doing? Any children?"

"No, Pete, I'm a widow." Usually undisturbed by death, Pete's face darkened with concern. "Bill was killed in an automobile accident eight years ago," she explained.

"I'm so sorry, Rosemary." He took her hand to console her. "What a fine person he was; we had a lot of fun together." Then turning to Dow, who appeared bored and ready to dispense with social amenities, Pete said, "Bill Cleaveland and I lived in the same house at Harvard. He was a genuine friend." Dow said nothing. "This is Detective Sergeant Mike Dow, Rosemary Cleaveland." Dow looked at Rosemary and nodded. "Dow here is a crime scene investigator. Let's sit, shall we?" He waited until Rosemary was seated at her desk, then sat in one of the chairs opposite her.

Mike Dow walked to the window behind Rosemary. He looked like Frank Grinnell's father for his skin was yellow and deeply wrinkled. Short, with stooped shoulders, he stood with his hands jammed far inside his coat pockets.

Although Rosemary was anxious to ask Pete about the investigation, she decided to wait. His renewed friendship would give her the support she needed during Felix's absence. "Do you have children, Pete?" she asked.

"Two."

"How old are they?"

"My son is ten, my daughter is eight. They're wonderful kids although I only get to see them on weekends."

"Why?" the word slipped out and she tried to correct her rudeness. "I'm sorry, Pete, it's none of my business."

"No, don't apologize. I'm divorced now." Pete lit a cigarette. "Damn shame," he continued. "I enjoy having a family life. But tell me about you. What did you do after Radcliffe?"

Rosemary told him that she had married Bill shortly after graduation, and about her masters degree from the Alfred P. Sloan School of Management at Massachusetts Institute of Technology, and about her positions in the health care field.

While she spoke, Pete looked as if time was his greatest commodity, with arms casually folded across his chest, legs crossed, occasional wisps of cigarette smoke slowly spiraling up. Sergeant Dow, however, had taken out his notebook and was drawing deep circles on the paper in an effort to get the ink flowing from his pen. He gave up and took a pencil from the cup on Rosemary's desk. As soon as Rosemary had finished, Dow asked, "What were you doing this morning, around seven o'clock?"

Rosemary considered him—a curt, no-nonsense cop. Probably because he had been roaming around the hospital without seeing her first, she didn't like him. "About seven this morning," she said, "I was parking my car."

"Where do you live?"

"Fifty-two Garden Street."

He wrote in the notebook. "Cambridge?"

"Yes."

"Aren't those apartments?"

"Yes."

"Which one are you in?"

Peggy knocked on the door and Pete went to open it. "I thought you might want some coffee," she said, carrying a large tray. She put it on a side table and began to pour coffee.

"Leave it," Dow ordered.

Peggy stopped, the carafe poised in her hand. "I beg your pardon, were you speaking to me?"

"Yes, are you stone deaf? Get out of here. Now."

Peggy put the carafe down and started for the door, her face red with embarrassment.

Rosemary stood up, and with hands on her hips said, "That was totally uncalled for. If you want to be rude, go home and kick the hell out of your dog. Do *not* take out your aggressions here."

"Sit down, lady."

"Peggy, don't leave. Apologize to her."

"What?"

"Apologize. You know, it goes something like I'm sorry."

"Look here, this is a police investigation, not a debutante party."

Looking at Dow and pointing to Peggy, Rosemary said firmly, "Apologize."

Pete sighed. All through the morning he had tried to keep Dow from becoming embroiled with members of the hospital staff. An intractable cop, Dow had worked on the force for nearly forty years. He was painfully punctilious, often extracting information from the most reticent of individuals.

"Say you're sorry, Mike."

The room was quiet; no one moved as Dow glared at Rosemary.

"Mike!" Pete repeated.

Dow looked over at Peggy. "I'm sorry," he said gruffly. That was Peggy's cue to leave and she raced from the room as if chased by a rabid dog.

Dow paced from the chair to the window while Pete poured the coffee and placed a cup in front of Rosemary, "For heaven's sake, sit down, Mike. Please answer his question, Rosemary."

"I forgot the question," she said as she sat down.

"Which apartment do you live in?"

"Four-eleven."

Dow picked up the interview. "Okay, what time did you get here?"

"Seven o'clock."

"Who can verify that?"

"The people who got off an elevator—Tom O'Leary, Dr. Ben Evans, Hank Downey, and a couple of nurses and aides." She told Dow each person's work area. "I got on the elevator with Steve Hammond and Maria Silva."

Pete sat upright. "Tell me exactly what happened."

"Steve Hammond from purchasing saw her taking syringes from the trash truck and he tried to retrieve them from her."

"Did he?"

"No, but she gave me three of them." Rosemary opened her desk drawer. "I believe she had more because her pocket was bulging."

"What did she say?"

"He accused her of stealing them and she denied it. She was Portuguese and I had a difficult time understanding her, but she said something like, 'See supervisor, see him and tell.' I realized what her problem was. Nurses are supposed to break off needles from syringes before discarding them in the trash. If they don't, then some poor housekeeper stands a chance of getting stabbed when the needles poke through the plastic trash bags. It's a constant prob . . . "

Rosemary was pushing the papers and pencils around inside the drawer. "Where are they?" she asked aloud. Bending down to take a closer look, she then pulled the contents out onto her desk. "I put them right here!"

Dow stood and peered over the desk.

She pushed a button on her intercom. "Peggy, did you remove anything from my desk?"

"No, Mrs. Cleaveland."

"What about that telephone repair man?"

"Not that I'm aware of."

"Thanks." She dialed Ted Fielding's extension. "Ted? It's Rosemary. Did you order telephone repairs for today? Would a man have come without an order? Well, did you see him? No, it's nothing. Yes, my phone's okay, thanks." She replaced the receiver and looked at Pete. "I think the syringes were stolen."

"Check it out, Dow. You said Maria had a pocketful of syringes, Rosemary, but there weren't any on her body or in either chute room. She did have a central supply requisition in her pocket for a carton of distilled water for the laboratory."

"She wouldn't be running an errand for the lab."

"The murderer may have removed the syringes and inserted the requisition."

"Why?"

"To put the heat on the lab. Certainly no lab person would leave that kind of calling card."

"Maybe that's what the murderer wants you to believe."

"Lieutenant," Dow said, "can we get on with this?"

"Sure."

Dow addressed Rosemary. "Where did you get off the elevator?"

"Steve and I got off on the second floor."

"What time was this?" Dow asked.

"Just a couple of minutes after seven."

"Are you usually in that early?"

"No, but we have an accreditation inspection coming up and many of the department heads and people in administration are coming in early."

"Did you see anyone at that point, like people getting on board, or walking by?"

Rosemary thought carefully. "Yes, some employees did get on. I recall seeing two or three maintenance men, an emergency medical technician, and Dr. Kreutzer, who was talking with Dr. Harris and an anesthesiologist, Nancy Goldberg. She's the head nurse of Concord Three. Maybe a nurses' aide. It's tough to recall. But all those people saw Maria give me the syringes."

When Dow finished scribbling, he asked, "Where did you and Steve go when you got off the elevator?"

"Steve went into fiscal services to pick up Ted Fielding for breakfast. They have coffee together every morning."

"Where did you go?"

"Into my office."

"Your secretary was in?"

"She arrived a few minutes after me."

"I'll check that," Dow said.

"Oh, for heaven's sake!"

Pete interrupted her. "When our boys were roping off the laundry chutes, they noticed signs of a fight in the fourth-floor chute room. A full laundry hamper was on its side with the contents strewn over the floor. It looked as if someone grabbed a patient gown tie from the hamper, strangled the woman, lifted her body, and pushed it down the chute, which must have taken some doing 'cause that lady weighed a ton."

Rosemary sat forward. "Why, Pete, when she was already dead?"

"I think the person wanted to lead us off the track," Pete explained, "although the job was sloppy; no, call it non-professional. The person was in a hurry and failed to clean up the area or consider the bruises caused by a fall down a chute."

Rosemary shuddered and squeezed her eyes closed, trying to block out the thought of Maria's body dropping through the black tunnel, flesh pared away and bruised as she banged against the metal tube, down four stories to the basement.

"What happened after you got to your office?" Dow asked.

Rosemary fell back into her chair with a hand on her brow. "I came in here, read some mail, and then Charlie Donovan, the head of maintenance, called. He was upset and asked me to join him immediately. He didn't say why but I knew he had a good reason." Rosemary talked to Pete rather than Dow. "I went down to the laundry room and saw them; hideous, awful sight. I called the police and then went to a department head meeting." She looked across the desk at Pete, who was watching her intently.

She continued, "I remember that Jake had been a patient here; I believe he had an M.I.—a myocardial infarction—so I asked Peggy to get me his medical record, and Maria Silva's too." Rosemary buzzed Peggy on the intercom and asked her to bring in the records.

She came in with one record. "Mabel up in the record room says that Maria was never a patient here; at least she can't find a record for her." Peggy handed the chart to Rosemary and, before closing the door after her, stuck out her tongue at Dow who was reading his notes. No one noticed.

Rosemary leafed through the pages until she came to the emergency department record. She read out loud, "Jacob L. Mason, Two nine three Third Street, Cambridge; hospital-paid Blue Cross and Blue Shield; came in at five twenty-five P.M. last January twenty-third; next of kin is Miss Louise Mason, sister, Ginger Hill Nursing Home in Concord, New Hampshire. Patient complains of chest pain, difficulty breathing, appears anxious and gasping for breath, blood pressure ninety over fifty-eight." She skipped down a few lines. "Admitted to the Intensive Care Unit at six forty-five P.M." She flipped over to the discharge notation, "Patient discharged on February sixth." She closed the record and handed it to Pete.

"So now you know the man had a bad ticker; good for you," Dow muttered.

"Listen here, Sergeant Dow, this is my hospital, not yours. You never gave me the courtesy of a visit or phone call to let me know where you were going or whom you were seeing. That may be your procedure, but I find it exasperating. You offered not one iota of guidance and so I took it upon myself to find Jake's medical record, hoping it might help in some way."

Pete interrupted. "It has. Jake Mason has an interesting address." He leafed through the pages. "We think Jake died of a massive coronary when Maria fell on top of him; probably scared him to death."

"Pete, wouldn't some of those people in the elevator have noticed Maria walking into the chute room, or heard a commotion in there?"

"We'll check it out, but please, Rosemary, try and leave this investigation to us."

Dow headed for the door. "We're wasting time here. I'm

48

going back downstairs, then over to the crime lab. You coming?" he asked Pete.

"In a moment; you run along." Pete looked up when Dow slammed the door. "Sorry for his behavior. He'll never learn."

"He's totally obnoxious."

Pete shrugged and put the record on Rosemary's desk. "We're not going to mention the fourth floor."

"Why?"

"For three reasons: one, it's best if the murderer thinks he tricked us into believing that Maria was never on the fourth floor; second, we may get more information from the lab staff if they're not frightened of one another; and third, we want this to appear an easy, open and closed case. Henceforth, I'd like you to say only that you believe Jake strangled Maria and died of a heart attack while doing it. His motive was financial need. He was stealing articles from the hospital, she caught him, and threatened to turn him in."

"No one will buy that story."

"Yes, they will because it's easier to swallow than the idea of a murderer on the prowl. People will grab onto anything that keeps them out of danger. Pretty soon you'll begin to hear the 'buts': 'Remember Jake? He was nice, but . . .' 'He wouldn't hurt a flea, but . . .' " Pete stood up and smiled. "It's nice to see you again, Rosemary. You're as beautiful as ever."

Rosemary watched him leave—a comfortable, warm, intelligent man capable in his position and apparently respected and heeded. She liked him and was pleased that he was on the case.

A knock interrupted her thoughts. "Mrs. Cleaveland." Peggy poked her head through the door.

"Yes?"

"Thank goodness they're gone! That sour-faced detective has a hermetically sealed brain. Thank you for making him apologize."

Rosemary stretched. "You're welcome."

"I have good news."

"Terrific."

"A secretary from the law offices of Sheriden, Tallow, Langenstern, and Friend has a dashing young lawyer on the phone, ready to cheer you up with romantic notions."

"Bob Friend? Oh, I was supposed to call him!"

"Line ten fifty-one."

Rosemary punched the button and waved goodbye to Peggy. Six months ago, Bob Friend had represented a patient who was suing a Riverside physician for negligence. He tried to date her but she felt that he posed a conflict of interest and refused until the case was settled. Although not certain if she loved him, she enjoyed his company and, for three months, they had dated frequently. He had just returned from a vacation in Martinique and she envisioned how he must look: a deep tan accentuating his blue eyes, jet black hair, and tight physique from daily jogging and weekend skiing.

"Hi, Bob, welcome back."

"Happy New Year. You missed me, didn't you?"

"What a narcissist you are; of course I missed you. How was Christmas marooned on an island?"

"Sunny every day, and lonely. Next year, I won't let you cancel out at the last moment."

"Next year, we won't have a Joint Commission survey. Anyway, I didn't cancel out at the last minute, I told you in November."

"Ah yes, over a fat turkey dinner with your parents. How are they?"

"Good. I spent Christmas day with them."

"You sound tired."

"I am." She brushed a hand across her eyes. "We had a monumental problem here this morning and my nerves are jangling."

"What happened?"

"A housekeeping woman and our laundry man were found dead in the terminal chute room. The hospital is swarming with brass-buttoned, very official officers of the law."

"Wow, that will make the news. Was it a Romeo and Juliet suicide?"

"I doubt it; they were in their sixties."

"Everyone's living longer and falling in love later in life. By the time I get you to marry me, the hearse will be waiting outside my door." Rosemary heard him chuckle. "It must be pretty wild around there, especially the grapevine."

"It is."

"Did they die of natural causes or did some maniac bludgeon them with a laundry hamper?"

"Neither. The old fellow was in financial straits. I guess she saw him steal something so he choked her." Rosemary felt sheepish about the lie, but then, Pete had been right; it was better thinking the lie than being frightened about a murderer. "An old school chum, Pete Tanner, is in charge of the case; matter of fact, he just left. He wants me to help him."

"Don't count on it. Most crime investigators have lips tighter than an oyster."

"But I know him." She began wondering if Bob was right. Pete had said enough to satisfy her immediate curiosity. He hadn't discussed the investigation at all.

"How about dinner tomorrow night?" he asked. "Seven o'clock. We'll get the corner table at Maison Robert and order up candlelight, kisses, and cream puffs."

"In that order? How about a secret rendezvous at Fifty-two Garden Street where, after dinner, the cook blind-folds the cat?"

"You don't want to cook, do you?" he asked with little conviction in his voice. "Not that I would mind a savory home-cooked meal."

"Good. Come at seven, I'm dying to see your tan."

He chuckled. "My un-tan is more interesting. Bye."

She hung up the receiver, smiling, and buzzed the intercom. "What's next, Peggy?"

"I don't know, but one thing's certain, another day like this and I'll be a patient at Metropolitan State Hospital."

Peggy was silent for a moment. "You know something?" she said. "People sure fool you. I always thought that Jake wouldn't even pull a knot tight if he thought the rope would wince." She paused. "You never know what goes on in people's minds, do you?"

"Don't fret over it, Peggy. Go on home now or I'll have to pay you overtime."

"You already do; it's six-fifteen."

Rosemary looked at her watch. "My heavens, you're right. Grab your coat and I'll walk out with you." She went to the closet for her own coat. The mirror behind the door reflected her face. Knowing the truth, she thought, knowing there's a murderer out there, with some strange motive, makes me very, very nervous.

As they left, Rosemary asked Peggy about the telephone man.

"I asked him where the regular guy was," Peggy said, "and he told me Benny was on a job in Cambridge, and that the company gets busy in January installing Christmas gift sets."

"What did he look like?"

"Ugly. He had a uniform on, but that face was something else, like he'd gotten hung up on barbed wire."

7

Activity in the emergency department was slowing down. The two staff nurses chatted idly with the ambulance drivers as they sat in the coffee room. The secretary wrote the last few names into the large logbook. The night nurses would arrive at eleven o'clock, which gave Mrs. Ewing, the charge nurse, half an hour to straighten the rooms. She wanted desperately to rid the department of patients and make the supervisors marvel again at her proficiency.

On her way to the minor surgery room, she plumped a pillow on a stretcher and asked the orderly to empty the trash baskets. Poking her head inside the door she said sternly, "Come on, Dr. Newbury, you're not a plastic surgeon. Get that laceration sewed up and get out of here fast; you've still got benches full of patients to see."

"How many?"

"Six and a repeater."

"Who's the repeat?"

"Aranda Lilly, the woman you saw last night with the pelvic inflammatory disease."

"Send her home."

"What?"

53

"Are you deaf?" he shouted. "I said send her home. Tell her that the culture report and penicillin take a few days. And Mrs. Ewing," he said, pinching the suture forceps in the air, "would you like an ear wax treatment for that deafness? Guaranteed to hurt."

Mrs. Ewing closed the door, turned on her heel, and wondered why Riverside Hospital had nincompoops for interns. "Harvard ought to save a buck and send the snots to sewing school," she muttered to herself.

She walked toward the seven patients who were lined up on straight metal chairs like ducks at a shooting gallery. Suddenly Aranda Lilly fell forward, and her head bounced off the chair in front of her with a loud knock. The other six patients watched her slide to the floor. No one got up to help for fear of losing their place in line. Mrs. Ewing yelled to the secretary, "Get Dr. Newbury out of that minor surgery room, fast, then come back and help me."

Mrs. Ewing pulled Aranda out from between the chairs and tried to roll her onto her back but she remained in a knot, holding her stomach. As Aranda's color turned gray, a fine mist of perspiration beaded on her forehead.

The secretary came back with a blood pressure cuff which Mrs. Ewing grabbed. She threw it around Aranda's arm and pumped furiously. When the gauge read one hundred and fifty pounds of mercury, she released the valve slightly and listened with her stethoscope. "Come on, come on," she said to the gauge. Finally she heard the heart thud at eighty-four and disappear at forty pounds of pressure. Aranda was in shock.

Dr. Newbury ran up, tossed his surgical gloves to the floor, knelt over Aranda, and pried open her eyes to check the pupils. As they lifted her onto a stretcher, he said, "Call the operating room team. This lady is going out fast."

8

After picking up the *Boston Globe* from outside her apartment door, Rosemary scanned the first few pages and found the story about Jake and Maria. Skittles followed her into the kitchen as she read. Just as Pete had promised, the article was brief and uninteresting. She placed the paper on the kitchen counter, put on the coffee pot, and filled a bowl with cat food. "Here you go, my dear, tuna crème de la crème for your fat body."

When the percolator stopped, Rosemary poured coffee into a mug and sat on one of the kitchen stools to reread the article. Her mind wandered back to the murder. Someone at Riverside had killed Maria, someone who either worked on, or had access to, the fourth floor, without creating suspicion, like maintenance men who wander freely throughout the hospital, or the computer electricians, or telephone repair men. Rosemary shook her head absently, less afraid of Riverside during the day-light.

She slipped on her coat, locked the apartment door, and began the short drive to the hospital. An early morning mist hung heavily over the city making the street lamps look like hazy dots of light.

Rosemary knew that Maria's pocket had contained many more syringes. Maria might have thrown them away before the attack in the laundry room, or perhaps her murderer removed them and inserted that lab slip Pete had mentioned. Assuming her murderer made the exchange, then he must have wanted the syringes for a reason.

She parked in the loading dock area and walked up the cement steps.

On the dock, cylinders of nitrous oxide stood together behind a wire mesh cage. Not only was the heavy protective chain not padlocked, but two valve protection caps were missing from the cylinders. She made a mental note to tell Charlie Donovan.

On the first floor of the Concord building she passed purchasing and the storeroom and walked by dollies loaded with supplies. John Kelley was already in the pharmacy refilling the drawers of the medication carts for the nursing units.

"Hello, John," Rosemary called, and waved at him from the corridor.

"Hi, you're in early this morning," he said while pouring pills into a container. When the pharmacy had been remodeled two years ago, the architect had used bright yellow and bright orange divider walls. John looked like a headless pharmacist for his orange hair blended in with the bright orange walls behind him.

"I couldn't sleep, John, there's too much to do."

"I know what you mean, I have two pharmacists out sick." He shrugged. "Someone's got to divvy the drugs."

She went through the doorway leading from Concord to the Main building, passed by the elevators and headed toward the cafeteria. Peggy wouldn't be in for a while and she wanted to take a cup of coffee to her desk.

She poured a cup, paid for it, and as she was leaving, someone called her name. Steve Hammond was motioning her over to his table. As she approached, he stood and pulled a chair out for her. "This is Romeo Fortune," he said, "from Fortune Autoclave Company. He's here to check out our new autoclaves. Romeo, this is Mrs. Rosemary Cleaveland, the world's most gorgeous assistant administrator."

Rosemary shook hands with the small, round man and sat. She enjoyed Steve's company, for he was personable and easy to talk with. On occasion, he had taken her out for a drink after work, but she refused to date him regularly, believing that hospital relationships eventually ended after torrid rumors had destroyed reputations.

"You're here early this morning," Steve said.

"I didn't sleep well last night."

"Me neither. That incident yesterday shook up my stomach and I'm taking Titralac pills by the handful. I told Romeo here about Jake and Maria and he's got an idea. Go on, Romeo, tell her."

Romeo lowered his head and looked at Rosemary over his glasses. "I think the administrator did it."

He looked so serious, and made his accusation with such conviction that Rosemary had to stifle a smile. "How did you come to that conclusion, Mr. Fortune?"

"Because all of a sudden his ticker started bothering him." He paused. "Don't you get it? If I murdered someone, it'd give me heart problems too." Fortune leaned forward. "He can't be reached for a few days, right? And by the time he returns, the heat's off."

Rosemary was losing her sense of humor. "Your idea is absurd, Mr. Fortune. Maria was strangled by Jake and that is that. False accusations have deleterious effects and I suggest that you keep your opinions to yourself."

Steve looked at her. "You're right."

"By the way, Steve, would you remind Charlie Donovan to chain those cylinders of nitrous oxide on the loading dock? I may forget to mention it to him."

"Sure will. How about going out tonight for a drink? There's a new place in the Square that might be fun."

"I'm busy tonight, Steve. Thanks, anyway." Rosemary stood and was about to leave when she turned back. "I was talking to Ted Fielding yesterday and he said that you got approval from Mr. Monroe to change computer companies."

"Yes, that's right."

"You have his signature of approval?"

Steve hesitated. "No, I didn't have the purchase order with me when we discussed it."

"Why would you even ask for approval?"

"Compulectrics can deliver the same equipment for a hundred thousand dollars less."

Rosemary glanced at Romeo Fortune, who seemed totally absorbed in the conversation. "I don't think we need to bore Mr. Fortune with the details of the decision to buy from IBM. Let me say, however, that the Board of Management approved the original order and they are the ones to approve changes. If Mr. Monroe received Board approval, I'm sure he'd tell me. I have your purchase order along with several others and I've told Ted to put a freeze on all new equipment spending."

"But the computer components have been ordered already; they're due on Sunday!"

"That's too bad. We're not changing companies so I suggest that you call and reverse the shipping."

Steve whistled softly. "There's a freeze on *all* capital purchases?"

"Yes."

"Dr. Kreutzer will be furious. He wants a new tissue transportation container, and an electron microscope."

"He'll have to find another source of funds." She left them sitting at the table and went to an elevator. She could ask Felix if he had approved those orders without telling her, but she did not want to bother him with hospital matters just yet.

Rather than go through Peggy's empty office, she unlocked the corridor door to her own office. A thin ray of sun cast a light across her desk and over yesterday's pile of messages, telephone return calls, and mail. She noticed that her first appointment was at eight-thirty with the Board of Management. Good, she would ask Mr. Highling, the chairman, if he knew about Compulectrics.

Ordinarily, she loved days packed with meetings, planning sessions, budget reviews, and appointments with community leaders, but after yesterday, her energy level was low. She dialed the maintenance extension number and talked to a man who had seen neither Pete nor Mike Dow this morning. Fine pair of investigators, she thought, they probably weren't out of bed yet. Discipline being the better part of valor, she sat and tackled the papers, signing her name, reading, making notations.

She didn't hear the door open.

"Hi," Jayne McCarthy said, and Rosemary jumped.

"You scared the wits out of me. I try to keep that door locked, to ward off spooky white apparitions."

"I'm not an apparition," Jayne said, "I'm a real live spook. What brings you in here before the eight o'clock whistle?"

"I couldn't sleep."

"Me too. I dreamed that Dr. Kreutzer reversed the natural growth patterns of the world so that eventually nothing would grow, no trees, no people, no nothing. I'm on my way up to see him about Lucy Bonnet's and Aranda

59

Lilly's negative culture reports. Want to come?"

"Wish I could, Jayne, but I have to prepare a report for the Board meeting this morning. Who's Aranda Lilly?"

"An emergency room patient treated a couple of nights ago for pelvic inflammatory disease. Dr. Newbury took a culture, prescribed penicillin, and sent her home. She came back last night and went into septic shock. They rushed her to the O.R. for a fast laparotomy but the woman died on the table. The interesting part was that her blood culture came back negative."

Rosemary looked up sharply. "You're kidding."

"No, aside from the laundry chute caper, you now have two dead patients. Who knows who will croak next?"

"That's not funny, Jayne."

"I know, that's why I'm seeing Kreutzer."

After Jayne left, Rosemary stared at the door. Death was no stranger, and he seemed to have taken a special interest in Riverside.

As Jayne walked down the hall, she smelled acid, base, and salt solutions, an odor associated with a laboratory much the same way ether is associated with a hospital. At Dr. Kreutzer's office, she knocked on the door and walked in. Karl Kreutzer, the chief of pathology and director of the laboratories, sat on a high wooden stool peering down the tube of a microscope. His office was in total disarray, with papers thrown everywhere.

"Dr. Kreutzer?"

"Wait a minute," he said curtly. His fingers riffled through his thick gray hair before they rested on the microscope knobs. She noticed that he wore surgical gloves. "What do you want? Disturbances slow me down." He looked down the microscope again.

The world of laboratory jars, stains, glass slides, and

solutions had always fascinated Jayne. She walked over to the counter and watched him. "What kind of cancer research are you doing?"

"You wouldn't understand."

"Try me."

"Basically, I'm studying the inhibitory values of certain enzymes and heavy metals on the growth processes of the cancer cell." His tall lanky frame straightened up and with a grandiose sweep of his outstretched hands he said, "The National Cancer Institute and the Potter Foundation are about to award me two sizeable grants for my studies with stages one, two, and three breast cancer." He looked at her. "But I have to get my papers to the Netherlands by Monday, so what do you want?"

"I heard about your two grants and I think your concern for cancer research is fantastic."

"It's more than fantastic, it's brilliant. We will be acclaimed the world's leading authorities."

"You and Dr. Harris?"

"Yes, and a fine friend, Dr. Malen Cristobal in the Netherlands. I'd never get the grants without his enzyme contributions." He jotted a note in a logbook next to his elbow. "What do you want?" he asked.

"Several areas of the hospital have reported unusual negative cultures which have possibly caused two deaths within the last twenty-four hours."

Kreutzer looked at her through narrow eyes. His voice was low. "Don't for a moment doubt our practices in the laboratory. Let me assure you that the fault, if there is one, lies with the nurses on the units who have no idea how to handle a culture." His voice rose. "Let me tell you what they do. They take a sterile cotton swab out of its nice sterile package and put it down on a filthy dirty overbed table. They sneeze all over the test tube, then they attack the infected area with the grubby swab, rub it in, swirl, and dig around just to make sure that it is completely covered with pus. Then they let the tube sit on top of the nurses' station desk for the messenger who picks it up at the end of the day. By the time we get it, organisms are marching in vast squadrons over the sides of the test tube."

"Dr. Kreutzer, listen to me. I am not blaming the lab technicians and I wish you wouldn't criticize the nurses. I was hoping that we could work on this together."

"I'm collaborating with enough people as it is. Research takes time, my dear, and if you have a problem, go see Tony Carasino. I've given him total responsibility for the labs."

"But this could turn into a serious medical problem."

"First off, Tony can handle anything; secondly, you have no right to assume that the difficulty, if there is one, rests with the laboratories. I would suggest that you evaluate your resources. If the problem starts on the nursing floors then work through each step of the culturing procedure. You may find that it's only a unit clerk failing to get the lab requisition on the right patient. Now please, Mrs. McCarthy, I'm a very busy person."

"But we could solve this much faster with your help."

"Again, you are assuming fault. No, you do your homework and then pay Tony a visit, if you even have to."

Jayne felt frustrated. She didn't like Tony for he never cooperated with her on interrelated problems. Furthermore, she had a few important papers waiting on her desk. Maybe she'd assign one of the supervisors to work on the problem. Yes, that's what she'd do.

"If I talk to my supervisors, would you get Tony to help them?" she said.

"No, you ask him."

"But you're his boss."

"My blood pressure is going up, Mrs. McCarthy."

"Okay, okay." She left him peering down his microscope. A lot of good he was. How could he seriously believe that his research was more important than the labs? And imagine, giving Tony Carasino all that authority. She stood outside the office door for a few moments to let her steam escape.

Rosemary's meeting with the thirteen members of the Board of Management had gone smoothly in spite of their many questions about the murder. They were satisfied that the case was closed and had praised her for adeptly handling the affairs of the hospital in Felix's absence. After the meeting she had spoken with Bernie Highling, who had not heard of a request to change computer companies.

Rosemary stopped by Jayne's office. The secretary, talking on the telephone, nodded her head and pointed to Jayne's door. Rosemary went in and found Jayne pacing the floor.

"The man is crazy," Jayne said. "His brain has been pickled in formaldehyde fixative."

Rosemary was astonished. "What's the matter?"

Her comment fell on deaf ears; Jayne was furious. "I'd like to gas him in an autoclave; give him a taste of his German heritage. If the autoclave had a window, I'd watch him scream as the pressure flattened his body. His juices would fill his lungs and drown him. Blood would pour from every pore in his skin as he was sucked inside out. His eyeballs would flatten . . . "

"Jayne!"

"Then ethylene oxide would flow in and scorch his remaining fragments."

"I'm getting sick."

"Just as the pressure was the greatest, I'd fling open the door and watch him bubble like opening a shaken soda pop bottle." She was clenching and unclenching her fists. "Do you think anyone would buy Kraut cola?"

Rosemary repressed a smile. "Sit down and tell me what went on."

Jayne sat in the chair; her frilly nursing cap had fallen to one side and she ripped it off. "He called me a liar."

"What did he say?"

"He insisted that those two deaths were not the lab's fault, oh, no, why they're all perfect up there. It's my nurses. Can you imagine? My nurses! He claims they intentionally destroy cultures by letting the tubes sit around all day. I have a few things to tell him about his lab techs sitting around on their fannies all day. Then he suggested that I work out the problems with that nincompoop Tony Carasino whose brain is as empty as the middle of a doughnut."

"Not a bad idea."

Jayne's mouth dropped open in amazement. "What?"

"Dr. Kreutzer could give us a medical evaluation of the deaths, but you shouldn't expect him to run quality assurance tests on lab equipment or performance evaluations on lab personnel; that's Tony's job."

"Maybe so, but I'm assigning one of my supervisors to work on the Kreutzer-Carasino escapade. Not me, no way will I talk to either of them." The intercom buzzed and Jayne picked up the receiver. "What do you want?" she growled. "Okay, put her on." While Jayne waited, she held the receiver against her chest and whispered, "The Kraut is so bug conscious that he even wears surgical gloves when he works. Hello? This is Mrs. McCarthy speaking." Rosemary noticed the fight drain out of Jayne for she

drooped forward and held her head. "I'll be right there."
Jayne let the receiver fall onto the telephone.

"What's the matter?"

After a few moments of silence, Jayne looked up slowly.
"We've had narcotics stolen from Sinclair Two."

9

WEDNESDAY MORNING
January 19

John Kelley arrived in the pharmacy just after Rosemary and Jayne. He was carrying the Sinclair Two narcotic book.

"What's missing, John?" Rosemary asked.

"A heap of stuff, look here." As John opened the book, other pharmacists and an aide came closer to hear. "Every narcotic cabinet throughout the hospital is stocked with two boxes of each narcotic; the second box is a spare in case the nurses run out during the night." He leafed through several sheets and stopped at Demerol. "The spare box is gone here . . ." He leafed to Dilaudid. "Here," and over to morphine. "Here. This morning, the nurse on Sinclair Two was preparing to give an injection of morphine. The box was empty so she looked for the spare and couldn't find it. That's when she noticed the other missing boxes." He looked up at Rosemary.

"Demerol, Dilaudid, and morphine," she mused.

"And a container of Seconal."

The pharmacy aide stepped up. "How did the thief get all that out of here without someone noticing?"

"Easy," Rosemary said. "People have walked out with much bigger items, like typewriters and desks." She turned to Jayne. "Why wasn't this picked up at seven o'clock this morning?"

"Maybe the nurses were busy. It's true, they're supposed to make a full count at the change of shift, but they don't often do it all at one time. The offgoing and oncoming medication nurses always count the boxes in current use, but sometimes the spares aren't counted until later."

Very rarely did Rosemary chastise one department head in front of another, but apparently Jayne was losing control of her nurses. Over the past few months, Rosemary had noticed Jayne's withdrawal as if something more important occupied her mind. Nevertheless, where drugs were concerned, Rosemary wanted an immediate resolution. "Why do you allow that sloppy practice?" she asked sharply.

Jayne's cheeks pinkened. "Well," she stammered, "I can't be everywhere."

"Starting at three o'clock today, and henceforth, I want you to make certain that all narcotics are counted on all three shifts, and I want a report on my desk every morning."

Although John appeared to be reading the narcotic book, he was listening intently, for the corners of his mouth were raised in a partial smile. Rosemary guessed that she was telling Jayne exactly what was on John's mind. She also guessed that John could add a few more items. But because of Rosemary's presence, or probably because he didn't want to alienate the nursing staff through Jayne, he changed the subject. "I spoke to the head nurse. She made a full count with the evening nurse at three o'clock yesterday, so my guess is the theft occurred last evening or night."

"Let's not guess," Rosemary said, and for the next hour, Rosemary, Jayne, and the pharmacists pored over the Sinclair Two medication records while they developed a strategy for catching the thief.

At one o'clock, John Kelley reluctantly went to the Infection Control Committee meeting with Steve Hammond and Frank Grinnell. They were the first members to arrive in the basement floor conference room and took seats at the far end of the long table.

"Two bits says the crazy Kraut won't show," John said, as he unfastened the top two snaps of his pharmacy tunic.

Steve lit a cigarette and blew a smoke ring into the air. "No bets. Kreutzer's missed the last two meetings."

"Someone should get rid of him," Frank said. "Ordering this, demanding that; I spend more time on his problems than on my own."

Since the day he started at Riverside, Steve had disliked Frank. Not only did he believe that Frank lacked intelligence and humor, but also that he was a pecksniffian pansy. He blew a smoke ring around Frank's nose.

"Damn it, when are you going to stop pretending you're the local incinerator?" Frank said, waving the smoke away. He was jealous of Steve and envied his position. As a consequence, Frank not only liked to put obstacles in Steve's way, but constantly criticized purchasing practices.

Peggy walked in with her steno pad, two medical records, and a stack of committee minutes.

Tom O'Leary came in next and wrestled his ponderous backside into a chair. "Sorry if I'm late," he apologized, "we've been busy planning the menus for the survey."

"Looks like you've been eating the menus," Frank said.

"Very funny, ha, ha, ha. You wouldn't begin to know the problems I've had." He held up his hand with his fingers outstretched. "First . . ."

Steve interrupted. "No one cares, Tom. We all have problems."

The conference room door opened again. Two nurses entered, followed by Dr. J. B. Harris, the chief of surgery and president of the medical staff, who looked like Peter Pan. He had just come from the operating room and was dressed in green from the gauze cap on his head to the green conductive booties on his feet. "The chief of the surgical medical staff has arrived," he announced pretentiously, "fresh from wrestling with a uterus. Where's Kreutzer? Hasn't this meeting started yet?" He looked around at the solemn faces, then sat down at the head of the table where the chairman usually sat.

Rosemary, Jayne, and George Jones, the head of housekeeping, came in and, just as Jayne was closing the door, Dr. Kreutzer burst through. "Meeting will come to order," he said, and scowled at J.B. for sitting at the head of the table. He sat and continued, "Because of the pending survey, I have been requested by administration to hold this meeting; however, it will be brief. Where's the infection surveillance nurse?" he asked Jayne.

"She's out with the flu, but Peggy here has the medical records we need."

"What's our old business?" he asked, looking over the minutes from the last meeting. "None? Good. Any new business?" Dr. Kreutzer would have been pleased to adjourn the meeting at that point but Frank Grinnell spoke.

"The O.R. supervisor called me Monday about an unsterile instrument pack. I guess they noticed that the internal indicator hadn't changed color. Well, I figured it was just one pack, probably got in the middle of a whole flash autoclave load, so I didn't worry. The supervisor then decided to culture a few packs that *were* sterile according to the indicator. She sent me the results." Frank pulled the lab slips from his yellow shirt pocket. "A chest tube pack grew out ē coli and a D. and C. pack grew out staphylococcus. We've checked out the spore indicator strips and tape and everything looks okay. I don't understand it."

"Strips hell," Steve said, "why don't you *fix* the autoclaves? You know so much about everything."

"Jiminy Christmas, a fellow can't even talk around this joint."

Kreutzer was growing impatient. "*What is your point?*"

"My *point*, Doctor, is that we have unsterile packs that may be infecting our surgical patients."

George Jones gingerly cleared his throat. "Excuse me everyone, but how does an autoclave work?"

Frank leaned forward. "They're large sterilizers. Some use superheated steam under pressure, others use ethylene oxide gas mixtures at high temperatures. Both kinds kill organisms."

Dr. Kreutzer was fidgeting in his chair. "This is a damn waste of time. Are we finished here?"

"No," Rosemary said. "We need to discuss our recent problems with negative cultures. We've had two accidental deaths and a series of complaints."

"And an unusual increase in the amounts of antibiotics ordered," said John Kelley.

Kreutzer glared at him. "What are you insinuating?"

Jayne answered for John. "The doctors are beginning to distrust the reports from the lab, so they're ordering a full spectrum of antibiotic treatment in case a report is incorrect."

Dr. Kreutzer did not need these problems just before his applications were due in the mail. He turned to J.B. "Dr. Harris? Do you trust the laboratory?"

With his gold Cross pen, J.B. had been absently filling in

all the O letters on his copy of the committee minutes. "Huh? What did you say?"

"Do you trust the laboratory?"

"Explicitly and unfalteringly."

"Are you prescribing unusually large doses of penicillin for your patients?"

"Of course not!"

"There, you see? Our laboratory procedures are impeccably performed. Furthermore, Mrs. McCarthy plans to investigate the two cases and will report to us at the next meeting."

"But why," Jayne asked, apparently trying to bait Kreutzer, "would culture reports be negative when both patients had clearly recognizable disease processes?"

"Negative cultures are no mystery. Basically, we have natural media like blood, urine, vegetable juices, and synthetic media like Trypticase Soy broth or high protein media like Lowenstein-Jensen egg. These are made specifically to support the nutritional requirements of what we want to grow. The problem is that often the organism is unknown when we're trying to identify the cause of infection. We don't have the patient there in the laboratory, the doctor never has time to write his suspicions or diagnosis on the lab slip, so off we go down genealogical paths of phyla, flora, and fauna.

"Now take the ē coli organisms," Kreutzer continued, "They're part of the normal flora of the intestinal tract. If I suspect salmonella organisms, then I don't want ē coli to grow. Tetrathionate broth is an enrichment media for enteric bacteria; its chemical composition will inhibit other organisms like ē coli and enhance the growth of salmonella."

If Dr. Kreutzer had looked around the conference table, he would have seen an assortment of reactions to his explanation. The two nurses yawned; Frank Grinnell nodded as if in agreement; Tom O'Leary frowned, he had gotten lost at the second sentence.

"That's an excellent explanation," J. B. Harris said, standing up. "I'm sure everything is correlating nicely. We have a breast biopsy at two o'clock, Karl, see you then. Ta, ta, everyone."

Rosemary excused herself and followed J.B. out of the door. "Can I talk to you for a moment?" she asked when the door was closed.

"Sure, sweetheart. You can do other things to me too if you'd like." He squeezed her arm. "Want to see if there's an empty bed?"

"I've never made it with a green Martian before; or are you pretending to be an avocado?"

"That's it, the green tree with the pendulous fruit. Want to try it?"

"You're impossible." She knew if she took him up on his offer, he would collapse from fright. Yet she played his game because it was easier to humor him than to fight him.

"Listen, J.B., I know you don't want those physicians suspended for their incomplete medical records, but the survey is less than two weeks away and we're way over our allowable percentage."

"I can't take away their admitting privileges, Rosemary. What am I to do when a pediatrician wants to admit a sweet two-year-old with triple pneumonia? Tell him to take her to Harvard Rehab? The mother would sue; it's bad for business."

"Get off it, J.B. A suspended doctor asks you to admit his patient under your name, then you call him in on consult. And you both make a buck."

"Why Rosemary Cleaveland, I would never . . . "

She touched his arm. "If the Joint Commission doesn't accredit us, all the doctors will be practicing at Harvard Rehab. Go along with me this time, please?"

"The touch of your delicate hand on my arm brings tears to my eyes. I'll do your bidding, but don't expect me to be around next weekend; those docs will bug me to death."

She continued. "I need you here the entire first day of the survey, J.B., and will you remember that we've done one hundred and three quality assurance studies for this quarter? I'll send the list to your secretary."

"Okay." He started down the corridor but turned back. "Have you heard from Felix?"

"His wife answered when I called the room earlier. He's starting through a full cardiac workup and taking it like a champ. She says that he's still talking about being back on Monday."

"That's great news. Tell him hello for me. Bye bye."

She watched him go through the door to the stairwell. An avocado, she thought, all pulp and no seed. She walked back into the conference room. Kreutzer was finishing the review of Aranda Lilly's chart and, by the expression on Jayne's face, emotions were volatile.

"When was the culture taken?" he bellowed. "Before the chill started? After?" Kreutzer glared at Jayne, who didn't answer. "See, you don't know. How am I to do a review when you never do your homework first?"

Jayne was trying hard to control her anger. "Doctor, the emergency room diagnosis says 'pelvic inflammatory disease.' I'm sure the physician had no other clues or he would have admitted her at her first visit."

"He had a blood culture drawn. Wouldn't that indicate to you that he suspected something more?"

"I left my crystal ball at home, sorry."

Rosemary interrupted. "These records will be reviewed by the Death Committee. Our purpose is not to criticize medical practices but to review infection control policies and procedures."

Jayne was annoyed. "I would like to recommend an audit of the bacteriology laboratory."

"Impossible," Kreutzer shouted as he stood up.

"Why?" Jayne shouted back.

"Some of us have more important things to do than put up with your folly, Mrs. McCarthy." He clenched his fists, then jammed them into his pockets as he tried to quell his anger. Months of tedious work had stripped the man of social amenities. "If you want an audit, begin with your own department which, in my estimation, needs an over-haul, starting at the top. I'm tired of needless interfer-ences and irrelevant committees and I will no longer tolerate polemicists, entrapped in their self-made web of hopeless mediocrity." He glanced at Rosemary. "The top includes you. I will get my electron microscope and tissue transport container, I will get my computer terminal in-stalled and those electricians will be out of the labora-tories within the week." He slammed the door after him.

Jayne's anger had risen to the boiling point. "That revolting, government inspected, grade A . . ."

"Wait just a minute," Rosemary interjected. "Diatribes are totally out of order. Dr. Kreutzer will have his grant applications finished soon and we must be patient. Let me know the results of your autoclave tests, Frank. Meeting is adjourned."

As the committee members filed out, Steve hung back and whispered to Rosemary, "Can we talk about the Com-pulectrics order?"

"No."

"But I called the company and it's too late to cancel. The

components have been shipped already, they're due in Sunday afternoon."

"You told me that and my answer is no. Listen, Steve, I have enough to do without standing around the loading dock waiting to cancel that order."

Steve shrugged and lowered his head. "I have another problem. Dr. Kreutzer is bugging me about that microscope. He told me to go ahead and place the order."

"Does he intend to pay for it?"

Steve shrugged again and Rosemary guessed the answer. "I'll find time to see him," she said.

As they left the conference room, Steve said, "Did you know that Jaundice and Maria Silva used to argue a lot?"

Rosemary stopped and looked at him. "First of all, his name is Frank. Secondly, that's a leading question. What are you trying to tell me?"

"Nothing, really. I've just had Maria on my mind. I know the police think that Jake strangled her, but couldn't someone else have seen them in the laundry room and killed them both?"

Rosemary had often arbitrated battles between Steve and Frank Grinnell and she sensed another one brewing. "I don't like your insinuation about Frank and, furthermore, Jake died from a myocardial infarction."

"Okay, I just thought it was interesting. Maria and Kreutzer used to argue too so I guess there's nothing to it."

Several residents and interns filed out of the next classroom. As Steve got on the elevator with them, he asked Rosemary for the two purchase orders.

"I'll send them to you," she said, "after you've canceled that shipment."

On the other side of the elevator, Rosemary saw that the dark terminal laundry chute room still had the crime scene rope stretched across the door. She heard voices and followed a dotted line of cigarette butts which trailed down the corridor to Charlie Donovan's office.

Amid a cyclonic array of clutter, Pete Tanner and Mike Dow were reviewing a list of employees. Wads of paper mounded around the wastebasket. Coats, boots, and hats occupied most of the available chair and floor space, and styrofoam cups were perched atop skyscrapers of notebooks.

Pete stood when he saw Rosemary. "Welcome to the clubhouse; have a seat."

She stepped into the room. "What a mess."

"This is the way men like it, good and lived in," Pete said. "It's the fashion, art disgust."

"Truly *House and Garden*."

Mike Dow propped his feet on the desk and stared at the ceiling.

"Where have you been this morning?" Rosemary asked as she cleared off a chair and sat.

"Working on another case."

Agitated, she asked, "This one isn't important enough? Never mind. Do you have any leads on those people who rode the elevator with Maria?"

"A few. Apparently the man dressed in a navy-blue uniform was not an emergency medical technician. No one seems to have recognized him. He got off on the fourth floor, as did Dr. Harris, Dr. Kreutzer, Dr. Fee, and a phlebotomist who had boarded on the third floor. By the way, we checked out that service man and he's a phony. The telephone company didn't have anyone here yesterday."

Rosemary was silent as she considered what measures the man might have taken if she'd been in her office. The thought made her shudder. "Could he have murdered Maria?"

"It's a possibility." He held out a piece of paper. "Here's a list of people who worked Monday night and those scheduled on duty Tuesday morning. Would you look it over for any discrepancies?" He handed her the list and leaned against the desk.

"How did you put this together?"

"From the time cards."

"Not everyone punches a card." She looked down the first page and turned to the second. "I've asked Ted Fielding for a computer listing. Let me compare the two."

"Be my guest. Now, from what you and the others have told us, Maria Silva was a loyal and dedicated employee. Over the years, she'd been assigned to clean various areas, and three years ago she was given the laboratories. Everyone up there liked her." Pete stopped to light a cigarette. "Within the past few months, Dr. Kreutzer's research intensified and his office became a maelstrom. Bent on duty, Maria overdusted, overcleaned, and apparently collected all his papers into neat stacks." He paused. "You know how frustrating that can be."

Rosemary nodded. "Kreutzer ordered her to stay out of his office."

"Yes, but now things get fuzzy. Dr. Kreutzer claims she continued going in, and he caught her reading his research papers. The lab staff claim that Maria wouldn't do such a thing, partly because of her dedication, partly because she had trouble reading English. At any rate, Kreutzer fired her. Tony Carasino came to her defense and, with your assistance, got Maria relocated to Concord One."

Rosemary nodded again, remembering the incident clearly.

Pete continued. "The housekeeping office is on the fourth floor. . . ."

"No, Pete," Rosemary said quickly. "Not Karl Kreutzer. He's too involved with his research."

Pete stared down at his shoes. "Are you aware of any other problems Maria had? Any other person who might have disliked her?"

"I don't believe so."

"Let's talk about syringes. I've learned that after an injection is given, the nurse breaks the plunger and needle. She's supposed to place the pieces in a heavy cardboard box, but sometimes she gets busy and just tosses them into the wastebasket, and sometimes she throws the intact syringe away. Are the medication rooms locked?"

"Yes."

Pete stubbed out his cigarette in a full ashtray. "Always?"

"Yes . . . I hope so."

"Keep in mind that new and used syringes are handled by many different departments. If used syringes remain intact, anyone can take them before they're emptied down the trash chute. At the bottom of the chute is a trash truck which, once full, gets wheeled out to the dumpster. Yesterday morning, a truck was sitting in the hall waiting to be dumped. Maria passed by and saw a needle poking through a bag. With concern for her fellow workers, she opened the bag and removed a handful of syringes to show her supervisor."

Sitting back in the chair, feet propped on the desk, Mike Dow closed his eyes.

Pete continued. "Now, I'm going to tell you something that you won't like, but your syringes could relate to another of my investigations."

She looked hard at Pete. "You really aren't concentrating on Riverside, are you?"

"We don't have enough policemen or detectives for a

one to one relationship with each case. I'm currently investigating seven other homicides."

With icicles in her voice, Rosemary said, "Your job would be easier, I am sure, if you had a partner who slept off duty."

Dow snapped forward as if hit by a land mine. "Listen here, lady, I get about two hours of sleep a day . . . " He was pointing a finger at her face.

"Stop, Mike," Pete said firmly, not relishing a confrontation between the two.

Rosemary bit her lower lip to choke back a counterattack.

"Can I continue?" Pete said.

She nodded.

"If Maria could take syringes out of the trash truck, someone else could also take them. Central supply and purchasing are located in the hallway where that truck sat yesterday morning. Maintenance men handle plastic bags when they throw them into the dumpster. Some employees come to work through the loading dock door."

Rosemary was quiet as she considered the possibilities. Finally, she asked, "Is someone selling used syringes outside the hospital?"

"It's a lucrative business. Used intramuscular syringes can bring five bucks apiece; new ones about ten bucks. Your nurses give hundreds of injections. We don't know the exact number yet, but assume five hundred per day, half of them unbroken, could realize twenty-five hundred dollars a day. Not a bad supplement to someone's income."

Dow stood up. "I'm going to see a few people, Lieutenant."

"I'll catch up with you this afternoon," Pete replied.

Rosemary watched Dow go and reluctantly asked, "What's your other investigation, Pete, the one that may relate to Riverside?"

"A drug ring in Cambridge. Someone is supplying drugs and used syringes to the pushers. As of today, your trash trucks will be under surveillance."

With a look of dismay, Rosemary asked, "Are the drugs like opium and marijuana?"

"Yeah, and morphine, Demerol, Dilaudid. Why?"

She hesitated. "A large narcotic theft was discovered this morning."

10

WEDNESDAY AFTERNOON
January 19

During the summer, three o'clock is the beginning of the afternoon. In the winter, it signifies only two more hours of daylight. Three o'clock at Riverside Hospital, however, is always the same, summer or winter. At three o'clock every day of the week, every week of the year, the day shift gets ready to leave while the evening shift reports to work.

Fran Porter chatted with several nursing friends as they rode the elevator up to the fifth floor of the Main building. As a float nurse, she had been assigned charge duty on the Gold Coast, the exclusive, expensive nursing unit which overlooked the Charles River and offered a panorama from Boston's skyscrapers west to the Harvard stadium.

She walked toward the nurses' station, past enormous private rooms that were adorned with antique furniture, large oil paintings, and crystal chandeliers. Only wealthy patients could afford the hefty price tag.

Haute cuisine such as filet mignon or lobster thermidor was served on English bone china and eaten with sterling silverware. Those patients on unrestricted diets could select from a gilded menu and wine list.

In addition to basic bedroom furniture, each of the

thirty rooms had a hospital telephone, a private telephone, color television, stereophonic radio, a writing desk which contained bar equipment, and a small refrigerator for ice.

"Pack it up, kids," Fran said to the day-shift nurses as she approached the nurses' station.

"Hi, Fran," the head nurse said, "be with you in a minute."

While the day-shift nurses finished with last-minute details, the evening nurses began to take over. Fran counted narcotics and the other three nurses organized the patient assignments, keeping the new admissions and fresh postoperative patients, and giving the less acute patients to the four nurses' aides.

When change of shift report ended, Fran approved the assignments, then organized the bulging medication cart and went out on rounds. She checked intravenous bottles, urine bags, and the general condition of each patient as she distributed medications.

Although Fran was new to Riverside Hospital, she had learned their nursing procedures quickly. Not only did her patients enjoy seeing her but her sense of responsibility had gained her the trust of the supervisors who now made rounds to the Gold Coast only once during the shift. That suited Fran nicely for, whichever nursing unit she was assigned to, she felt the supervisors' visits were an intrusion into her private domain.

"Hello, Mrs. Stormer, I'm Fran Porter, the evening nurse. How are you feeling?" Emma Stormer had been admitted earlier that day. She was huddled in the bed with the sheets pulled up under her nose. She didn't answer.

"May I call you Emma?" Fran said as she walked closer to the bed. Emma stared at the young nurse with tears in her eyes.

Fran consulted the patient kardex. "You've had a mammogram and I see you're scheduled for surgery tomorrow morning. What is Dr. Harris going to do?" No answer. Fran decided to use another tactic. She sat on the edge of the bed and started talking about the weather, her new car, hospital procedures, anything that came to her. Finally, she said, "I bet you have three children."

Emma's blue eyes sparked momentarily. She lowered the sheet and whispered, "I have two fine boys."

Fran saw a small, round, rosy face surrounded by curly gray hair. Emma looked like Mrs. Santa Claus. "Why are you nervous? Is it the surgery?"

Emma grabbed Fran's hand as a dark shadow passed across her face. "I have a friend . . . " She paused while tears welled up in her eyes and stood on her lower eyelids, ready to drop. "I mean I *had* a friend. She had a breast removed only a year ago but they didn't get it all, you know, all those bad cells, and it came back." Emma began to weep. "She's dead."

Fran patted Emma's hand. "There, there now. Tell me. You have a lump in your breast, too, right?"

"Yes. I discovered it last week."

"And you're having a biopsy done?"

"Yes. What will Henry think? Having a wife with just one breast?" Emma's tears rolled down her cheeks.

"But you may not have your breast removed, Emma. That lump could just be an enlarged cyst."

"They'll find cancer, I know it."

"No, no. Many of these lumps are perfectly normal."

Relief flashed across Emma's round face. "You mean he won't take my breast off?"

"Don't misunderstand me. If it's malignant, well, yes, he'll have to remove your breast. Let me explain it to you. While you're on the operating room table, Dr. Harris will take a tiny piece of tissue from that lump. He'll send the tissue to the frozen section laboratory, just down the corridor, where the pathologist will freeze it and look at it under a microscope. He then tells the surgeon what he sees. If it's benign, Dr. Harris removes the lump and presto, you're in the recovery room. Let's pray that it's benign; you must keep the faith, Emma."

"I have faith."

Fran patted Emma's hand. "Good."

"Can Henry, my husband, have breakfast with me?"

"Henry can eat your breakfast for you because after midnight, you can't put anything in your mouth. You'll be N.P.O., which means no food and no liquids. At seven in the morning, the O.R. people will pick you up for surgery but I'll see that a tray is left for Henry."

"I hate pain. Will I be in pain?"

"We won't let the pain bother you because every three hours we'll give you pain medication."

The door opened and Henry Stormer minced into the room. He carried his hat in his hands and looked like a timid gnome.

"Oh, Henry, this nice nurse just explained the surgery and I feel so much better."

Fran got up, said hello to Henry, and continued on her medication rounds.

At the next door, she felt a thrill of excitement. Rip Easterbrook was in room five fifteen; a soap opera star who, when he first arrived as a patient, had the nurses vying to take care of him. But in spite of his good looks, he had created havoc, complaining about the food and the nurses. He was a spoiled brat and most of the nurses couldn't wait for his discharge day.

Fran knew their feelings, yet she couldn't help the tiny knot of anticipation from tightening in her stomach. She pushed the door open. "Hello, Rip, how . . . "

He was standing beside the bed, his hand working underneath the skirt of a tall brunette. They both looked quickly at Fran, then Rip removed his hand.

More disillusioned than repulsed, Fran said, "Do you want a pain shot, Rip?"

"Nope, doc is springing me this weekend so I'm cutting out the shots."

"You're feeling better?"

After his appendectomy, Rip had developed pneumonia, which he blamed on the hospital. "Yup."

"Eating solid foods now?"

Rip looked back at the brunette, slid his hand up her dress again and smiled. "I'm eating a lot of solid food now." The brunette giggled.

Fran closed the door, and as she wheeled the cart back to the medication room she began to agree with the other nurses: Rip was a slob.

She opened the narcotic book and recorded: 5:00 P.M. R. Easterbrook, Demerol 100 mgm, IM for pain. F. Porter, R.N.

She subtracted one from the count, then took an ampul of Demerol from the plastic box, dropped it into her pocket, and went to the nurses' station. A group of interns and residents passed by with the chief of medicine. She declined their invitation to go on rounds, sat at the desk, and began stamping laboratory slips with the patient's addressograph cards. Several patients had been discharged on the day shift, and she knew their plastic cards had been thrown in the wastebasket.

When the area was quiet, she bent down under the counter and sorted through the papers in the trash basket until she found the cards.

"Are you all right?"

The voice startled Fran and she banged her head on the

counter as she sat up. "Ouch, damn it."

Ilse Jensen, the evening supervisor, stood on the corridor side of the nurses' station.

"Hi," Fran said, rubbing her head.

"Do you feel faint?"

"No, I dropped a card on the floor," she lied.

"Listen, the heat is on from nursing service," Ilse whispered. "I guess some of the nurses are not breaking needles off syringes and Jayne McCarthy's in a flap about it. Would you pass the word to the night shift?"

"Sure."

"Anything to report up here?"

"No, it's quiet."

"How's Mr. Easterbrook tonight?"

"No problem so far. He's playing nursery rhymes with a brunette."

"What do you mean?"

"Humpty dumpty."

Ilse smiled. "See you later."

Once Ilse was gone, Fran bent down quickly, grabbed the addressograph cards from the trash basket and put them into her pocket, along with several of yesterday's lab slips, and the stolen ampul of Demerol.

11

When the doorbell rang, Rosemary winced. After taking a hot shower, she had avoided looking at the bed and its promise of tranquillity, for depression and fatigue were overshadowing her desire to be with Bob Friend. She shook her head, squared her shoulders, and opened the door.

Bob's dark hair and coat were sprinkled with melting snowflakes. The twinkle in his eyes, and a broad smile made Rosemary forget her weariness.

"It's good to see you, Bob. Come in and get warm."

"You look delicious," he said, closing the door. He placed two cold hands on her cheeks and gave her a lingering kiss. "You taste delicious too; are you for dinner?"

"You're somewhat lewd for a Harvard lawyer type," she said facetiously. "Do you make obscene phone calls too?"

"Yes."

"Good. I could use some hard-core raunch."

Laughing, he reached into his coat pockets and removed two bottles of wine. "I read your mind. This is Saint Émilion raunch and this one here, a special Pouilly-Fuissé raunch." He saw the smile spread across her face. "I know, I know, I bought the raunch."

Bob removed his coat and followed her toward the kitchen. Her apartment abounded with antique furniture, oriental rugs, overstuffed chairs, and paintings. Blue, her favorite color, ran through the living room and dining room, melting with other soft pastel colors.

"What are we having?" he asked.

"A new recipe I clipped from the newspaper. It won the December recipe award: pork toenails marinated in turnip juice and aged sauerkraut mash."

She pulled the casserole from the oven, lifted the lid, and a puff of steam escaped, carrying with it the savory aroma of steak and vegetables.

He breathed a sign of relief. "Beef Bourguignon, my favorite."

"Would you make us a drink? I could use one." Rosemary replaced the casserole and when she turned, he was still behind her. Placing his hands on her shoulders, he said gently, "You look tired."

"I am."

He kissed one of her eyelids, then the other, and held her tightly.

"Do you feel like telling me what happened yesterday?"

She glanced at him as if he'd read her mind, then told him about the murder, describing the detectives and their investigations, and ending with Jake's motive for killing Maria.

"Charlie Donovan discovered the bodies?"

"Yes."

"He must be their prime suspect."

"Not really. He was in dietary shortly after seven o'clock, arguing with Tom O'Leary."

"What about?"

"The dietary sprayers. Charlie wants Tom's people to turn off the hot and cold water valves under the sink when they're not using the sprayers. I guess pressure can build in the hoses and if the rubber tubing explodes, dietary people have to haul out the ark again. Anyway, Tom was defending his people and Charlie was defending his workload; many people heard and saw them. On his way back to maintenance, Charlie stopped by the laundry chute room to see if Jake had arrived. Apparently the laundry trucks were not out on the dock at the usual time. Anyway, he found the bodies and called me to come down. . . . " Her voice faded away.

Bob found her hand and clasped it. "We don't have to talk about this anymore if you're uncomfortable."

"It feels good to unload." She smiled at him.

"Still want that drink?"

"Yes, a tall red raunch sounds delicious."

He was pouring the wine, when they heard a loud knock on the door. "I'll get it," Bob offered.

Rosemary was lighting the candles on the table when he returned. "Who was that?"

"Some creepy guy looking for apartment four-eighteen."

"There is no four-eighteen."

Bob glanced back at the door.

"What did he look like?"

"Huge, olive-skinned, probably the ugliest bastard I've ever seen."

Terror washed over Rosemary and she stopped breathing momentarily. Heaven help me, she thought, he knows where I live. She stood wide-eyed, fear penetrating through to her heart.

"What's the matter?" Bob asked.

She caught his look of concern and pointed at the door. "Go after him, please, catch him, get his license plate number, anything."

"Why?"

"He could be Maria Silva's killer!"

Bob came over, put his arm around her shoulder, and began leading her toward the kitchen. "Not on your life, young lady. One thing I don't do is chase killers. Anyway, I wouldn't want to leave you alone. Why don't we call the police and have *them* find the guy?" Bob dialed and spoke to the desk sergeant.

Before he was finished, she took the receiver, explained who she was, and asked that Pete Tanner be notified. She dialed another number.

"Who are you calling?" Bob asked.

"The manager of this place."

"He'll only tell you that the guy rang all the apartment buzzers until some dumb ass let him through the lobby door."

Rosemary knew he was right, but she listened to the ringing at the other end until finally she hung up.

As they ate, Bob told her about his vacation in Martinique and invited her on a ski trip to Stowe. His law practice involved long, tiresome hours in court and he enjoyed getting away on weekends.

"I can't go this weekend, Bob. I plan to be at the hospital both days."

"You should get away for a while."

"I know. How about the weekend after the survey; the pressure will be off by then, I hope."

"It's a date." He sat back. "Rosemary, you're an excellent chef."

"Thank you."

After clearing the table, they went into the living room. A dying fire glowed in the old marble fireplace. The cat, Skittles, opened an eye when Bob stirred the fire with a brass poker, then licked a paw and went back to sleep on the ottoman.

"How do you keep your sanity in court?" she asked.

"You can't let people get to you, that's all."

"I try to be objective, but it's difficult."

"Tonight, you are my objective." He wrapped an arm around her shoulders and led her to the couch. "What else is happening at the hospital?" he asked, pulling her down beside him.

"The usual everyday headaches."

"Yes, but didn't you mention something about a negative culture?"

She looked up at him. "No, I didn't."

"Sure, you said something about a problem with negative cultures."

Astonished, Rosemary sat up. "I never mentioned it, Bob, and I'd like to know how you found out."

"I got a call this afternoon from a Mr. Dick Bonnet."

"Lucy Bonnet's father?"

"That's the one."

"And?"

"Now don't get riled up." He tried to pull her close.

She pushed his hands away. "Tell me!"

"Well, he and Mrs. Bonnet were in pediatrics about to sign the death release and make arrangements; needless to say, they were quite upset. Dr. Farrah didn't know that the man standing at the nurses' station was Mr. Bonnet and he picked up the telephone and yelled at the lab people. He carried on about poor laboratory practices; poor culturing to be exact." Rosemary stood up and glared down at Bob. He continued, "I'm sure his comments weren't meant to be overheard. Anyway, Mr. Bonnet called me."

"He wants to sue the hospital and you're going to represent him," she accused.

"He wants me to look into the circumstances of Lucy's death."

Her anger flared. "Are you going to take the case?"

"Come on, Rosemary, I haven't decided yet."

"If you take that case, we'll be in opposition again." Totally frustrated and annoyed, her voice became strained. "I imagine you'll decide once you know how much money you might win from the hospital."

"That's not fair."

"You're not being fair. Why doesn't Sheriden, or Tallow, or Langenstern represent him?"

"Because Mr. Bonnet asked for me. Anyway, he may not even have a case."

"And you will make that determination?"

"Yes."

"I'll be damned. Why didn't you tell me this earlier? You let me discuss my problems on the pretext of having concern for me, ate my dinner, and all along I was being interrogated." Rosemary stood and began pacing the living room. "I am very, very tired and I'd like you to go home." She grabbed his coat from a chair. "I need time to think."

Bob patted the couch. "Why don't you sit down here and I'll get you another glass of wine. Come on."

"I don't need wine and I don't need any more conversation." She held his coat up.

Reluctantly, he stood and took the coat. "I had a very nice evening, Rosemary. I don't understand you, and I know you don't understand me, but you will. I'll call soon."

"Don't call until you decide, and if you go with Mr. Bonnet, then don't call at all. Goodnight." She went to the door and held it open.

Bob looked at her, shrugged, and walked out.

Tears flooded down her cheeks the moment the door was bolted. She went back into the living room, picked up Skittles from the ottoman, and sat on the couch. "He means nothing to me, Skittles," she cried, trying to convince herself. "He's just a friend, used to be a friend anyway, more interested in court, and cases, and money than in our relationship. He didn't even think about giving the case to another trial lawyer."

Tears abated as her thoughts turned from Bob to the man at her apartment door. He must have found out where she lived, and come when she would be relaxed and vulnerable; he couldn't have expected to see Bob.

Why? What did he want? She had nothing of value . . . except her life. Suddenly, she jumped up, raced to the window, and peered outside. She saw a man leaning against a street lamp. She couldn't see his face, but his head was tilted as he looked up at her.

12

THURSDAY MORNING
January 20

Dressed in a green scrub suit, J. B. Harris walked out of
the O.R. locker room and headed for the surgeon's lounge
where Karl Kreutzer and two anesthesiologists sat drink-
ing coffee.

Seven-thirty in the morning was always a time of sys-
tematized confusion as nurses and scrub technicians set
up operating rooms according to the daily schedule.
Transporters brought patients down to the anesthesia
holding area while aides autoclaved last-minute instrument packs. Miss Pickle, the stiff, unflappable supervisor,
snapped orders over the intercom, a system that connected every room in the O.R. including the bathrooms.

J.B. winced as he walked into the lounge. "A good screw
would loosen up old Picklenik in a minute."

One of the anesthesiologists snorted in agreement,
"Yeah, J.B., why don't you tickle her pickle?"

"He can't," the second anesthesiologist said, jabbing the
first with his elbow, "it's shriveled from soaking in brine."

J.B.'s sense of humor had its limitations and the two
young doctors had pushed him to the edge. He enjoyed
sexual provocations from the ladies but not physically

94

demeaning insinuations from anyone, jokingly or not. "All right," he said, "let's cut the crap." He poured himself a cup of coffee from the urn and sat next to Karl, who continued to read his journal. "How're you doing, Karl? Ready for our case?"

Karl pushed back his gray hair with a gloved hand. He looked distraught. "Yes, I'm ready. This won't take long, will it?" he asked impatiently.

"No, no. We'll be finished in no time. This is a sixty-six-year-old woman with a two-centimeter, subareolar mass at three o'clock in her left breast. I'll get the tissue to you within five minutes after the incision." J.B. picked up a large, jelly-filled donut from the box of pastries on the coffee table. "I shouldn't but I will." As his teeth clamped down, a spurt of raspberry jelly hit his cheek. He wiped it off and licked his fingers.

One of the anesthesiologists saw him and commented under his breath, "A moment upon the lips is a lifetime upon the hips."

J.B. glared at the young doctors. "Don't you two have anything better to do? Why don't you blow your laughing gas into a few patients? Maybe one of them will think you're hilarious."

The two doctors got up and left the lounge. They didn't respect the chief of surgery, but they didn't want to hassle him either.

Once the two doctors were out of the room, J.B. leaned forward in his chair. "How's our project going, Karl? Will we make the deadline?"

Karl considered his questions. He hated the fat, pompous man but he needed surgical tissues for his research. "I don't know, J.B. That new bacteriologist has a gelatinous mass for a brain, damn it. And I need at least four more surgical tissues before Monday. I promised Cristobal that he'd have my papers a week ago. We're going to miss the damn deadline."

"Can't you send in our application and research now, and his when it arrives?"

Kreutzer stood up abruptly. "No, you can't get any of this procedure into your head. Cristobal needs my heavy metal research to conclude his enzyme studies." Kreutzer gazed toward the ceiling. "A half million dollars going down the drain."

"Don't worry." J.B. saw a stretcher go by the door. "That's my patient." He patted Kreutzer on the shoulder and left the lounge. At Emma Stormer's side, he said hello, asked how she felt, and continued into the inner operating room area to start his five-minute hand scrub.

Karl Kreutzer walked quickly to the frozen section lab, just outside the surgical rooms, anxious to get the frozen section done and get back upstairs to work on his research papers.

The lab was a small room which contained an array of pathology equipment and supplies. A cryostat freezer and a biological refrigerator were against one wall, and opposite was a long stainless steel counter with forceps, slides, microscope, jars, scalpel, and an assortment of multicolored solutions.

Kreutzer perched on the stool and thought about his two grants. He and Malen Cristobal were on the verge of obtaining a National Cancer Institute grant of two hundred and fifty thousand dollars, and another for three hundred and twenty-five thousand dollars from the Potter Foundation in New York. The money, allocated over a three-year period, would support Cristobal while he was in the United States, pay for his office space, a research lab in a building adjacent to Riverside, and subsidize their elaborate studies of the cancer cell.

To the grant specialist of the research branch of the National Cancer Institute, Kreutzer had demonstrated that he had a full team of specialists ready for the program: a breast cancer surgeon, namely Dr. Harris; a radiotherapist, medical oncologists, technologists, and clerical staff. The new computer, MOM III, had the capacity to provide the necessary pathology reference center and large data bank. Allocation of the federal grant was contingent upon a letter of financial support from the Potter Foundation, an item Kreutzer would pick up on Sunday, and receipt of the full research application by January twenty-eighth.

After many meetings with the vice president of Potter, he was assured of receiving the letter and the grant money, provided his proposals were submitted two months before the March meeting of the Foundation's board. The thought of meeting both deadlines was eroding Kreutzer's physical and mental well-being.

When Miss Pickle's voice came rasping over the intercom, he absently reached up and switched the button from an open line to O.R. 5 where Emma Stormer's operation was about to take place. He overheard the nurses talking among themselves as they prepared the tables. He heard the anesthesiologist ask Emma to count backwards from one hundred. After a few moments, he heard J.B. greet the O.R. team. Karl opened the journal and continued to read.

Ten minutes later, a knock startled him. He opened the door, took the tissue from the circulating nurse, and kicked the door closed.

The room temperature tissue was as tough as a piece of red meat. Kreutzer placed it on a metal disc, then put the disc in the cryostat freezer where liquid carbon dioxide froze the tissue instantly. While frozen, he sliced off many paper thin sections with a microtome, then removed the slices and stained them with hemotoxylin and eosin solutions.

Kreutzer looked at the first slice under a microscope and saw normal tissue. The next slice was normal and the next and on to the last. The breast showed a pocket of thickened tissue, but it was benign. He sat back and thought for a moment. To thoroughly complete his studies, he needed four more malignancies, but J.B. had no further biopsies scheduled between now and Sunday when Kreutzer was flying to New York for the Potter letter of support, and then on to the Netherlands.

He had called J.B.'s last seven cases malignant although three had been normal, rationalizing their surgical removal for the sake of scientific progress. He'd injected the normal nipple areas with various dilutions of his dimethylated mixtures and kept them incubated and nourished in plasma baths. Expecting the nipples to turn black from deterioration within an unusually short period of time, to his surprise, the tissues remained brown, and decayed at a normal rate. He had planned on demonstrating this to Cristobal, using Cristobal's research tissues, but here was an available breast, and in its entirety, he and Cristobal would have enough to run a few dozen fresh experiments.

He made up his mind and pushed the intercom button. "J.B.? That tissue is loaded with intraductile carcinoma."

"Okey fanokey, Karl. Thanks."

Kreutzer heard J.B. say to the O.R. team, "Off she comes, we're doing a radical." He switched off the intercom, wrote his diagnosis on the frozen section consultation report form, and signed his name. Because the slides of Emma's breast tissue would become permanent records, he wanted them up in the lab where he could exchange the normal tissue for old leftover pieces of intra-ductile carcinoma. He found Miss Pickle, gave her the consultation report and with the slides went to his office on the fourth floor, satisfied that, within an hour, Emma's normal breast, normal underarm glandular tissues, and a sheet of fascia over her rib cage would be sent to him in a plastic bag.

13

THURSDAY MORNING
January 20

"Mrs. Cleaveland," Peggy said over the intercom, "Mrs. McCarthy would like to see you about the narcotics."

Rosemary hesitated. Not only was she tired from sitting up late the night before but she had a busy schedule and had barely finished reading the morning financial report, census figures, operative surgical case reports, list of VIPs who were patients at Riverside, and other bits of daily information accumulated for her each day by fiscal services. "Okay," she said, "tell her I'll see her." Rosemary opened her compact, looked at her tired face, and pushed a curl into place. She hoped Jayne had good news about the theft; she hoped everyone she saw today had good news, particularly Pete Tanner. Closing the compact, Rosemary resolved that in spite of her busy schedule, she was going to get a few answers about Jake and Maria from Pete Tanner and about negative lab cultures from either Tony or Kreutzer. She would wait before she bothered Felix about that Compulectrics order. Her thoughts turned to the accreditation inspection. The surveyors were due in eleven days, not much time.

The door opened. "May I come in?" Jayne asked. "You look pooped," she said and sat in a chair opposite Rosemary.

"Thanks." Rosemary glanced at Jayne's rumpled uniform. "So do you."

"I know. I'm whipped from hopping around like a flea after a dog." She smoothed her white dress. "And of all things, the laundry forgot to starch my uniforms." Her black hair was pulled back into a bun and on top of her head sat the frilly nursing cap.

"What can I do for you?" Rosemary asked.

"John Kelley just called to report that he found boxes of Demerol and Dilaudid missing from the Sinclair Three narcotic cabinet late yesterday afternoon."

"Damn."

"That's astute. Wait till I tell you the rest. You know that the pharmacy stocks the medication bins in the carts with a three-day supply of patient drugs?"

"Yes."

"Well, the carts were down early this morning and one of the pharmacists saw that a patient's bin was low on Valium. As he was adding a three-day supply, he happened to notice on the patient's profile that a three-day supply had been added yesterday. Now one would think we have a very nervous patient, who needed a lot of Valium, right? Not at all. He checked through other drawers and sure as my panties are white, someone is pilfering from the drug bins. One of our illustrious nurses is very nervous." Jayne pinched the bridge of her nose. "When I get my hands on her, the only things she'll be lifting are rocks in a penitentiary."

Rosemary listened patiently to the news. Outwardly, she appeared receptive and calm but inwardly, a slow, angry boil of emotions was beginning to rise. "What are you doing about this?" she asked.

"John's pharmacists are doing gymnastics trying to pinpoint the unit, shift, and nervous nurse."

"That wasn't my question. What are *you* doing to help him?"

"Me? Well, I have my supervisors checking the staffing sheets. Speaking of supervisors, I just got word that the grand master key is missing from one of the supervisor's key rings."

Rosemary stood up and walked to the picture window. Don't explode, she told herself, just be patient. She buttoned her suit jacket as a blast of January wind rattled the picture window. "How did that happen?"

"I don't know. Probably one of them took it off the key ring for some reason and plans to return it when she comes on duty again."

Rosemary turned. "Absolutely not. You know hospital policy on narcotic keys. The same holds true for grand master keys, even more so. If someone copies that key, he'll have access through every door at Riverside. I want you to call each and every supervisor and find who has that key. She must return it immediately."

"Okay, okay, I'll find it."

Peggy knocked on the door, then came in with two steaming cups of coffee. "I thought you might want to caffeinate your corpuscles."

"Thanks, Peggy," Rosemary said. "You win the gold medal of thoughtfulness award."

"You're welcome, see ya." She went back to her office.

When the door closed, Jayne asked, "We must look half dead, huh?"

"Guess so," Rosemary said, and sipped her coffee. "What about central supply? Has Frank Grinnell come up with a reason for the unsterile packs?"

"No. He was running all six autoclaves through continuous cycles until that new gas autoclave malfunctioned again, and refused to go into an initial vacuum phase.

Frank got a call from Miss Pickle this morning. She's beating her jungle drums about another unsterilized pack of chest tubes. When the scrub nurse opened the pack on her table, she saw that the internal indicator hadn't changed, and they had to break down the whole field and start over. Frank's going to check the O.R. packs and flash autoclaves this afternoon."

Rosemary banged her fist on the desk. "Damn it." She began to pace the office. "The O.R. autoclaves are growing droves of bacteria while the laboratory can't get a normal everyday germ to sprout. So far, no one has died because of an abundance of bacteria, but two have died from negative cultures. I want you to help John Kelley and Frank Grinnell. Offer them manpower, whatever they need, and get that key returned. Let's go."

Jayne stood and followed Rosemary into Peggy's office.

"Mrs. Cleaveland, before you go I have some messages and things," Peggy said.

Rosemary stopped. "Jayne, I want to make rounds with you and Charlie Donovan at two o'clock." Jayne nodded and left.

Peggy referred to her stenographer's notebook. "I know you probably don't want to hear all this. . . ."

"Go on, Peggy. Maybe someone on your list wants to carry me off to the land of honey and bliss."

"Not from the looks of it. Do you want to hear about Charlie Donovan?"

"Sure."

"He called to complain about the new wheelchairs. Says that the last order was fit for a . . . well, I won't say exactly what he said, but they have to be sent back; all the wheels are falling off."

"Tell him to call physical therapy. Sam's the one who ordered them."

"Okay, next, Charlie wants to turn off the water line in the main building for an hour either today or tomorrow. Says a toilet mechanism on this floor needs replacing."

"That will affect dietary, physical therapy, the lab, and the Gold Coast. Have him check with the department heads, and with Jayne. She'll know when the Gold Coast can ease up on the patients' bath water."

"Miss Pickle called . . . "

"My goodness, she's been busy this morning."

"Yeah, she wanted you to know that Dr. Harris is at the end of his rope." Peggy looked up. "I don't know why that should bother him, he uses the rope for his Peter Pan act. Anyway, in the middle of his operation, the circulating nurse noticed that the D. and C. pack wasn't sterile. The indicator didn't do whatever it was supposed to do."

"Type that up and give it to Jayne's secretary for Jayne to look at soon. You'd better tell Frank Grinnell too."

"Jaundice?"

"That's not nice. His name is Frank."

"But he's so yellow and icky." Peggy made a face. "His eyes are like two optic yellow tennis balls."

Rosemary smiled. "What else?"

"Tanner wants to see you sometime, no rush."

"He's at Riverside today? Tell him I'll be down in an hour."

"John Kelley wants to know if he can call the bomb squad in to dispose of the half-used cans of ether."

"No. Tell him to take them outside and pour them onto the ground. They'll evaporate safely; he should know that. Anyway, tell him to write that into his procedure manual."

"Here's a corker for you. The emergency room head nurse reported some negative cultures. Seems as though two no-growths are on patients suspected of having gonorrhea."

Rosemary groaned. "Tell her to call bacteriology for an explanation, and to send me a report along with the two medical records. Better put that in your note to Jayne McCarthy."

Peggy turned a page in her notebook. "Next on the list . . . "

"More?" Rosemary asked wearily.

"Oh, Mrs. Cleaveland, this is just volume one." Peggy grinned as Rosemary looked at her with consternation. "Not really, just two more things. Dr. Kreutzer has switched from mad Nazi to Geronimo, and in his oh-so-pleasant manner, he shouted war whoops over the telephone. He would like to see you, not in a minute or two, but exactly this very instant."

"I'm going up to see him now."

Peggy referred to her notes. "The head nurse on the Gold Coast says that Rip Easterbrook, the soap opera star, brought in a tape recorder for his voice lessons. She explained the electrical safety policy but he doesn't care. And he won't give up his recorder."

Rosemary was thoughtful. "Someone around here has a tape recorder with a three-pronged plug. Who is it, the in-service department?"

"I dunno." Peggy scratched her head with the pencil eraser.

"Ask Charlie Donovan; he'll remember. When you locate it, take it up to Mr. Easterbrook for me."

Peggy's jaw dropped open and her eyes widened as big as saucers. "Oh, Mrs. Cleaveland, can I? I'd love to meet him. He isn't married and he loves brunettes. It said so in my movie magazine. Oh, thank you. I can't wait." She picked up the telephone to call Charlie.

"Wait a minute. I want you to do something for me."

Peggy put the receiver down and sighed heavily. Rosemary gave her a friendly squeeze on her shoulder. "Come on, sport. I won't take too much of your time."

"I'm sorry, I just got so excited that my brain scrambled."

"When you call Charlie, ask him to go on rounds with Jayne and me at two o'clock. How is Miss Truslow doing with the medical staff bylaws?"

"She's typing them now. Not much more to go."

"When she finishes the appeals mechanism section, have her get Dr. Harris to read and sign it, then I want to see the entire thing."

"Where are you going in case I need you?"

"To see Dr. Kreutzer, then Pete Tanner."

The telephone rang and Peggy picked up the receiver. "Hello, Mrs. Cleaveland's office. Hi, Tony. I don't know, why? Oh *yeah*?" She covered the receiver with her hand. "Mrs. Cleaveland? This is Tony in the lab. He wants to know how old a woman can be and still get pregnant." Peggy tried to stifle a smile.

"He doesn't know?"

"He knows, but he's got some requisitions to run pregnancy tests on ninety-year-old biddies."

14

THURSDAY MORNING
January 20

"Phew," Rosemary said as she walked into the chemistry lab, "smells like rotten eggs in here."

Tony glanced up from his mixtures. "Hi, Mrs. Cleaveland. You're right. It's the sulfuric acid for this Scott-Williams reagent. Dr. Kreutzer needs it immediately." He carefully added silver nitrate to a solution of sodium hydroxide and mercuric cyanide. Large amber bottles, marked "Poison" over a skull and crossbones, were in a row on the counter top. Once the reagent was mixed, he placed it in a spectrophotometer and took a reading. "There. I tell you, this whole thing is archaic." He turned on the stool and looked at Rosemary. "You look terrific."

"Thank you. What's this about pregnant old ladies, Tony?"

"Yeah, isn't that a new one? Look at these slips over here." He got up and walked over to another long counter. "They were *so* weird that I called the nursing supervisor earlier and asked her about them. She thought I was joking and laughed. So I said, ha, ha, ha, just to amuse her. After going over the names, she told me that these women had been discharged yesterday afternoon. I got to thinking and decided to check *all* our recent requests for preg-

107

nancy tests. Look at this one." He held up a slip.

"Joanne May," Rosemary read from the addressograph imprint. "Ninety-three."

"She was discharged yesterday, back to a nursing home," Tony said.

"Incredible."

"You said it. Now I ask, why is a ninety-three-year-old woman worried about being pregnant? She isn't, unless the world of science fiction came true overnight."

Rosemary took the lab slips from him and checked the name of each patient. "How many are there?"

"Seven, but one looks legitimate. She's a twenty-four-year-old patient on the maternity unit. You know what I think?"

"What do you think, Tony?"

"That you'd better figure out a better way to discard the Addressograph cards when patients go home. Someone is using the cards to requisition pregnancy tests. Probably a small business for outside friends."

"May I keep these?"

"Sure, except for the twenty-four-year-old. I have to run that one."

Rosemary slipped them into her pocket. "Can we go into your office? We have to talk for a minute."

"Okay, but I know what's on your mind." He led her down the hall, past several labs, to his small, windowless office.

"Sit here," he motioned. "I'll call Penny Abbott in."

"Not yet, Tony. Tell me what she said."

"She wrote that letter to the Joint Commission because she hates Dr. Kreutzer and wants to get rid of him."

"That's pretty serious. Why didn't she seek your help?"

"She was afraid."

"Of you?"

"No, of him." Tony sat at his desk. "She claims that his demands are not on her job description. He's been ordering her around and she's sick of it, but being a new employee, she doesn't want to lose her job so she thought someone from the outside could help."

"If I could get Dr. Kreutzer settled down, would she rescind her request for an interview?"

"I think so."

"Tell me what you know about those negative culture reports."

Tony scratched his head. "I honestly can't figure them out. We've both put in a few overtime hours but can't find a thing wrong."

"Could Penny be the problem?"

"She's an excellent technician and her credentials are super. We're lucky to have her."

"That may be, but it doesn't solve our problem. I recently heard from the emergency room that culture reports on several highly suspicious cases of gonorrhea came back negative."

"Wait a minute," he said, picked up the telephone, and called the bacteriology lab. They could hear the faint ring of a telephone down the hall. The ringing stopped.

"Hi, Penny," Tony said. "Come on down to my office, will you?" He hung up and, within seconds, Penny walked in. She lowered her eyes when she saw Rosemary.

Tony pointed to a chair. "Sit there, Penny. Mrs. Cleaveland wants to know about these negative cultures and I figured you're the best person to tell her."

Penny looked quickly from Tony to Rosemary.

"I . . . I haven't any idea. I haven't done anything wrong. I haven't changed anything." She started wringing her hands.

Rosemary leaned toward the girl. "Something has

changed and I want to know what. Are you running quality control checks?"

"Yes."

"Against standards?"

"Yes."

"Every week?"

"Yes."

"Every morning and between tests too?"

A forlorn look settled on Penny's face.

"Are you?" Rosemary demanded.

Penny shrugged her shoulders.

Rosemary leaned back and crossed her arms in front of
her. "Did you know that Lucy Bonnet died?"

Penny nodded her head.

"And a patient named Aranda Lilly?"

Penny nodded again.

"Don't you care? What's the matter with you?" Rosemary felt like shaking the girl. "Don't you care if several
patients walk out of here with undiagnosed gonorrhea?"

"It's . . . it's just . . . " Her eyes widened and she sat up.
"Dr. Kreutzer is giving me too much work and I haven't
time for my regular job. He doesn't even know my name.
'Here,' he demands, 'do this, do that, do it now.' I've tried
to explain my job but he won't listen."

"I see. Because of him, you aren't running proper
checks?"

"I can't."

"You can and you will. The hospital hired you and pays
your salary, not Dr. Kreutzer. You are to do your full-time
job first, and if you wish to help him, do it on an overtime
basis, on his payroll. I have to see him now and I'll get this
straightened out." Rosemary stood and left the tiny office.
She didn't see Tony shrug, nor did she see Penny begin to
cry.

In the corridor opposite the elevator was a short, yellow biological refrigerator with a logbook on top. Curious, Rosemary stopped and opened the log. Personnel bringing specimens for culturing left them in the refrigerator, then recorded the date, time, type of specimen, patient's name and room number, and their initials in the book. She casually flipped the pages to Tuesday morning, hoping to find an entry between seven and eight in the morning, hoping for a possible witness to Maria's demise. The time was blank. She opened the refrigerator door. Several plastic containers filled with urine sat on sticky racks inside. Tony had obviously overlooked the refrigerator on his latest cleanliness-is-next-to-godliness rounds with housekeeping. She noticed that not only did the racks need a scrubbing, but sitting between two urine bottles was someone's ham sandwich. She grimaced and closed the door.

Dr. Kreutzer's back was to her when Rosemary reached his office door. He sat on a stool at a counter under the window. The office looked as if a blizzard had passed through. Reams of white paper blanketed every surface and undulated over filing cabinets, under chairs, and over what she guessed was the trash basket. Like hailstones, paper wads dotted the white terrain. The only break in the whiteness was the top of Kreutzer's desk, which was spotless. A box of sterile gloves sat in one corner.

Kreutzer was slicing a piece of surgical tissue. "Damnation," he said, threw the tissue over one shoulder, and made another slice. Much to Rosemary's horror, pieces of human tissue covered the white papers behind him. "Damn it to hell, damn it *all* to hell."

She cleared her throat.

"What? Just put the specimen on the counter," he said.

"Dr. Kreutzer, I'd like to speak to you for a moment."

He glanced up, saw Rosemary, and went back to his dissection. "I want approvals for the microscope and specimen container," he growled.

"The hospital is short of funds and no one's getting approvals for anything."

Kreutzer remained silent as she went over to the counter and watched him put a tiny piece of tissue on a glass slide. Casually she asked, "What kind of tissue is that?"

"Intraductile carcinoma of the left breast." As he dabbed the tissue with gentian violet, she noticed that his gloved hands were trembling. Kreutzer enjoyed teaching medical students and, before his time-consuming research studies had started, he taught histopathology at Harvard Medical School. "Ninety percent of breast cancer arises from the epithelium of the lactiferous ducts. A malignant tumor may remain confined to the ducts by connective tissue or it may spread locally, thus obfuscating the site of origin. Under the microscope, the tumor can have an orderly or disorderly pattern, a variation in the cell size and shape, and many mitotic figures. This cancer infiltrated the ducts, so we call it intraductile."

"Who's the patient?"

"Stormer."

She noticed Kreutzer's face drain of color. Suddenly, without looking, his hand reached over toward his log book. Rosemary read part of the last entry just before he snapped the book closed: "514 . . . Stormer, Emma . . left breast . . ." Small beads of sweat had risen on Kreutzer's brow and upper lip. She looked down again at the cover of the logbook and saw, handwritten in large red letters, the words *Confidential—Private Property.*

He stood suddenly. "No one seems to appreciate my tight

schedule, nor the esteem Riverside will acquire if I can get these grants."

"Dr. Kreutzer, many people are proud of your work, your devotion to Riverside, and particularly your interest in developing a cure for cancer."

"Not a cure, my dear, but total obliteration of the disease. A few years hence words like cancer, tumor, malignancy, will be dropped from the everyday lexicon." He looked down at her. "What can I do for you?"

"I came to ask you about negative culture reports."

His eyes narrowed. "Didn't I see you at the infection meeting yesterday?"

"Yes."

"Then you know what I said about putting additives into media to stop the growth of normal flora."

"I heard you. But isn't spinal fluid considered sterile?"

"Of course." He brushed a hand through his hair.

"Then why would the bacteriologist plant sterile spinal fluid in a medium containing additives? Wouldn't she want to see if ē coli or any other normal bacterium was present?"

"Yes, yes, yes. It *was* placed on pure media. Look, Mrs. Cleaveland, several of my studies haven't grown correctly either." He walked to the desk, sat heavily in the chair, and stared at his folded hands. Deep lines stretched across his forehead and two deeper furrows ran from either side of his nose down past his thin lips, pulling his face into a look of forlorn dismay. When he finally looked up, his eyes focused, not on Rosemary but on a thought buried inside his brain. "Cristobal," he whispered.

"What, Dr. Kreutzer?" she asked.

His eyes found hers. "We met three years ago in the Netherlands, Dr. Malen Cristobal and I. We had been working on the cancer cell independently but research was slow and tedious. He was studying the effects of enzymes and I was researching heavy metals. We realized that together we could develop the right combination and consequently end malignancies."

Rosemary sat on the stool and listened while Kreutzer explained his work and his dreams. While he talked, he sat, got up and paced, and sat again, like a tiger in a cage, unaware of her presence. Sometimes he spoke with extreme animation, his eyes sparkling, hands moving. Sometimes he fell into the chair and spoke in whispered tones, his eyes downcast and dull. She felt an unexplained sadness for the man. He hoped for success and he expected fulfillment.

Rosemary had witnessed hope many times before; the expectation of final fulfillment, an inner knowledge that things will eventually, absolutely get better. She had seen hope on the faces of young graduating nurses as they walked the long aisle toward the podium and their waiting diplomas. She had seen hope radiating from the faces of patients on kidney dialysis machines and from the foggy eyes of patients on their way to surgery. She had seen, had felt, the hope of terminal cancer patients who believed that if they waited long enough, and prayed, they would eventually get better. She knew hope and she saw it on Kreutzer's face. He finished his explanation with an exhausted plop into the chair.

"I thought Dr. Harris was working with you too."

"He is, but Cristobal and I are doing the most work."

"Well, I truly hope that you receive your grants."

"We *will*." He stood suddenly and went to the counter. Pushing through an array of slides, he found one, inserted it under the microscope stage clips, and adjusted the knobs. "See there?" He stepped aside for Rosemary. "That used to be cancer. See how the tissue looks? Normal, *normal*."

"It looks normal, but to tell you the truth, I wouldn't be able to tell, it's been such a long time since I . . . "

He brushed her away and resumed his dissection.

"Dr. Kreutzer, I understand that Penny Abbott is falling behind on her work."

"She doesn't know how to organize her time."

"She's a hospital employee and cannot put aside her regular work to help you. Recently, she hasn't had time to run daily quality control checks."

Kreutzer whispered, "I must use her. My papers . . . "

"Could I send you some help?"

"Like who?"

"Another secretary to help with typing."

"It would take a week to train her."

"How about letting someone from the nuclear medicine lab set up your slides and help with notations?"

"No."

Rosemary's patience was gone; he was behaving like a two-year-old during the height of negativity. Trying hard to keep from screaming at him, she said slowly, "It appears as if we have parallel problems. Some of your culture plates have failed to grow while two of my patients have failed to live. You need an electron microscope; I need the funds for its purchase. You have grant deadlines; I have the Joint Commission arriving in eleven days. You want Miss Abbott for your research; I want her to do her regular job." She hesitated, expecting a reaction but, when he didn't speak, she continued. "We can do nothing about our deadlines, and I can't produce overnight funding for your microscope. That leaves culturing problems and personnel shortages. I've offered to send you help from other departments but you declined. If you would prefer that I hire temporary technical assistants, fine, I'll do it. But I'm neither a pathologist nor a bacteriologist, and can offer only support for a thorough investigation of the lab's culturing equipment and procedures. I need your help on this."

Kreutzer had been staring down the microscope and she wasn't certain if he had heard or absorbed any part of what she'd said.

Finally his gaze met hers. "That's very nice, but both you and Mrs. McCarthy have prematurely jumped the fjord. The old-fashioned method of problem solving seems to have mutated into fault-finding where people, with over-grown index fingers, enjoy pointing at problems other than their own."

"I disagree."

"Your opinion makes no difference. Your method of solution does. Now, please, as I explained to Mrs. Mc-Carthy, go talk with Mr. Carasino. He's responsible for the labs and all that goes on."

"You've given him full responsibility?"

"Yes."

"You're no longer involved with the daily operations of the lab?"

"Correct."

"Excellent. Now we can get to the heart of the matter." She headed for the door.

Kreutzer swiveled around on the stool. "What are your intentions?"

"I intend to call Dr. Swanson from Mass. General for assistance. His chief technologist could give Tony and Penny a hand with quality control evaluations."

"You will do no such thing. Not while I'm the chief of pathology—" His voice stiffened. "—and not while I'm working on my papers."

Rosemary's temper broke loose. "And just where do you draw the line between Tony's responsibilities and yours? Or perhaps you have him on a management yo-yo, letting him dangle by a thin string when everything is going your way, then jerking back in when something interferes with your work. That's not the best way of maintaining morale."

"Enough! Get out of my office and stay away from my laboratories."

"I will honor your first request, but not your second." She closed the door behind her but, within seconds, Kreutzer jerked it open.

"I'm warning you, Mrs. Cleaveland, I will not allow outsiders poking around the lab."

As she walked down the corridor, Rosemary felt his eyes burning holes in her back. She was furious and refused to acknowledge his words by looking back. When the elevator arrived, she pressed the button for the first floor, leaned against the cold steel walls of the cab, and watched the door close gently, like the inner lid of a cat's eye, closing out the natural light.

Damn it! Chased by the rabid jaws of time, Kreutzer was running circles around himself and upsetting the entire laboratory. He hadn't time for his work and yet he wouldn't stop long enough to train new people. He's nuts! She felt her body relax slightly. I'm nuts to let him get under my skin. She shook her head. If someone were to walk up to *me* and say, "Gee, you look terribly busy with your important work, why don't you let me train another secretary for you, and let me help troubleshoot . . . " That kind of old-fashioned individual had mutated into a union steward. On the other hand, she thought, I wouldn't want interference if I happened to be hiding something.

She thought about the logbook and the words *Confidential—Private Property*. Rosemary knew that the hospital's regular pathology record was a long, black hardcover journal with Riverside Hospital imprinted in gold letters on the cover. In it were documentations of all patient tissues removed in surgery or anywhere in the hospital. The notations correlated with permanent slides and, as with all hospital documents, logs and slides could be reviewed by hospital officials. Not so with private papers. What worried Rosemary now was the extent of Kreutzer's work, his use of Emma Stormer's tissues, and the gray area between what was considered ethical research and what the government considered illegal human experimentation.

She wanted to read that log.

15

Hands on his hips, deep in thought, Pete Tanner was at the entrance to the terminal laundry chute room when Rosemary stepped into the corridor.

A silence hung in the air—not the noiseless silence of inactivity, but more, a feeling of emptiness and foreboding. Rosemary reacted with a shudder. She walked toward Pete. "Brr, it's cold down here. Feels like a subterranean crypt."

"Yeah." He turned and dropped his arm around her shoulders. "Hi, Rosemary, I'm glad you came down."

Although she appreciated his physical warmth, she was exasperated with him. He seemed interested in juicier cases, preferring those junkheads who, in her estimation, could be caught buying, selling, shooting up, sniffing, or smoking after he'd found Maria's killer. Over the past two days, she'd seen Pete only twice and her elation at having him on the case had been dimmed by his absences.

"Did your desk sergeant tell you about a prowler in my apartment building last night?" she asked.

"He may have tried, but I was out all night."

"Good for you."

"Come on, Rosemary, I've already told you that my time isn't my own."

"Sorry."

"Who was the prowler?"

"I think he was the telephone repair man."

Pete looked at her sharply. "Tell me about it."

As they walked toward Charlie's office, Rosemary told Pete about the man at her door, the time of night, his appearance from Bob's description, his lie about the apartment number, everything she could remember.

At the office door, she turned to look at Pete. "I have to get two things off my chest."

"Do it."

"Don't you have a better method for receiving phone messages? I could bleed to death on my living room rug and you'd never know about it."

"Yes, I would. The first policeman to arrive at the scene of your demise would notify me immediately."

Rosemary was silent, unable to lift her spirits enough to enjoy his humor.

"Sit down here," he said, holding the back of a chair for her, "and tell me the second thing."

"You spend no time at Riverside. One would think Maria had been a gun moll for that drug ring."

Pete looked astonished. "Rosemary, baby, you know better than anyone that my flesh and bones don't have to be physically evident for me to get the job done and, anyway, the essentials of the crime are no longer here."

"People are, and in particular, the man who killed Maria. I'm not asking for a bodyguard, but can't you be more accessible?"

"I'll try." Pete sat at Charlie's desk. "I need some additional information about your syringe supplies, Rosemary. Will you help me?"

120

"What do you want to know?"

"From talking to Steve Hammond, I know that he orders syringes on a regular weekly basis according to departmental need. Most departments get their syringes directly from purchasing except the nursing units, which requisition from central supply where Frank Grinnell receives about ten cases of intramuscular syringes per week from purchasing. What I need to know is exactly how many syringes are dispensed from central supply and purchasing each day, where they go, and if the amounts have increased lately."

"That's easy," Rosemary said, "but why do you want me to find out?"

"Because I don't want anyone to know that I'm interested."

"Damn that drug ring," she said, more to herself than to Pete.

He pushed a hand through his brown hair. "We had a narcotic raid in Cambridge last night, picked up four addicts and a pusher. The police grilled the pusher until he was writhing in agony. It helps, sometimes, to let them start into cold turkey. Anyway, it seems as though the guy who is supplying the drugs is atypical."

"What do you mean?"

"We don't think he's an addict. He's called Smoke by the junkies, appears out of nowhere—no car, no bus, no taxi, just appears. He and the pusher make a brief exchange of junk and money, then Smoke disappears into the night. He apparently never talks. If the pusher has no money, Smoke delivers no goods, just fades away. They've tried following him but he's pretty good at his disappearing act. Anyway, according to the pusher, Smoke is the one who sells them syringes."

"Did the pusher describe him?" Rosemary asked.

"He dresses like one of them—you know, faded jeans, jacket, sunglasses."

Rosemary's patience was slipping away. "Why are you trying to link Riverside with this Smoke person? Every hospital uses syringes."

Pete swiveled the chair around, stood up, and poured two cups of coffee from the urn behind the desk. "Correct. We're checking Cambridge Hospital, Mount Auburn, several nursing homes, even a few pharmacies. Some use your vendor, some don't. As coincidence would have it, Riverside is the only one where a housekeeper died shortly after handling used syringes." He swiveled back and handed Rosemary a Styrofoam cup. "We've studied the trash coming from each nursing unit and we know approximately how many syringes the nurses are discarding each shift. Now I need to know how many they're receiving."

"It would take the mentality of a pithed toad for someone to continue swiping used syringes."

"He isn't. He's now selling new syringes."

"He?"

"Or she. That's why I want you to get me the distribution lists. In fact, I'd like to know how many syringes, all types and sizes, are ordered initially, how many arrive, who signs the receipt, where they're stored, how they're distributed, and by whom."

Rosemary's depression deepened. "How do you know that new ones are being sold?"

"During the raid last night, we found syringes still enclosed in their paper wrappers." He picked up the coroner's report and skimmed through the pages. "Maria had a piece of skin under a fingernail. The piece was tiny, almost a soft scraping from some area like the inner elbow. If it had been from the face, it would have had

122

hairs or large pores. We know her killer is right-handed from the way he knotted the gown tie. We know he was strong enough to lift her two-hundred-pound body, and we know he was familiar with the hospital." His voice trailed off.

Rosemary had been watching Pete's face; frank blue eyes with no veil of secrecy, the lines in his forehead deepening as he spoke, the corners of his mouth pulling back in a straight line, indicating his disgust, and she softened. "I'm sorry for getting so upset. What else can I do to help?"

"How about getting me a date with Riverside's assistant administrator tonight?"

A smile slowly grew on Rosemary's face. "She only eats medium rare steaks."

"And baked potato slathered with sour cream?"

"And a glass of wine?"

"Sure, and maybe I'll get her a Brigham's banana split afterwards."

"She'll go with you on one condition."

"Name it."

"That you return your bloody phone messages."

They both stood and Pete escorted her to the elevators.

"I almost forgot," she said. "Jayne McCarthy told me that Demerol, Dilaudid, and Valium were stolen last evening from Sinclair Three. Also, the grand master key is missing from one of the supervisor's key rings, which is odd because supervisors usually carry the rings."

"How many are there?"

"Two."

"Are they ever left unattended?"

"Yes, in a locked cabinet in the supervisor's office." She envisioned the cabinet and the door always standing ajar. "But they don't lock the office door."

An elevator arrived and several maintenance men got off.

"Don't worry," Pete said. "It'll show up. I'll come get you in your office at six o'clock."

Pete turned from the elevator and started back to Charlie's office, feeling frustrated. Rosemary had every right to be angry. He *was* spending too much time on the drug ring, yet he couldn't shake the notion that an im- . portant aspect of the ring was closely related to Riverside, and was just waiting for him to recognize it.

16

"O.R., Galvin here."

"This is Mrs. Cleaveland. Is Miss Pickle there?"

"Yup, hang on."

Rosemary glanced out her office window. In the west, the black billowing clouds parted slightly and a single shaft of bright sunshine poured through and danced briefly across the frozen river.

"Hello, Mrs. Cleaveland, may I help you?"

"Yes," Rosemary said. "Mrs. Emma Stormer had a breast biopsy done this morning. Could you tell me the results?"

"She had a left radical mastectomy for intraductile carcinoma. Mrs. Stormer will be leaving the recovery room shortly."

"Thank you." Rosemary pressed the telephone button, released it, and dialed again.

"Central supply."

"Is Frank Grinnell there, please?"

"Speaking."

"This is Mrs. Cleaveland. What have you found out about the unsterile O.R. packs, Frank?"

"Nothing yet, but all the autoclaves will be checked out once the case load clears a bit."

125

"Why wait?"

"Because Miss Pickle won't let us traipse through her inner parlor until her guests leave."

"You will check them today, though?"

"Oh sure."

"Also, will you send me a list of the number and variety of syringes you send daily to each nursing unit?"

"Why do you want to know?"

"I just do. Have any of the units increased their daily order lately?"

"No."

"Have you increased central's order?"

Frank hesitated.

"Have you?" Rosemary repeated.

"Steve Hammond just put in an extra large order," he admitted.

"Why?"

"I don't know."

"Send me that list as soon as you can, Frank." Rosemary pressed the telephone button, then dialed the number for purchasing.

"Good afternoon. This is Freda Felton in purchasing and supplies. May I help you?"

Rosemary wrinkled her nose at the girl's sugary salutation. "This is Mrs. Cleaveland; is Steve Hammond there?"

"Yes, Mr. Hammond is right here; just a moment, please."

Rosemary heard the girl cover the receiver and call for Steve, her voice dripping with confectionery overtones.

"Hi, what can I do for you?" Steve said.

"I need some information."

"Let's see. The Sack Cinema is showing *The Last Tango in Cambridge,* want to join me?"

"That movie was replaced today by *No No Not Yet.* Listen, Steve, can you send me a list of the number and variety of syringes you send daily to each of the departments?"

"Jaundice has that information."

"I know. I need all the other departments. I also need to know how many cases you order per week, all sizes, who signs for receipt, how that person checks the number ordered against the number received, where you store the cartons, who distributes them, and how."

"I place the order on Fridays and receive it on Mondays. It doesn't vary too much. I get thirteen . . . "

"Steve," Rosemary interrupted, "dictate it. I haven't time to listen now."

"All right."

"Have you increased your total order lately?"

"Yes, I ordered three additional cases of IM syringes."

"Why?"

"Because the doctors are shoving antibiotics into their patients, to protect them against negative culture reports."

"Send me the information as soon as you can."

Rosemary pressed down the telephone button. If doctors were ordering more antibiotics, then the nursing units had to be ordering more syringes and yet Frank had said he hadn't increased central supply's order. She was tempted to call Frank back but the clock on her desk read one-fifteen. She dialed extension ten ninety-two and listened as the telephone on Dr. Kreutzer's desk rang six times; he was at lunch. Replacing the receiver, she quickly left.

Feeling like a prowler, Rosemary opened the stairway door leading to the fourth floor, saw no one in the corridor, and went swiftly to Kreutzer's office. She tried the door but found it locked. As she pulled her personal grand master key from her pocket, she realized that her hands were trembling.

While trying to drum up an excuse for breaking into the office, should he be there, she silently unlocked the door, waited a moment, and then with a finger, gently pushed it. As it swung open, she scanned the room. Kreutzer was not there. Pushing it closed, she went swiftly to the counter where his private logbook was half hidden under notebooks and papers. Brushing them aside, she opened the book and leafed through to Emma Stormer's entry.

Jan 19, 514, Stormer . . . left breast . . . all specs benign. Path. no. 77428, slides 249-257. (intraductile carcinoma taken from Levine, Path. no. 77397, slides 154-163)

Benign! It couldn't be; Emma had had radical surgery. Confused, Rosemary read the entry again, her mind racing for an answer. Why would Harris do a radical if the tissue was benign? Why would Kreutzer call the tissue malignant? . . . Her eyes widened. He needs cancerous tissue for his research . . . but . . . maybe he also needs benign tissue! A sensation of horror prickled over her skin. She found the official hospital journal and opened it to the most recent entries. "Stormer . . . left breast . . . intraductile carcinoma . . ."

"Dear God," Rosemary whispered. She looked around quickly. If he caught her . . .

She grabbed the logbook, carefully opened the door, and glanced both ways down the corridor, then raced for the stairwell and, as if chased by ghosts, bounded down the stairs to the second floor.

"Peggy," she said, gasping for breath, "get hold of the chairman of the board, Mr. Highling. I *must* see him." Rosemary hurried into her office and sank into the chair. Both doctors were using Riverside's surgical patients as guinea pigs . . . for how long? With shaking fingers, she opened the logbook and scanned through the female names.

Jan 14, 342, Nikas, Nicole . . . left ovary . . . all specs benign. Path. no. 77398, slides 164-171.

Jan 14, 497, Levine, Henrietta . . . right breast . . . intraductile carcinoma. Path. no. 77397, slides 154-163

Here it is, she thought. Levine's slides were used to authenticate Stormer's fictitious malignancy.

Jan 13, 211, Cote, Mary . . . left breast . . . all specs benign. Path. no. 77396, slides 148-153. (Cystosarcoma phyllodes taken from Vaillancourt, Path. no. 64963, slides 99751-99756).

Another one! She grabbed a pencil and wrote down the names of patients with altered slides. Disgusting bastards, both of them, taking innocent, frightened women to surgery and intentionally hacking out normal tissues. They were outrageously violating their patients and scarring Riverside's reputation. She buzzed Peggy on the intercom. "Have you located Mr. Highling yet?"

"His secretary said he's still out for lunch. Do you want me to get you a sandwich or something?"

"No, I'm sick to my stomach."

"You are? Should I tell Mrs. McCarthy and Mr. Donovan to come back later?"

"Have them wait. I want you to come in first."

A moment later, Peggy was standing in front of Rosemary's desk.

"This logbook is extremely valuable, Peggy. I don't want anyone to know you have it." Rosemary inserted the book into a manila envelope. "Take it to the machine in fiscal services and make a copy of every page; then call me when you're finished. Also, would you get those medical records for me?" Rosemary handed her the list she had made of the research victims.

"What if Mr. Highling calls when I'm out?"

"Ask Miss Truslow to cover your phone."

"Okay." Peggy turned to leave.

"Remember, don't let anyone know what you're doing," Rosemary warned.

Peggy held a finger to her lips. "Trust agent 007."

"I do, explicitly. You can send Charlie and Jayne in."

Rosemary stood, smoothed her dress, and walked over to the window. According to the medical staff bylaws, she had the authority to suspend both physicians immediately. With Felix gone, her only source of support and direction was the chairman of the board, who would undoubtedly ask for evidence, which she had, as well as another medical opinion, which she would get.

Charlie Donovan cleared his throat. "Are you ready for rounds?" he asked.

"In a minute. Please have a seat."

Jayne and Charlie sat across from Rosemary's desk. She thumbed through several papers and found the lab requisitions. "I need your opinion on a laboratory problem." Rosemary handed Jayne six slips. "Take a look at these."

Jayne leafed through them quickly. "They look okay to me."

"Look at Joanne May's slip."

Jayne found and scrutinized the Addressograph imprint. "She's ninety-three!"

"And went back to a nursing home yesterday." Rosemary added.

Jayne looked at Charlie in disbelief.

Charlie smiled. "Maybe she was afraid of a positive test so she packed up her bedpan."

Rosemary turned to Jayne. "The Addressograph plates of discharged patients are not being destroyed and I think some member of your nursing staff is using them to run pregnancy tests for her friends."

"Horse manure," Jayne said. "One more damn thing to worry about. I'll have the unit secretaries turn the plates in to the front office."

Rosemary thought for a minute. "No, if we make a change she, or he, might devise an alternate scheme. I'd rather catch the person and put an end to it. Tell me, Jayne, once lab request slips are filled out how and when do they get up to the lab?"

"The messenger, who is supposed to make rounds every hour, picks up all the slips and urine specimens, puts them in the lab's biological refrigerator, and records them in the data book."

"Then could we have the supervisors check the refrigerator every hour or so? They could check the names on the slips against the discharge list."

"Sure."

"Let's see who we get."

"Oh, here," Jayne said and handed Rosemary several papers from her pocket. "My supervisors went over Lieutenant Tanner's list of employees on duty Monday night and Tuesday. We omitted the people on sick or vacation leave. And here's the list of float personnel you wanted. We eliminated the weekend and day shift floats because they wouldn't have been on duty when the narcotics were stolen."

"How many are left?"

"Fourteen. I've asked the supervisors to watch them all."

Rosemary put the papers on her desk. After rounds, she would go through both lists, read Dr. Kreutzer's log again, and look through the medical records of his victimized patients.

17

"When would be a good time to turn off the water supply to the Main building?" Charlie asked as he followed Jayne and Rosemary onto the elevator. "I need it off for an hour while we replace a worn toilet mechanism on this floor."

"How about a month from now?" Jayne replied. "That's all I need to worry about."

"How about tomorrow morning?" Charlie asked.

"How about Saturday morning, after the discharges go home?"

"Many of my regular men are off on Saturday. I only have a skeleton crew." He scratched his head. "I suppose we could wait but . . . "

"Good," Jayne said before he had a chance to change his mind, "let's do it Saturday morning."

On the first floor, they turned right and went into the Concord building. Like a rainbow, areas in a hospital cast their own colorful mood; red hot activity in the emergency department, mellow greens in the operating room suite, comforting blues in delivery, myriads of plaids and executive stripes in administration, juicy yellows and oranges in the pharmacy. One area, however, had no

definite color or mood, not because of personal prefer-
ence or hospital uniformity, but because of the nature of
the place. All plastic and cardboard, the purchasing and
storeroom area seemed bland.

Rosemary asked the secretary if Steve Hammond was
available to show them around his department. She
learned that he was busy with a salesman.

Back in the corridor, Jayne, Charlie, and Rosemary
stopped briefly and looked into the storeroom where
three workers were putting supplies from cardboard
boxes onto the shelves. Proceeding on to central supply,
they saw Frank Grinnell standing in front of a bank of
autoclaves, pointing and talking furiously with a service
repair man. When he saw them, he walked over,
scratching the hair on his yellow head. "Welcome. As you
can see, we're into round three with Lulu."

"Who's Lulu?" Jayne asked. "That serviceman?"

Frank missed her humor. "No, that's what we named the
new autoclave." They walked over as the serviceman disappeared behind the autoclave wall with his box of tools.

Frank patted Lulu's large closure wheel, then pointed to
the indicator dials. "See where she's supposed to start with
a vacuum phase? That's our problem. A twenty-six-inch
mercury vacuum must be drawn to prevent the dilution
of gas. Depending on what we've got inside, the vacuum
time ranges from five to forty-five minutes. Currently, she
won't click in."

Rosemary passed down the autoclave bank. "Will these
others take the load for you, until Lulu is repaired?"

"Yes, this one here does the same thing." He patted
another large gas autoclave. "But he's old, about fourteen
years, and I hate to put the pressure on him; he could go
any day too."

"How long will it take to fix this one?" Charlie asked.

"Serviceman says today, if it's not too complicated, and if she doesn't need new parts." They could hear the man pounding on Lulu's gas intake valves.

While Frank discussed Lulu's problem with Charlie and Jayne, Rosemary put a paper gown over her dress and went into a large room adjacent to the autoclaves. The room contained sterile supplies which were requisitioned to personnel through a dutch door leading to the corridor in the Main building.

On one row of stainless steel shelving, Rosemary found cases of assorted syringes. "Frank," she called, "would you come in here?"

Inserting his arms into a paper gown, he joined her amidst the rows of shelving. "Yes?"

"Is this your total supply of syringes, Frank, or do you store cases elsewhere?"

"Steve ordered a pile of extra syringes this week."

Frank was being as elusive as the home port of a space shot lost in the great void. "Damn it, would you answer my question?"

"Sure, sure."

"Well?"

"Yeah, that's all we've got. What you see is what you . . . "

"Steve told me that he ordered three extra cases to compensate for an increase in antibiotic injections."

"He said that?"

"Yes. If it's true, why hasn't *your* order increased?"

"I guess you could say it has."

Exasperated, Rosemary bit her lip for fear of saying something demeaning.

"Yeah, I guess you could say that," Frank repeated. "We've just changed to a three-day schedule," he explained. "Now we get them on Tuesdays, Thursdays, and Saturdays, so it's increased."

"Thank you. Get me that syringe list as soon as you can."

Back in the corridor, Jayne said, "That's cute. He really loves his autoclaves."

"Yeah," Charlie agreed, and kicked a wooden wedge out from under a door. "Damn things. I've told everyone down here not to prop doors open with these." He put the wedge into his pocket. Still upset with Frank, Rosemary pretended not to notice.

When they got to the pharmacy door, John Kelley was standing in front of the orange partitions dispensing pills.

"Our headless pharmacist," Jayne said. "Honestly, John, why don't you get that wall painted another color?"

"I like it," he answered, "makes me feel mysterious. What brings this triumvirate here on a visit?"

"Rounds," Rosemary said. "How are you doing?"

"Okay. The ether is gone and the procedure is written."

"Anything new on the narcotic theft?" Rosemary asked.

"So far nothing. My boys are going through doctors' orders now. I'll let you know if anything turns up."

As they crossed through the Main building and into Sinclair, Rosemary listened for her name over the public paging system. Certainly Peggy had found Mr. Highling by now, or at least knew where he could be reached. The waiting was putting a harder strain on her nerves. Proceeding down a flight of stairs, they stopped in front of the morgue door while Charlie looked for the key on his large ring.

"That reminds me," Rosemary said. "Have you located the supervisor's grand master key yet?"

"No," Jayne answered, "none of them took it off the ring, or so they say. I'll have another one made up."

Rosemary looked at her sharply. "No, you won't; you'll find the one you had."

"Okay, okay, we'll keep looking."

Charlie unlocked the door and they went to the autopsy area. Two stainless steel tables sat on wide pedestal bases in the middle of the room. Near the sink along the wall were two stainless steel rollaway tables, each with an array of basins, instruments, and orthopedic saws.

"Charlie," Rosemary said, and the word ping-ponged from one white tiled wall around to the others.

"I know, I know," he said. "They were supposed to be moved last week." The three stood in front of the wall shelving which was loaded with boxes of Christmas ornaments.

"I want you to get them moved right now," Rosemary said.

"Okay." He picked up the wall phone and called maintenance, furious that his men had failed him.

Jayne ran a finger down one of the autopsy tables. She looked at her finger. "Aranda Lilly was autopsied this morning. I heard she hemorrhaged from a ruptured ectopic pregnancy *and* that she had an IUD in place."

Charlie scratched his chin. "How can that be?"

"An IUD prevents the fertilized egg from implanting in the uterus, but not the tubes," Jayne explained. "If the egg, for some abnormal reason, can't pass from the tube down to the uterus, then it stays and grows and soon, pressure notwithstanding size, the tube explodes."

"Did she have a pregnancy test done?" Rosemary asked.

"No. Aside from Dr. Newbury being a lazy bastard, he accused Aranda of malingering!"

"Damn it!" Rosemary said angrily. "What is going on around here? Isn't anybody responsible for anything? I'm sick and tired of seeing and hearing stupid problems. How long have you known this about Dr. Newbury?"

Astonished, Jayne had taken a step backward. "Just this morning," she faltered, "I heard the nurses complaining about his lackadaisical attitude. He apparently knows all there is to know about medicine and considers the patients a bunch of sniveling hypochondriacs."

Rosemary looked from Jayne to Charlie. She was seething inside, a volcano on the verge of eruption, and slowly, with clipped words, she said, "As we continue on our rounds, I pray that we encounter no further difficulties in either of your departments. By the end of the day, Charlie will have removed the Christmas ornaments and the wooden wedges under doors." She stared at him. "The fire extinguishers will have current inspection stickers, the nitrous oxide tanks will have protective caps, and there will be a padlocked chain around them. Jayne will have information on autoclaves, narcotics—" Rosemary looked at her. "—the grand master key, and Dr. Newbury."

Jayne protested. "What can I do about him?"

"Talk to the medical director of the emergency department for starters."

Jayne shrugged.

"Let's keep going," Rosemary said. They left the morgue and went up one flight of stairs. She felt thwarted by Jayne and Charlie. Rather than helping her prepare the hospital for the accreditation inspection, they seemed to be throwing obstacles in her way; yet she needed their assistance and tried to suppress her anger.

The emergency department waiting area was jammed with people. While patients were hurried in and out of the treatment rooms, others waited on the straight metal chairs, lined up like pews, in front of the secretary's glass enclosed cage. Several loving mothers clasped frightened children to their breasts, while others smacked their already bruised children into pitiful complaisance.

A bright-eyed, expectant girl, arms wrapped around her

large abdomen, sat next to a slumped alcoholic whose head rolled around on his shoulders. When it rested on her shoulder, she shrugged and he let out a snort. Asthmatics wheezed and old tracheotomy patients whistled. A man holding his bleeding nose sat next to a boy massaging the thigh above his cast.

Suddenly an ambulance pulled up and two emergency medical technicians quickly wheeled in a stretcher upon which was a girl with the bone in her thigh completely broken so that her ankle rested close to her ear.

The secretary tried to stop them but they banged through the inner door and disappeared.

"Gad," said Charlie, "I've seen some bad breaks but that takes the cake."

"It's too busy for us to look around now," Rosemary said. "Furthermore, it's four o'clock. Let's go to one patient unit, then quit for today."

"Mrs. Cleaveland call ten fifty please. Mrs. Cleaveland, ten fifty."

"That's Peggy. You two go on up to Concord Five. I'll meet you there." Rosemary went to the secretary's telephone and dialed the extension number.

"Hi, Peggy, did you locate Mr. Highling?"

"Yes, I'll transfer the call. Where are you?"

"Extension ten eighty-one. Have you copied the book yet?"

"I'm still working on it; that stupid machine keeps breaking. Hang on."

Rosemary waited as Peggy transferred the call.

"Hello?"

"Hello, Mr. Highling, this is Rosemary Cleaveland. Thanks for returning my call."

"You're welcome, dear. What can I do for you?"

"I need your support on a grave problem involving two

of our physicians. Can you come to the hospital this afternoon?"

"If it involves the medical staff, shouldn't you discuss the problem with Dr. Harris?"

"He's one of them."

"One of whom?"

Rosemary chewed her lip and looked down at the secretary, suspecting that both his ears were perked. "Mr. Highling, I'm not in my office and can't talk freely right now. Can I call you back in five minutes?"

"I'm already late for an appointment, dear. As a matter of fact, I have three more appointments before a speaking engagement tonight."

Rosemary felt him slipping away. "Could I meet you somewhere between your appointments? This is a serious problem and I'm afraid more harm will be done if I don't take some action."

"What kind of action do you have in mind?"

"Suspending their clinical privileges."

The phone was silent for a moment. "How about ten-thirty tomorrow morning? I'll meet you in Felix's office."

Rosemary agreed, not pleased about waiting, but feeling somewhat assured that soon she would be able to stop Harris and Kreutzer from performing any further surgery. But on her way to Concord Five, she began having misgivings. Although Highling always seemed interested in hospital matters, she wondered how effective he would be without the full board around him. Well, she had Kreutzer's log, and would ask Pete for the name of a good forensic pathologist to substantiate her evidence.

She found Jayne and Charlie talking with the evening charge nurse. The four of them spot-checked the nursing unit, noting that aside from a few minor problems, the area appeared organized and tidy. As they returned to the nursing station, Jayne pushed open the clean utility room door and glanced inside.

"Wait a minute," she said and went in. "Look at this!" Jayne held up two douche bottles containing a green liquid. "What's in these?"

Fran Porter took a bottle, twisted off the cap, and smelled the contents. "Get Grit," she said. "Housekeeping uses the stuff to clean tile and windows."

Jayne yanked the bottle from the nurse's hand and sniffed. "What the sweet hell is Get Grit doing in a douche bottle?"

"Hard telling," Fran replied.

"How would you like to take a douche with this? You wouldn't, honey, nor would any of our patients. Get rid of it!" Jayne pushed the bottle at the nurse.

"Mrs. McCarthy, I have no control over house . . . "

"You have one second to pour that stuff down the sink."

Fran quickly opened the bottle and let it drain. She was angry with Jayne and her stomach churned as she clenched and unclenched her teeth.

"If I ever again find another unlabeled container up here . . . " Jayne grabbed the second bottle, opened the step can, and threw the bottle inside. "If I ever see douche containers filled with cleaning fluids, you're through." Jayne stormed out of the utility room.

"But Mrs. McCarthy . . . " Fran's words trailed off when Jayne pushed through the door to the Main building and disappeared. "Mrs. Cleaveland, honestly, I'll never let that happen again."

Rosemary patted the nurse's shoulder. "I'm sure you won't. Your nursing unit looks good, thank you."

Wearily, Rosemary and Charlie rode the elevator down.

After a period of silence, Charlie spoke aloud while he continued gazing at the floor. "You know, those detectives have been bugging everyone and I'd just love to know where Jayne McCarthy was early Tuesday morning."

Rosemary was astonished. "I hope you realize the seriousness of your implication, Charlie. Jayne was in early, but I doubt if she had a motive for being in the terminal laundry chute room."

"Not there, but maybe on another floor. Well, don't look at me so funny. It doesn't take a mind whiz to figure out that Maria went down the chute. Jayne's been acting weird lately, and keeping strange company," he added. "She could have been carrying a grudge against Maria."

The elevator door opened onto the second floor and Rosemary stepped off. "Goodnight, Charlie."

Plush navy carpeting which ran the length of the executive hallway deadened her footsteps. Several potted Schefflera with their outstretched green umbrellas broke the long expanse as did the spill of light from offices where she heard coat closets open and close and snatches of conversation.

The other doors were closed, including Jayne's, and Rosemary assumed she had departed in a fury. Jayne's sudden, violent reaction hadn't surprised Charlie. She wondered what he meant by strange company. Rosemary realized that she no longer knew who Jayne's close associates were.

In Peggy's office, she noticed a scribbled note on the desk.

Dear Mrs. Cleaveland:
   The you-know-what is in my bottom drawer. I'll have to finish copying it tomorrow because the machine finally quit altogether.

Peggy

Damn! Why hadn't Peggy used the machine in medical records, or the one in purchasing, or the mail room? Now she'd have to keep Kreutzer's log overnight. She removed the book from the desk, feeling repulsed as if she were handling putrefied flesh.

Far down the corridor she heard the elevator doors slide shut as the last of the secretaries left. All the sounds of a busy work day were gone and a strange quiet filled her ears.

18

With Dr. Kreutzer's log on her lap, Rosemary leaned across the desk and noted her appointment with Mr. Highling on her desk calendar. Her date with Pete Tanner was in half an hour, giving her time to look through Ted Fielding's computer run which sat on top of several stacks of papers. Opening the run, she noticed that Ted had condensed the information for her. With his blue accountant's pencil, he had crossed out the names of people who were not on duty Monday night or Tuesday morning. He had even programed the computer to spit out an A-to-Z run and a departmental run which included: name, job title, regular hours worked, and actual hours worked for the past seven days.

As she slowly turned the green and white striped pages, she heard the winter wind whip the building and whine as it tried to penetrate the windows. She was alone and although she had worked late many times, this evening the lack of human sounds was disturbing. She thought about the long corridor outside her door and realized that the plush carpeting muffled footsteps, that the vacant dark offices offered refuge to prowlers, that the stairwells gave access to the second floor from anywhere in the building, that the master key was still missing. She wasn't safe.

From her chair, she stared at the knob on her corridor door, trying to guess if it was locked. Not certain, she raced over and tested it. Satisfied, but feeling no safer, she surveyed the room, then opened the log to the middle pages and lowered it over the wire in the back of her Hudson River painting. The left side jutted out slightly. She pushed and jiggled until it hung straight. She then took the few copied pages, lifted the edge of her oriental rug, and pushed them around until they were flat against the floor. Satisfied that both log and pages were well hidden, Rosemary sat down at the desk.

After trying to compare Jayne's employee list with Ted's computer list, she realized that a thorough analysis would take several hours. Furthermore, Peggy could do it. She picked up the purchase orders for Compulectrics components and an electron microscope. With a red marker, she wrote *cancel* across each one. She found the medical staff bylaws freshly typed and signed by J. B. Harris, M.D. and began reading the section on summary suspension.

Kreutzer and Harris would lose their clinical privileges at Riverside the moment she imposed the suspensions. Within fourteen days, they could request a hearing before the medical staff executive committee. If this group of physicians decided that the suspensions must remain in effect, they would form an ad hoc committee to collect supportive evidence and to examine witnesses. At the same time, Harris and Kreutzer would have an opportunity for challenge by trying to prove that the charges lacked factual basis and the suspensions were, in some way, arbitrary, unreasonable, or capricious.

Rosemary stopped reading. The procedure was endless. The Joint Commission surveyors would have come and gone months before the governing board reached a final decision. If, of course, the executive committee agreed with her findings in the first place. She had to be very sure of her grounds. Could she possibly have misread the log?

Something shuffled in the corridor.

Looking up briefly, Rosemary listened, heard nothing, and continued reading the bylaws. In a way, Kreutzer didn't surprise her for he bordered on the totally absorbed, mad scientist. But J. B. Harris, fun-loving and gregarious, who joshed the physicians into completing their medical records, or chairing committees, or abiding by medical staff rules and regulations, he surprised her. Both men had a lot to lose, but . . .

The knob on Peggy's corridor door was being turned back and forth violently. Rising quickly, she ran into Peggy's office and listened. Someone was inserting a key into the slot.

"Peggy?" she called out.

Silence. She looked at the crack between the rug and the door and saw the shadow of two feet, standing perfectly still. "Jayne, is that you?"

No answer.

Rosemary's imagination went haywire as she had visions of Maria's murderer jamming the fat body into the laundry chute opening. The murderer! Quickly she returned to her office, and pressing the locking mechanism, slammed the interoffice door. Stumbling to the desk, she tried to extract the letter opener from its leather sheath. She heard desk drawers being flung to the ground.

The letter opener came loose and she held it between both hands, ready to attack. Peggy's filing cabinet drawers were yanked open and smashed closed. He was looking for something. Kreutzer! It had to be Kreutzer in search of his personal log. No, it can't be . . . he doesn't know I have it. He doesn't have the key to Peggy's office . . . unless . . . no, the key was lost yesterday. The slamming and banging stopped, followed by a disquieting silence.

She guessed that he was standing on the other side of the interoffice door, listening. Certainly he saw the light through the cracks, knew she was there. Rosemary's knees almost buckled when she noticed the knob turning slowly, a millimeter at a time. She tried to scream but her throat had constricted in fright.

Suddenly the door vibrated with a smashing thump. He was ramming it down! She whirled around the desk and was headed for the corridor door when the telephone rang. Her nerves jumped. She grabbed the receiver and tried to speak but her voice caught in her throat.

"Hello, Rosemary? It's Pete. Are you ready for dinner?"

Although the ramming had stopped, she heard heavy breathing. "Pete," she mouthed. "Pete, Pete." Her voice was returning. *"Lieutenant Tanner!"* She shouted more at the door than into the phone.

"Rosemary, what's the matter?" Pete demanded.

"Come quickly. Someone has broken into Peggy's office. He's . . . "

"On my way." He hung up but Rosemary held the telephone to her breast like a child unable to release her security blanket.

Within minutes, she heard Pete rattling the doorknob. "Rosemary, let me in."

She ran over, flung open the corridor door, and fell into his arms, tears beginning a rapid path down her cheeks. "Someone is in there," she said, pointing to Peggy's office.

Pete threw down his coat and drawing his revolver he turned the knob, eased the door open a fraction, then flung it back. Holding the gun with both hands, he crouched low and looked inside.

The person was gone. File drawers stood open, papers

flung everywhere, the desk on its side. Pete straightened up and walked in, followed by Rosemary who cautiously glanced behind the door.

While Pete checked the area around Peggy's desk, Rosemary closed the door, then stood with both arms wrapped across her chest.

"Edgy?" Pete asked.

"My skin is standing a foot out from my bones." She watched him make mental notations and, without moving, did the same. Her eyes caught a glimpse of something unusual poking out from under several books on the floor. "Pete?"

"Hmm?"

"Come look at this. Underneath those notebooks, see, that brown thing that looks like a hand."

Pete brushed aside the books and with his handkerchief, picked up a surgical glove and set it on the desk. "I'm getting Sergeant Dow over here."

While Pete was on the telephone, Rosemary returned to her office and removed the log from behind the painting. She placed it, and the copies from under the rug, into a manila envelope.

"What's that?" Pete asked when he finished speaking with Dow.

"Will you give me an honest opinion?"

"Sure."

She told Pete about Kreutzer and the log entries, then opened the book and pointed to Emma Stormer's notation. "Why would he record that all specimens were benign, then write that note about Levine's intraductile carcinoma slides?"

"I don't know. Maybe his research involves cross-checking tissues."

"Pete, the woman had her breast removed! This clearly

says to me that although her tissues were benign, he diagnosed them as malignant."

"Frozen sections can be wrong."

"True, but the tissue committee would know about them and they don't. False positives should be rare, but look how many we've had in the past few months."

She waited while Pete carefully studied page after page of the log. "You'll need more evidence, like Stormer's medical record, and that series of slides."

"If I get them, would you take everything to the crime lab?"

"Don't you have another pathologist who could give an objective evaluation?"

"Yes, but I've lost trust in our physicians for the present time, and I want this log out of the hospital."

Pete thought for a moment. "The crime lab doesn't handle this type of thing, but a buddy of mine is a forensic pathologist; he may agree to offer an opinion. You'll have to locate slides . . ." He looked at the entries. ". . . two-four-nine through two-five-seven and one-five-four through one-six-four."

They heard a knock on the door. "Hey, Lieutenant, let me in." Dow had arrived.

"Thank goodness," Rosemary said. "Let's get out of here."

While Rosemary put on her coat, hat, and lipstick, Pete explained the intrusion to Dow and two other officers. "I want every print lifted from this room." He handed the surgical glove to Dow. "This was on the floor near the door."

Pulling on his coat, he tucked the manila envelope under one arm, put his other around Rosemary's shoulders, and took her out through the loading dock area. Neither saw the tall figure, hidden between two laundry carts, watch them leave the hospital.

19

Rosemary followed Pete's car through the snowy streets of Cambridge and pulled into a parking space behind his. They trudged along the sidewalks of Harvard Square, Pete's arm around her shoulders as he recounted his Harvard days.

The maitre d' at Ferdinand's Restaurant led Pete and Rosemary to a cozy back room where dark purple swags and jabots lay heavily over the windows, where red-flocked wallpaper was toned deeper by dark wood paneling, where candles in the wall sconces cast a warm glow over the room and over the diners. Absorbed by the room, the myriad conversations created only a low hum.

The maitre d' placed menus and a wine list on a corner table and helped Rosemary remove her coat.

Rosemary brushed a hand across her brow, then searched through her purse for a bottle of aspirin. "Join me?" she asked Pete as she shook two tablets into her palm.

"No thanks."

"I have an exploded nuclear warhead inside my skull." She swallowed the pills with a sip of water.

A thin light from the wall sconce touched their faces. Pete leaned over and placed his hand on top of hers. "Intrusion is a terrifying experience, especially when you're not certain what the person wants."

"It had to have been Kreutzer, after his log. I wish I'd had a chance to return the damn thing." Rosemary's eyes widened. "Where *is* it?"

"In my car; it'll be safe there. Now tell me why you suspect Kreutzer."

"Because the man is desperate; he's working against time. The National Cancer Institute application must be submitted by January twenty-eighth, that's next Friday. And he won't get funded without a letter from the Potter Foundation guaranteeing their matched support. He hasn't received the letter, nor has he gotten some contributory papers from a Dr. Cristobal in Amsterdam. Added to that is the loss of his personal log which I'm sure he needs to keep his research in order. He may have seen Peggy at the copy machine and, not wanting to create a scene in fiscal services, waited until the second-floor personnel had gone home."

"Was Peggy's door locked?"

"Yes, but the person used a key to get in; I heard it."

"Who carries master keys?"

"Housekeeping. They usually clean offices in the evening."

"What about grand master keys?"

"I have one; Felix, Charlie, Jayne, and the supervisors have one on each key ring—six altogether. I told you one of theirs has been missing since yesterday."

"Do you think Kreutzer took it?"

The waiter placed martinis on the table and took their dinner order.

"Maybe, although I didn't take his log until today."

"Does Peggy keep anything valuable in her office—personnel checks, money, incriminating documents, anything like that?"

Rosemary looked at Pete. He obviously wasn't convinced of Kreutzer's guilt.

Pete continued. "It looked to me as if the intruder was after something filed in her drawers or cabinets . . . Would Charlie Donovan be after something in Peggy's office?"

"No. I'd give him almost any information he needed. Anyway, Riverside is his second home, sometimes his first when a major catastrophe gets him out of bed in the middle of the night."

"What about Mrs. McCarthy? Her temper is outrageous. She flew at Dow like a meteor."

"He's tough."

"She's tougher."

"I have noticed a recent change." Rosemary told him about the scene over the douche bottles. "With the inspection coming up, I thought she was displaying a case of nerves like the other department heads. She was right, but her reaction was too strong."

"Would she want something filed in Peggy's office?"

"I don't know what."

"Look, Rosemary, you've got an important job at the hospital, one of which is to keep a smooth ship, but you've got to roll around in the muck with me. Someone's been murdered, narcotics have been stolen, and now an office has been overturned. Forget your kind thoughts and consider everyone's ugly side. Charlie, for example, may not be the hospital homebody you take him for. He cheats on his wife, or so he brags. He also carries keys that open office doors and narcotic cabinets, and he's pretty crafty about his whereabouts. Jayne McCarthy is a bitch. Her silver tongue is devastating and I'm sure she's got more enemies than friends. She too can get into narcotics and offices, and she has no alibi for yesterday morning, at least none that anyone can substantiate. Don't get me wrong, I love your appreciation for humanity but this is a stinking world. Until the case is solved, you must believe that everyone you know is Maria's murderer. What's the worst thing you know about Jayne?"

"She picks on people."

"That's a start. What about Charlie?"

"He picks his nose."

Pete smiled. "Very suspicious; never trust a nose picker, he rarely knows where to hide the evidence."

The waiter placed their dinner on the table, poured the wine, and retreated into the kitchen.

Pete changed the subject and asked Rosemary about her marriage to his old friend Bill Cleaveland. "Do you mind telling me how he died?"

"No, although it's not my favorite subject. He was driving home one evening and some jerk ran a red light."

"A drunk jerk?"

Rosemary nodded; the remembrance was painful to her.

"How long had you been married?"

"Three years."

"It's a shame. Bill was one hell of a guy."

"What about you, Pete? Did you join the police force after graduation?"

He smiled broadly. "No indeed. My old man would have had a coronary even earlier if I had. He was priming me for president of his bank. I clerked and jerked through all the departments, counting money, buying up securities, and listening to overextended housewives give me crap about our faulty computer. It took years before I realized that banking wasn't my bag. When I quit my job, unfortunately my family quit me, flock, stock, and deniro."

"I'm sorry, Pete."

"Don't be. I see the kids now and then, and I love my job."

Rosemary detected a certain loneliness in his voice, despite his casual sarcasm. She looked down at her plate, wanting to tell him that she was lonely too, that their relationship was important to her. Since Bill's death, the years had built up layers of protective shielding, keeping out the hardships of life and straining her ability to love freely. Pete was like the sun; his warmth, understanding, and good nature were peeling away the heavy layers and it felt good.

As if he were reading her thoughts, he said, "Rosemary, I don't know if you're dating anyone, but I'd like to see you. My life gets involved and sometimes I forget that I need a personal life, away from police work. Could we get together this weekend?"

He was leaning close and she could see the sincerity in his eyes. "I'd love to, but can we leave it open? I don't know what tragedy will occur next at the hospital."

"We'll find time. Actually, we're planning another drug bust and I'm not sure which night it'll be."

"You haven't caught that Smoke fellow yet?"

"We're close. We have the pusher and the lab's going over a syringe we found during the raid last night."

"What kind were they?"

"Baker-Volk."

"We use that company," Rosemary moaned.

Pete nodded as he finished the last sip of his wine. "We can't figure how Smoke disappears after a drop-off. Anyway, he'll be selling to the pusher who'll have a high-powered rifle aimed at his head."

"You'd kill him?"

"He's junk, Rosemary. How sympathetic can you be with someone who pumps heroin into high school kids? If the

153

bastard beats tracks, he'll be back on the street within a day or two. A rifle shot would spook Smoke away, so to answer your questions, no, we're hoping the pusher will cooperate, with a rifle as an incentive."

He was right, she thought, right about those who maliciously took advantage of innocent people. "What have you found out about Maria Silva?"

"I think her inability to communicate easily in English kept her out of trouble. She was a hot-blooded Portuguese woman who enjoyed two or three friendships at the hospital, Jake's being one of them. She kept to herself, always came in and left on time, never missed a day of work; she was a classic hard worker. When her husband died several years ago, she moved in with her parents in Somerville. They live on Social Security and food stamps. Her father is hard of hearing and her mother is crippled with arthritis. They weren't too helpful."

"Poor woman," Rosemary murmured. "I feel bad for her and her parents and for all those women who had needless mastectomies. Imagine if those women ever knew their cancers were benign." She shook her head. "Medical ethics be damned. We've got a problem with false negatives in the lab and yet Kreutzer, who should be concerned, doesn't give a sweet damn. He's too busy hacking off normal tissues. Dr. Harris, who should be overseeing Riverside's surgical practices, is aiding and abetting Kreutzer. Meanwhile, the medical staff suspension bylaws are so complicated that it's almost impossible to get rid of the bastards. They protect each other, and even if some doctor knows first hand about another's evil doing, do you think he'd step forward and say, 'Gee, Mrs. Cleaveland, that Dr. Doe hasn't been sober for going on three months now.' They hide behind each other, like that game of match the pairs. You keep searching and searching

154

but someone keeps changing the boxes around. How can I build enthusiasm or dedication or group cohesion when the core is rotting out? I should tell those poor women about their omnipotent surgeon and pathologist."

"You won't."

"No?"

"No, because at this point, you'd only be acting on your own moral judgment. You haven't any solid evidence of misdoing."

"Maybe you're right, but for better or worse, my morals are what I want for Riverside."

"In the right dosage for the right disease. You can't always rely on your morality of good versus evil unless you've learned all there is to know about the situation, and even then, you can't ignore your own personal feelings. What if your mother shot a purse snatcher?"

"That's not fair. I'm not a bleeding heart liberal."

"But you get my drift."

After the waiter had removed their dinner plates, he returned with two steaming glasses of Irish coffee, Rosemary's favorite after-dinner drink. They sipped the whiskey-laced coffee, relishing their newly found friendship, finding comfort in being together.

"Thank you for being my psychiatrist tonight," Rosemary said.

"I'm not finished with you."

"Oh?"

"You haven't tried out my couch."

Rosemary laughed. "Where is your couch?"

"In Cambridge, on Buckingham Street."

"That's near me."

"Very close to you."

"Are you in an apartment or a house?"

"A small house—bedrooms, living room, the usual. Best

spot is my screened-in porch where the most delicious shish kebabs are grilled. You'll have to taste my cuisine sometime."

"I'd love to." Rosemary wanted to tell him how comfortable she felt with him, how much she appreciated his concern, but she decided not to disclose her feelings; not now, not with his concentration on the murder case and her problems at the hospital. Perhaps there would be a time.

In their separate cars, Pete followed to her apartment building, parked in front, and escorted her to the apartment door on the fourth floor.

"Headache gone?" he asked.

"Yup."

"Nothing else bothering you?"

"Yup."

"What?"

"You look like you're not going to accept my invitation for coffee."

"You're right, I'm not. I have an early day tomorrow."

"But I promised Skittles that I'd introduce you two. She has to approve my dates, you know."

"Skittles? Let's see. Is that your roommate?"

"No."

"Your crotchety mother who beats your dates with her fry pan?"

Rosemary was laughing. "Wrong again. Skittles is a very serious young lady who claws anyone she doesn't like."

Pete tapped his forehead. "How could I be so dumb? Of course, Skittles has to be your pet rat."

"Cat."

"Oh. Well, please give the young lady my regards and tell her not to worry. I'm only going to kiss you." He did, warmly, tenderly, but quickly. "If I kiss you any longer,

Skittles would disapprove."

"She might find herself temporarily locked in a closet."

Pete whistled as he ran down the stairs; the evening had been terrific. He crossed the street, stopped at his car, and searched his pockets for the key. He bent to unlock the door just as a familiar loud crack broke the snowy silence of the night. The bullet missed his head, shattered the side window, and exited through the opposite window. In an instant, Pete was flat on the street, looking furtively for movement from the buildings. He waited until the snow underneath him began melting and the slush seeped through his clothes, making him shiver. He raised his hand, opened the car door, and slipped onto the floor. He felt for his gun under the front seat, then turned on the two-way radio and summoned help. Remembering the manila envelope, he reached under the passenger seat until the edge of the envelope caught between his fingers. He let out a long sigh and pulled his hand back. That left another alternative. If Kreutzer wasn't after his log, then Smoke must be after him.

A moment later, he slid out of the passenger door and crawled behind a low brick wall. His mind began racing. Shit, he thought, I'm sitting here like the number one candlepin. Wherever he is, he can see me. He spotted a quick movement across the street, in the shadows of Rosemary's building. His hands and feet were frozen but he lifted his gun and aimed. Don't shiver, he told himself. The figure moved out of the shadows and onto the street. A dog, a silly damn dog. He felt like laughing.

Two cars sped quickly down Garden Street. When he saw the blue overhead lights, he jumped the brick wall and ran over. He climbed inside the first cruiser, appreciating the warmth. The officer of the second cruiser got in too and Pete explained the situation to them. With guns held tightly, they left the car, quickly circled the building, and met back on the street, all agreeing that the person had disappeared.

One of the officers called for an all-night watch of the building before the three cars drove off.

From his hiding place, a man watched the cars pull away. No one was was there to see the hatred in his eyes.

20

FRIDAY MORNING
January 21

Rosemary felt a tapping on her eyelid. "Go away, Skittles, let me sleep." The cat batted Rosemary's nose, then snuggled under her chin. "Honestly, you are nothing but a mangey, sawed-off, biodegradable hank of hair."

She peeled herself from between the sheets, flicked on the lamp, and peered out the window. "Triple trouble," she said. "First off, it's snowing. Secondly, my dear kitty, I think we're out of Nine Lives tuna, in which case you get leftover Beef Bourguignon; and third, I think I'm falling for Pete Tanner."

She journeyed into the bathroom. "Yes, indeedy," she said to the mirror, "Pete is a very, very nice fellow and if you're not careful, you'll fall head over pantyhose for him."

I haven't felt like this since Bill died, she thought. Pete's handsomer, less rugged, not the large athletic build. He's intelligent, he's polite, he's funny, he . . . I wonder what he's like in bed. She felt a tingling between her legs. I wonder if he's ever been raped by a horny assistant administrator. Trouble, Pete Tanner, you are in trouble.

Back in the bedroom, she pulled on a beige wool dress, threw the matching jacket over her arm, and went to the

159

kitchen where she fed Skittles before putting on her boots, jacket, coat, gloves, and hat. "I feel like the stuffing in a sausage casing. Goodbye Skittles, be sure you dust and vacuum today." She patted the cat on the head and left.

The hospital felt steamy as she passed through the Concord building and went up the stairs. Peggy wasn't due until eight o'clock, giving her time to glance through the papers on her desk and to organize her day. She unlocked Peggy's door and turned on the lights.

The office was in greater shambles than last night. Although probably thorough, Mike Dow had not straightened up before leaving. Peggy's desk was on its side, the chair was overturned, and papers lay strewn on top of the cabinets and on the floor. She shook her head. Reading and filing the papers would take Peggy a number of days.

She passed into her own office, switched on the lights, and hung her coat in the closet, glancing into the mirror at her face and deciding that the beige dress would look better hanging on a thrift shop rack. As she closed the door, she saw her desk and sucked in her breath. The contents of the drawers had been pulled out and flung across the floor. Paper shreds lay like confetti after a wedding.

Behind the desk, she knelt and tried to find Ted Fielding's computer sheets and the list of float personnel. They were gone! What the sweet hell did Sergeant Dow do? Damn you, she swore. He had no right . . . But Dow wouldn't shred her papers, he'd read or take them. An aura of suspicion mingled with the same nervous sensation that she'd felt last evening. She glanced around, half believing that the prowler still remained.

Her eyes wandered back to the shredded papers and she tried to remember what other items had been on her desk: Pete's list of personnel revised by Jayne, along with another listing of the fourteen float personnel on duty when the narcotics were stolen. Picking up the shreds, she placed them on her desk and bent over to examine them. She couldn't understand what anyone would want with personnel lists, but then other items had been on her desk too, like the financial report, purchase orders, Joint Commission notations, minutes of the last executive committee.

As she concentrated, a glint of light caught the corner of her eye, unusual, shimmering, causing her to glance over toward her chair. Rosemary leaned over to look again. Imbedded in the padded backrest was her brass letter opener.

Fear surged through her body and choked off her breath. She clutched for the edge of the desk, unable to take her eyes off the knife. Beginning to pant, she fumbled for the telephone, dialed, erred, redialed.

"Tanner here."

Silence.

"Who's on the phone?" he asked.

"Me, wait," she panted, trying to regain her voice. "Oh, Pete, someone has ransacked my office. . . . "

"Rosemary?"

" . . . there's a knife . . . "

"Don't touch anything. Is Peggy there?"

"No."

"When she arrives, take her for coffee. Are you all right?"

"Yes."

"Good, when we're finished, I'll call."

"Mrs. Cleaveland?" Peggy called from her office, loud enough for Rosemary to hear. "I know this is going to sound funny, but if you've been trying to straighten up around here, you did a lousy job."

Rosemary tried quickly to compose herself as she headed into Peggy's office. "Hang up your coat and let's go; I'm treating you to a full-course breakfast."

"No kidding? I'm famished." She hung up her coat and glanced at Rosemary. "Right now, huh?"

"Yup, I'm famished too." Rosemary wasn't at all hungry; in fact, she wondered if she could get coffee to her mouth without shaking it out of the cup.

"Well, let's hit the stainless steel trayway." They walked down the stairs and into the cafeteria. Breakfast aromas intermingled in the warm, steamy air. Rosemary ordered two breakfasts of eggs, bacon, and English muffins while Peggy filled the coffee cups, adding cream and sugar to her own.

Rosemary paid and followed Peggy to a table by the windows. Soon Peggy would ask about her office and Rosemary's mind raced for an answer. She wanted to be honest, yet she didn't want a secretary frozen in terror. She needed Peggy, and she loved her. Despite the twelve-year generation gap, they had grown to understand and respect each other.

"Unpique my curiosity," Peggy said. "How come a free breakfast?"

"It's be-kind-to-secretaries week."

"Nope, that's in the spring."

"Oh, well, let's see. My great aunt passed away and left me her millions. You're my first charitable donation."

Peggy put grape jelly on her muffin. "If your great aunt passed away, you'd be sailing the high seas. Furthermore, you'd be in mourning. I have this notion that we're here because some catastrophe occurred in my office, maybe the window caved in, or the pipes broke. You can tell me, I'm tough."

"Someone broke in and turned our offices upside down,

but fortunately I had taken the logbook with me when I left yesterday." Rosemary explained what had happened last night and this morning.

Peggy fell back into her chair. "Your letter opener? Are the detectives up there now?"

"Yes."

"So that's why we're here." Peggy thought for a moment. "Was anything stolen? Like my brand new, absolutely terriffic, IBM selectric that took approximately eight months to wheedle out of your budget? The nerve! If my typewriter is gone, I'll stick poison pins into the bastard. And my rainy day money! I had fifteen dollars in my drawer."

"Hold it, sport. I don't know what's missing, but if your supersonic Selectric, or your money, or anything is gone, I'll see that it's replaced."

The cafeteria telephone rang. Rosemary watched the cashier lift the receiver, nod quickly, look over, and point to her. She almost ran to the telephone.

"Hello, Pete?"

"No, it's John Kelley. I think we've caught our narcotic thief."

The news took Rosemary by surprise. "Who is it?" she asked him eagerly.

"An evening float nurse named Fran Porter. She's new at Riverside, been here about two months. Anyway, after checking through stacks of doctors' orders and not finding a clue, we then talked to a few patients. Nothing like a little pharmacy P.R., you know. I put two of my pharmacists on it yesterday. They worked through a list of four- and five-day-old postoperative patients; we figured they'd be easier to check than patients who really need pain killers, like for cancer. They visited each patient on the list and asked them questions about their medications, any side effects, things like that. They rechecked allergies, then zeroed in on their pain meds. Quite a few hadn't taken anything for pain in days, although their medication record indicated a regular evening dosage. Beside each notation on the med sheets were the initials F.P. and in the narcotic book, her name, F. Porter, R.N. Do you remember those medication carts with the missing Valium?"

"I remember."

"I kept a record of the nursing units and the dates. Well, once we had the staffing sheets from Ilse Jensen, I compared the staffing with the dates, and Fran Porter worked the prior evening shift in every single case."

"Nice work, John." Rosemary's spirits lifted slightly and she sighed. Someone was helping her, finally. Maybe the avalanche of insane problems was over; maybe now she'd be able to get a grip on things again.

"Are you there?" John asked.

"Yes, just thinking. Tell Jayne McCarthy. If you get those records together, the three of us can meet with Fran Porter when she comes on duty."

"I don't know how airtight my evidence is. Nailing someone on a narco rap is serious business. Ilse and I would like to catch her either stealing an ampul, or with one in her purse."

Rosemary was thoughtful. As much as she wanted the thief, she didn't want to endanger John or Ilse. Fran Porter, if she was into narcotics, might carry a gun.

"Mrs. Cleaveland?"

"Yes, John?"

"I know what you're thinking and it's okay. Ilse and I'll be careful. We want to assign Porter to the Gold Coast because it's full, and eight of the patients are anywhere from three to seven days postop, and there are six patients on Valium."

"It sounds like you've already worked out a plan."

"Yup," he answered with pride in his voice. "Want to hear it?"

"Not on the telephone. I'll stop by later today. Thank you, John. Thank you very, very much."

Rosemary hung up the receiver and went back to the table.

"That's nice," Peggy said.

"What's nice?"

"The smile on your face. Someone must have given you some good news."

"Excellent news." Rosemary told Peggy about the narcotic thief. She would hear about it soon enough and the news was best coming from Rosemary.

"Will you be there when they catch the nurse?"

"Absolutely." Rosemary remembered that Pete was planning a narcotic raid in Cambridge over the weekend and hoped it wasn't tonight. "Are you finished?" she asked Peggy, who nodded. "Then let's get going."

In the office, Pete had the telephone receiver resting on his shoulder as he dialed a number. He looked up when Rosemary arrived. "I was just about to call you. We're all finished here."

"What did you find?"

"We got several good prints but they could belong to you or Peggy."

Peggy's voice came through the door. "Hey, Mrs. Cleaveland, this man wants my fingerprints!"

Rosemary looked at Pete. He walked over to the door and said, "It's okay, Peggy. We need your prints for comparison." He looked back at Rosemary. "Yours, too. It'll only take a minute."

As the man rolled their fingers on an ink pad, Rosemary described the papers missing from her desk, then asked

Pete the significance of the letter opener, but he was evasive.

"The turkey was frustrated, Rosemary. He may not have found what he was after."

"I think it was a warning."

Although Pete answered no, he avoided her glance. She was about to suggest Kreutzer and his log but the telephone rang.

"It's Mabel Goldstein from medical records," Peggy said. "She says it's about a lawsuit."

Rosemary picked up the phone, not at all anxious to speak with Mabel. "What's this about a suit?" she asked.

"He wants the medical record, and it's incomplete. He wants it today. What am I going to do?"

"Mabel, who wants that record?"

"Some lawyer, a Mr. Robert Friend, wants Lucy Bonnet's record."

Rosemary glanced up at Pete who was leaning against the doorjamb, smoking a cigarette. His eyes were moving slowly up her body from her ankles toward her face. She blushed and, not wanting Pete to notice, she said quickly into the phone, "Does he have a court order?"

"He didn't say," Mabel replied.

Rosemary knew that Bob could get a court order or subpoena before the day was out, but Mabel needed time to complete the record. "Call him back and tell him that you're having trouble locating me, that you'll let him know in a short while. Then around two o'clock this afternoon, call him and ask him if he has a court order. If he doesn't, you'll have today and all weekend to finish the record. If he does, well, you'd better get busy."

"That gives me time." Mabel paused; she was not one who was easily satisfied. "But working on one record will mess up my whole day. I'll have to reorganize my staff, put a dictationist on filing, put my file girl on finding the doctor, put myself on . . . "

"Mabel, stop worrying. Just get Lucy Bonnet's record finished."

Rosemary replaced the receiver with a smile on her face. "That's hard-core dedication."

Pete pushed himself off the doorjamb and walked over to her. "What's the court order for?"

Rosemary briefly explained the incident.

"Does the father have a case?"

A dark shadow passed across her face. "He may. It depends on the lab. I understand that meningococcal meningitis can be mistaken for another disease process. The child was initially put on Erythromycin, the wrong antibiotic for meningitis, but a good one for an ear infection. Doctors don't usually perform spinal taps in their offices so they send patients to the emergency department. And once at the hospital, the patient becomes our responsibility." Rosemary sank into her chair. "I believe Lucy's medical care was adequate. I'm not sure, though, that our lab procedures are correct. Our new bacteriologist hasn't been running quality control checks because of Kreutzer's demands on her time."

Pete rested a leg on the edge of her desk and watched her.

Rosemary continued, "I can't figure out why Tony Carasino hasn't found the negative culture problem and called me back. Something must be going on up there." She looked up quickly. "Did you get the log over to your friend, the forensic pathologist?"

"I dropped it off last night. He'll phone me when he's looked it over. We can both go to talk to him about it."

"Good. Where will you be during the day, in case I get the slides?"

"Here until noon, then at headquarters, then out. Call the station; they'll locate me."

Rosemary's eyes widened. "I almost forgot to tell you. John Kelley and Ilse Jensen found our narcotic thief."

"Who?"

She told him what John and his pharmacists had done, and that Ilse and John had devised a plot for her capture that evening. "This could be significant. Fran Porter may also be the person who's been selling our syringes to outsiders. She may be connected with Maria's murder. . . ."

"Where does Porter live?"

"I can find out; wait a minute." She dialed the extension for personnel. "Betty? Look up an address for me. The name is Porter, Fran Porter." Rosemary listened intently to Betty's reply, then hung up. "Two-nine-three Third Street, where Jake Mason lived."

Pete whistled under his breath.

"What's the significance of that address?" she asked.

"It's a hot place for a lot of drug exchanging." Pete shook his head slowly. "I never considered that Smoke could be a woman."

21

"Damn the person who stole my log!"

"Calm down, Karl." J. B. Harris tried to pat Kreutzer's arm, but he pulled away.

"Don't you have any idea what this means? Without my personal log, I can't complete my studies."

"*Our* studies, Karl. Anyway, why can't you use that one?" J.B. asked, pointing to the hospital logbook. "Isn't the information the same?"

"No, my notes are more detailed."

"Have you looked around?"

"Of course. I've looked everywhere."

"Did you leave it at home?"

Exasperated to the point of smashing J.B. in the face, Kreutzer lashed out at him. "Cancel your surgery today; you're going to help me find my log."

"I can't do that, those patients need me."

"*I* need you and when we've gotten over half a million dollars, you'll need *me* even more."

J.B. hesitated. "No one would intentionally take that book and furthermore, your office is atrocious. The log is here somewhere, unless you threw it out by mistake."

"Someone *took* it, I know it."

"Ridiculous!"

Kreutzer whirled to face J.B. "Find my book. Now!"

Her thoughts still on Fran Porter, Rosemary opened the interoffice door and saw Charlie Donovan helping Peggy stuff papers back into file folders. Jayne was watching from Peggy's side chair, not helping, not talking, and looking as white as her uniform. They had planned to finish rounds this morning although each, for his or her own reasons, would have preferred to cancel until later, particularly Rosemary who intended to monitor Kreutzer's moves througout the day; at some point, he'd have to leave his office and his slides.

"What a bloody mess," Charlie said to Rosemary. "Why didn't you tell me? I'd have sent my men up to help out. This is terrible, terrible." He shook his head. "Peggy said some nut broke down the door and tried to steal her money. Now I tell you, destroying an office for a lousy fifteen bucks." He shook his head again.

Rosemary was relieved that Peggy had not mentioned the letter opener imbedded in the desk chair. With her emotions hanging one notch above a flood of tears, she didn't need an onrush of questions. As she watched Jayne and Charlie settle into her office chairs, she realized that her suspicions were totally centered on Kreutzer. Why not Jayne? she thought. Did she really not have an alibi as Pete had suggested? Could she be going on rounds with a murderer? What about Fran Porter? Could she have killed Maria Silva? Nothing made sense anymore.

"Where should we start?" Charlie asked.

His question brought Rosemary back to the present. "We should visit rehabilitation, intensive care, and dietary."

"The boiler room," Charlie added.

"Okay. Any areas of concern to you, Jayne?"

"No."

"How's the intensive care unit functioning while the electrical outlets are being converted?"

"With double A batteries."

"That's not funny."

Charlie interrupted. "We're using the emergency generator, when necessary." He looked at his watch. "Think we'll be finished by noon?"

"We must be. Several members of the Ladies Auxiliary are coming for lunch; they're bringing a large donation for the hospital."

With a bitter tone in her voice, Jayne said, "Those old farts? How do you stand them?"

"Jayne, I'm surprised at you. They volunteer thousands of hours each year, and they help to support not only the hospital but your nursing units as well."

"I wish they'd donate their mink coats to me."

Rosemary walked silently to the elevators with Jayne and Charlie and the three watched while the indicator flashed the floor numbers; one was descending. During the wait, Rosemary thought about Jayne. Whatever was wrong with her was growing worse. In the past, Jayne had thrown a few barbs at the Auxiliary, but always with humor, always knowing in the back of her mind how much the Auxiliary did for the hospital, and how much the employees counted on their volunteer hours.

The elevator took them down to the ground floor. They walked past the terminal laundry chute which was still cordoned off.

"Pain in the ass," Jayne muttered under her breath.

They went past Charlie's office where Pete was interrogating an employee. Mike Dow sat nearby, tapping his pencil on a note pad. Pete waved as they walked by.

171

"Shit," Jayne said, "this whole damn thing stinks. It's disrupted every nursing unit."

"Yeah," Charlie agreed, "maintenance too."

"Did you see them sitting on their butts? I thought they were supposed to be solving the crime of the century, but oh no, they hang around with nothing to do."

"In *my* office," Charlie said.

Rosemary was growing impatient with their attitudes. "Come on, you two. We have a job to do and we're *not* going to do it as usual; we're going to be one hundred and ten percent ready for that inspection." Charlie opened the boiler room door and led them down the steps.

Rosemary continued, "I want this hospital in shape. No more overlooking small details, Charlie. If we see anything amiss, I want it taken care of immediately. Same with you, Jayne. If you're doing your job, you won't have time for juvenile outbursts, or inflammatory remarks. Got it?" They nodded.

The boiler room was enormous and hummed with activity. Multicolored pipes labeled cold water, hot water, air, steam, ran in organized pathways along the ceiling. Red fire extinguishers dotted the walls, and on the support columns were control boxes which clicked periodically. At the end of the room, a fireman could be seen in his glass-enclosed office. He was reading printed sheets which ticked out from a computer.

Sheepishly, Charlie asked, "Do you want to see the preventive maintenance records? Over here, I have the humidity logs, want to see?" He started for the small office.

Rosemary stood still. "Do you have a problem?" she asked.

"No."

"Well, then, let's get out of here." Rosemary turned to go.

"Umm."

"What is it, Charlie?"

"We're going to turn off the water supply to the Main building tomorrow for an hour. Is that okay?"

Rosemary looked at Jayne. "I thought you agreed yesterday."

"I did."

Rosemary put one hand on Charlie's shoulder and the other on Jayne's. "I'd like you to meet Jayne McCarthy, Charlie. Apparently since yesterday you've forgotten who she is and what you'd planned."

Rosemary knew they were getting more aggravated and it was just what she wanted. She was giving them an alternative for their irritation, like closing the flue on one chimney and opening another. She wanted them to stop rechecking and start looking for problems and she was offering herself as their source of irritation for she believed it was better for them to criticize her than spend fruitless hours stewing about trivia.

"Let's go visit rehab, shall we?"

On the way, Rosemary asked if the Christmas decorations had been removed from the morgue and Charlie said they had.

Rehabilitation services consisted of physical therapy, occupational and speech therapies, audiometry, rehabilitation nursing, glaucoma screening, rheumatology, orthopedic services, and home care rehabilitation. The department occupied most of the third floor and, as a separate financial cost center, netted a sizable annual income, unlike nursing services, which had to spread its costs over medical and surgical charges and room rates.

Where nursing viewed itself as an unchallengable unit of professional expertise, other departments boasted their ability to support themselves financially and, as such, could afford additional personnel and equipment with ease while nursing had to beg for additional help. The air was always astir with undercurrents of rivalry.

In the whirlpool room, Jayne stuck her finger in a tub to check the temperature, and then casually opened a laundry hamper. "Look at this!" she bellowed. "Look at this, will you. Damn it!" She slammed the lid down and went from hamper to hamper. "Someone in this department is stealing our linens."

Rosemary had been waiting for an opportunity to bait Jayne; aggravate her to the point of disclosing what had recently changed her from a humorous wit to a cranky bitch. Rosemary quickly walked over to the linen closet and opened the door. "You're absolutely right, Jayne, look in here."

Jayne looked. "Underhanded bastards," she whispered. The shelves were stacked not only with physical therapy's pink towels and sheets, but white towels used on the nursing units. She turned on her heel and yelled, "Where's Sam Crowell?" Patients in the whirlpool baths looked at her, patients on the parallel bars looked at her, a patient learning to walk up the stairs of the wooden platform looked at her, therapists giving massages looked at her, but no one said a word.

Jayne glared at them, then stormed into the chief therapist's office where he was talking with a patient. "Excuse me," she said in a loud voice, "but I want to know why you've got our linens." She stood over him, hands on hips, her mouth in a thin straight line.

Sam Crowell had dealt with Jayne many times during his years at Riverside. She was tall, but he was taller and he stood up, placed his hands on his hips, and stared down at her.

"Well?" Jayne asked.

In a soft voice, Sam said, "Mrs. McCarthy, I understand you're upset but I don't ordinarily discuss problems in front of patients and I'm sure it's not your practice either." He waited while Jayne glanced down at the patient sitting in a chair next to Sam's desk, then continued, "If you will be so kind as to take yourself back to the closet, I'm sure you will notice rehab's stamp on each white towel. I am sorry that we also have white towels; however, pink ones are getting too expensive. When we're closed over the weekend, you have my permission to remove the white towels and dye them pink, as long as you dry, fold, and replace them by Monday morning. If that isn't satisfactory with you, then we can discuss this later today. Not now."

"Mr. Crowell . . . "

"Not now, Mrs. McCarthy, goodbye." Sam stood over her until she turned and marched out of his office.

Jayne kept marching until she reached the elevator. Rosemary and Charlie came up behind her. Jayne smashed the signal button with her palm, then turned. "What right does he have to talk to me like that? Who the hell does he think he is, implying I don't know about patients' welfare?" She started to pace. "Did you hear him? Rosemary, what are you going to do about it?"

Rosemary winced. Of all questions, that one irritated her the most. "No, Jayne, what are *you* going to do about it?"

"You're the acting administrator around here. I'm not in charge of him nor his nasty department."

"But you're the director of nursing and it's your problem."

"I know. Oh, he makes me mad."

Rosemary wanted to pursue the matter but she heard Peggy paging her. "That's my ten-thirty appointment. I'll catch up with you in the intensive care unit."

On her way to the office, Rosemary tried to review exactly what she would say to Mr. Highling.

"Mrs. Cleaveland," Peggy said, "I hated to bother you but Mr. Monroe is on the telephone and he said it was important."

Rosemary's heart sank and she whispered, "Where is Mr. Highling?"

"I'll find out."

"Hello, Felix, how are you feeling?"

"Fine, fine. The doctor still doesn't want me to work on Monday but I told him I'd sign myself out."

"That's not wise."

"Wisdom, my dear, is not the issue. How's the investigation?"

Rosemary glanced down at Peggy. As far as she could tell, both Felix and Peggy still believed that Jake had murdered Maria. She chose her words carefully. "The detectives are wrapping things up. They should be out of here by the first of the week."

"Good. I imagine their tedious interrogations have disrupted everyone's schedule." Felix paused. "I hate to bother you with an insignificant problem."

"What is it?"

"Well, I had a phone call from Dr. Kreutzer this morning and he's upset with you. As a matter of fact, Dr. Harris, according to Dr. Kreutzer, isn't too pleased either."

Rosemary bristled and caught herself before blurting out her findings. Felix would hear about the two doctors on Monday and she anticipated an overly solicitous attitude toward them. He would flatly refuse to hear the sordid story, claiming that physicians of such high esteem and position would never engage in unethical practices. "Dr. Kreutzer should know not to unburden his problems while you're a patient."

"I don't mind."

"That may be, but . . . " She stopped again, trying hard to control her temper. "Did he call just to complain abut me?"

"No, he wants an electron microscope."

"I canceled his purchase order."

"He told me, but why don't you put it through? It certainly would appease him."

Rosemary would have liked to appease Kreutzer with an immediate suspension of privileges. "I'll think about it, Felix. By the way, do you recall telling Steve Hammond that he could order Compulectric components instead of IBM?"

"I remember we talked about it."

"Did you give him approval?"

"Let's see. He was telling me all the pros and cons of both systems. I may have, Rosemary, I don't recall."

"Well, I canceled that one, too. When you get back, I think we should go over it with Steve."

"Okay."

They talked, and after a while, Felix seemed assured that all was running smoothly.

"How is he?" Peggy asked as she continued to collate medical record forms.

"Okay, I guess. He still insists on being here Monday morning."

"Is that bad?"

"I just don't want him to have a relapse."

"Well, you sound just like a mother hen."

"Cluck. Where's Mr. Highling?"

"The ever-so-efficient Miss Truslow doesn't know."

Rosemary turned on her heel and stormed down the

corridor to Miss Truslow's office. "What do you mean you don't know?" she said sharply to the older woman, who was wiping her nose with a tissue.

"What on earth are you talking about?"

"Where is the chairman of the board?"

"I haven't seen him. Oh, wait a minute, his secretary did call about an hour ago. I didn't think anything of the message because Mr. Monroe isn't here. She said that Mr. Highling had an important meeting with the Mayor and couldn't stop by this morning."

"Did she say when he *could* come in?"

"No."

"Miss Truslow, would you be kind enough to call Mr. Highling's office and find out when and where I can see him? I will meet him in the Mayor's office, I will even fly to Hong Kong to see him."

"Okay, dear, I'll see what I can do."

"It's extremely important. Page me when you get an appointment time."

Back in the corridor, Rosemary silently cursed the woman. She had to reach Highling and she had to get those slides. Stopping by her office, she used Peggy's phone to dial Kreutzer's number. When he answered, she hung up. "Damn it!"

"Naughty, naughty," Peggy said.

"Do me a favor. Call Miss Truslow every fifteen minutes and ask her if she's gotten me an appointment with Mr. Highling yet. Page me the minute she gets one, or has any news of his whereabouts. Give the woman one lousy project and she can't stop blowing her nose long enough to concentrate on it."

Just as Rosemary was about to leave, the telephone rang and Peggy said, "It's for you. Tom O'Leary."

"Ask him what he wants."

Peggy did. "It's important," she said to Rosemary and handed her the phone.

"What can I do for you, Tom?"

"Housekeeping won't respond, and I have a canister of soda exploding all over the storeroom."

His voice was low and scratchy. "Do you have a cold?" she asked.

He hesitated. "Yes, but that's not my problem."

"Have you called maintenance?"

"No one is helping me out, and I'm afraid more canisters will go."

"Okay, I'll be right there."

She hung up. "Peggy, please call the intensive care unit and if Charlie and Jayne are still there, tell them to wait for me. I'll see you later."

She walked by the cafeteria and kitchen and into a rear corridor. Two large metal doors were marked *Storeroom, Authorized Personnel Only*. She pushed them open and went inside. A series of ceiling mounted fluorescent tubes spread a glaring light over the enormous room and the dozens of industrial metal shelvings and beige tiled floor and walls. Unlike a neighborhood grocery store with colorful decorations and food displays, this room held large number-ten cans of food products and packages of dry goods.

"Tom?" she called, as she walked past several rows of shelving, looking down each aisle for his sturdy frame. At the end of the room, she stopped. The canisters were stored against the far back wall in a metal frame, which looked like an oversized wine rack. Aside from the hiss, the room was quiet. Where was he? This is certainly no emergency, she thought. Just as she started to leave, a series of fast footsteps from inside the room made her stop again. Click. The overhead lights went off.

Rosemary's heart skipped a beat. She strained to look through the items on the shelf. At the door, the figure of a man, slimmer than Tom O'Leary, was silhouetted by the outer corridor lights. He kicked the doorstop up and as the metal door swung shut, she saw that he remained inside the room with her, the two of them, alone. Her pulse quickened, and in the silence she could hear her heart throbbing in her ears. Why had she acted so irrationally? Why hadn't she brought Charlie? What did this man want?

With no windows to the outside, the storeroom was pitch black. The man was unable to see either, she rationalized, until she saw a small dot of light two aisles away. He had a flashlight. She began running down the aisle, toward the canisters, away from the light, hanging onto the shelving to guide her. At the end, she turned and stopped. He was coming down. She quickly kicked off her shoes and ran stocking-footed across the tiled floor, three aisles down, turned, and headed back up, but the light had also turned and was scanning each row. She might make the door if she hurried. The flashlight went out. Running her hand along the shelving, she went quickly toward the door, but a brace caught her left index finger and almost tore it from her hand. She cried out in pain. Taking a step backward to release her finger, she put it in her mouth and tasted the salty blood pouring out.

The canister had stopped hissing and, in the deadly silence, she heard a low chuckle. The hair on the nape of her neck bristled. She was about to make another run for the door when the flashlight snapped on again, one row over, between the canned goods. It shone directly into her face. She froze from fear.

"You're dead," she heard him say in that same low, scratchy voice.

The flashlight went out again and Rosemary wasn't certain which way he would head. She picked up a can and threw it in the direction of the entrance door, then turned and raced down the aisle away from the clatter. At the end, she turned left and ran by two rows, darted between and stopped. The light came on and she watched it move slowly across the back wall, across a red metal box, then down across the floor. He was bending down to peer under the shelves for her feet! She stepped up quickly. Hanging on tightly with her injured left hand, she found another smaller can and flung it over the tops of several rows. It was distraction enough, for he jumped up and began walking away from her. She held her breath and waited. Once he turned up a row, she stepped down and went toward the red metal box, inching along, careful not to knock over any supplies. With fingers feeling the wall tiles, she prayed for rescue. Suddenly, the gash on her index finger caught on something sharp and she almost screamed out in pain. But she had found it. Fumbling for the metal handle, she grabbed it with both hands and pulled.

Instantly, the bell above the fire alarm pull box resounded with a deafening blare. She ran into the opposite aisle and started for the door. It opened and she saw the man disappear into the corridor. By the time she got there, the door had closed again. As she pulled frantically on the knob, the door was flung open, almost knocking her down. A mob of dietary personnel, maintenance men, and employees poured through, some carrying fire extinguishers, all of them shouting orders to one another.

"Did anyone see a man leave this room?" she shouted, but no one heard her through the commotion.

22

"Go away."

"But I just want to help," Peggy said to Rosemary with the look of a child trying to soothe an angry adult.

Rosemary sat at her desk, left hand raised to keep down the swelling from ten stitches placed in her index finger. The novocaine was beginning to wear off, and intermittent jabs of pain dampened her spirits. She was alive, that helped. But Pete had been unreachable, her beige dress was blotched from scrubbing out the blood stains, the man had escaped unnoticed by any of the would-be firefighters, Miss Truslow hadn't found Highling, and she still did not have Kreutzer's slides.

Peggy stood by Rosemary's side and said, "Mrs. Vandervoor of the reputable society known as Riverside Hospital Auxiliary called to let you know that she's here and will greet all the ladies as they bustle into the private dining room. Mrs. Vandervoor sends her sympathies for your unfortunate mishap with your finger, but of course, nothing is more important than her hard workers who have coughed up twelve thousand dollars to be put toward wall furnishings in the pediatric unit."

Rosemary was smiling. "Enough prattle. Please tell her

that I'll be down in half an hour and to go ahead with the singalong, opening prayer, and fruit cup."

Alone, Rosemary's spirits fell again. Now she knew how Maria must have felt when confronted with her assailant. Was it the same person, she wondered. If so, what did she and Maria have in common? Maria was somehow involved with syringe thievery, while she was involved with Kreutzer and his log. Kreutzer would kill to get his personal journal back, but would he kill Maria for a handful of syringes? And would he actually kill, or buy off someone like that phony repairman.

Rosemary grew more confused. It can't be the same man, she thought. I know who's trying to kill me, and the patients in my hospital. He duped me once; it won't happen again. Standing up, she said aloud, "Okay, Pete, I'll get off your murder investigation; you go ahead and solve it. I intend to save my own skin, starting with our immaculately clean, but ever so deadly, laboratory."

She left her office and rushed up the stairs two at a time until the jarring increased the pain in her finger and she slowed down. Cautiously passing Kreutzer's office, she saw his back as he peered down the microscope, and a sudden fright bristled her skin. She hastened on to the lab, looking in bacteriology, chemistry, and finally spotting Tony Carasino in his office, eating a sandwich.

Rosemary closed the door and sat. "Tony, I haven't much time but I need to know if you've learned why those culture reports were negative."

He sipped his coffee, wiped his mouth again, and sat back. "I talked to Penny after you left yesterday and, honestly, I don't know what the problem could be."

"Have you talked to her today?"

"I haven't had time."

"Why not?"

"We're doing all those chemistries manually now, and I've been busy mixing solutions for Dr. Kreutzer."

Rosemary felt like punching him. Apparently the mixtures had taken precedence over more important matters. "You do remember, don't you, that we had two deaths because of faulty lab work."

"Wait a minute," he said indignantly, "those weren't our fault."

Rosemary couldn't believe her ears. He had cooperated yesterday and now he was denying the problem. "How do you know?"

"I just know."

"That is the dumbest thing I've ever heard you say. What's the matter with you? What's going on up here?"

"Nothing." He pointed to his sandwich. "Do you mind?"

"Yes, you can eat that later." She leaned forward. "I intend to call in a quality control specialist to check over this lab."

"I don't think you'll do that."

She looked at him carefully. "Oh, I see. You've been talking to Dr. Kreutzer."

"He mentioned that if anyone from the outside came snooping around the lab, I was to notify him immediately."

Exasperated, Rosemary asked, "Does Kreutzer pay your salary?"

"No."

"You work for the hospital and you take orders from me and I'm telling you right now, I want to know what is going on in that bacti lab. I want you to find out today, and I want you to call me before you leave." She stood up. "If one more patient dies, you might as well stay home Monday morning."

Tony slumped over and placed his head on his hands. "I guess I'd better tell you."

"Tell me what?" She sat down again and waited for him to continue.

"It's the Kraut. He's got everyone at their wits end, demanding this and that. Everyone wants to quit and it's all I can do to keep them coming back to work each day. He's still got Penny Abbott mixing up strange culture media for his experiments and I'm blowing my budget on the supplies." He looked up at Rosemary with tears in his eyes. "You know how much I love this laboratory, and everyone here. You've been patient with me, and Mr. Monroe has, too. I just hate to let you down but I can't break away from the man. I'm sure he'll be at Riverside for many years, especially if he gets those grants, so I've started looking for another job. We all have."

Through the years, Rosemary had learned how to cope with a weeping woman but she had difficulty comforting a tearful man. She waited patiently until he had blown his nose and dried his eyes.

"I didn't realize it was that bad, Tony."

"I couldn't begin to tell you how bad it really is. Behind his back, we talk about nasty things, like spilling lye on . . . I shouldn't be telling you this."

"You can tell me anything you want. I won't say a word."

"Even to the Kraut?"

"Even him. As a matter of fact, I agree with you. Only it wasn't lye I was thinking of. Something even more painful like burning all his research papers."

"That's not a bad idea." His thin smile turned to a broad grin. "We'll help you; just say the word. I've got an army of technicians who will go into action immediately."

She patted his arm. "I don't think Dr. Kreutzer will be bothering you much longer."

"Why?"

"You'll know soon enough, just believe me."

She left Tony and retraced her steps down the hallway. Kreutzer was not at the counter. She slowed and looked in the room. He could be in the men's room, and about to return, but it was her only chance. She slipped in and raced over to the counter. Picking up boxes of slides, she read each one for the series numbered one-fifty-four through two-fifty-seven. They weren't there.

Rosemary went to Kreutzer's desk and was about to open the top drawer when she noticed his briefcase half hidden under the desk. She stooped down and opened it. The boxes of slides were inside along with a KLM airline ticket. She opened the envelope. Kreutzer had booked a flight to Amsterdam, leaving Sunday evening. Tucking the two boxes under her arm, she quickly replaced the ticket and was sliding the briefcase under the desk when she heard someone enter the room. Her heart skipped a beat.

"Hi," a housekeeper said.

Rosemary tried to conceal a look of guilt, but her cheeks reddened. "Oh, hi," she answered.

"You looking for the doc?"

"I was but he must be at lunch. I'll come back later."

"Suit yourself." The woman was staring at the two boxes under Rosemary's arm.

"I was going to leave these . . . " She stopped, not wanting to incriminate herself further. "Are you in charge of cleaning this office?" she asked abruptly.

"Land sakes, no. He won't let any of us in here, but that's okay by me. Who wants to pick up them bloody skins? Not me, that's for sure. Did you see them? Over there on the floor." The woman was pointing to bits of human tissue around the stool.

"I see them," Rosemary mumbled as she brushed past the housekeeper. Once in the stairwell, she flew down to the second floor and prayed that the housekeeper would button her lip. Feeling nervous and guilty, she deposited the slides deep inside her desk drawer, called Pete, then went to join the Ladies Auxiliary in the dining room.

They had finished eating and were waiting impatiently for her. When she arrived, Mrs. Vandervoor swooped down on her as if she were the fatted calf.

Rosemary plastered a smile on her face as she accepted the Auxiliary's check in front of popping flashcubes. When the ceremony ended, she led them to the ambulatory services parking lot where, she noticed, Mrs. Vandervoor had parked in a space reserved for the handicapped. She waved goodbye and went to join Pete Tanner who had left a message for her to meet him at the forensic pathologist's office.

23

FRIDAY AFTERNOON
January 21

Invigorated by the crisp winter day, Rosemary waved goodbye to Pete and then bounded up the front steps of Riverside Hospital after visiting Pete's friend, Dr. McArdle, the forensic pathologist. The doctor's analysis of the slides and log had given her a sense of relief and accomplishment. But, typical of most peer reviewers, not only had he wanted to remain anonymous, but he also would disavow any knowledge of the problem should Dr. Kreutzer, Dr. Harris, or any investigator call him for clarification of his opinion. Rosemary didn't care. At least she had an objective opinion and it was enough for the present.

Peggy was leaning on her typewriter talking with Steve Hammond when Rosemary dashed in. "Bring your note pad," she said to Peggy.

"Can I see you for a moment?" Steve asked.

"In about ten minutes. Come in, Peggy." She closed the interoffice door, motioned Peggy to sit, then hid Kreutzer's journal, slides, and the photocopied medical records in her closet. "Has Miss Truslow found Mr. Highling yet?"

"No, but John Kelley has been trying to reach you."

"In all my born days, I have never met a man so totally exasperating." She leaned over and whispered, "You

188

haven't told anyone about my trip to the pathologist's office?"

"Not a peep."

"Good. I have two letters I want you to get ready. The first is to Kreutzer.

Dear Dr. Kreutzer:

As evidenced by your pathology logbook and slides numbered one-five-four through two-five-seven, you have breached your medical ethics agreement with Riverside Hospital and you are endangering the lives of certain female patients by misdiagnosing the incidence of malignant carcinoma.

Effective Monday, January twenty-fourth, by the authority vested in me by the executive committee of the board of management, I hereby revoke your clinical privileges at Riverside Hospital and summarily suspend you from your position as chief of pathology and the medical laboratory department.

An executive committee meeting will be held on Thursday, January twenty-seventh, at which time the committee will review the terms of the suspension and, thereafter, will inform you of their decision. In accordance with the bylaws of the medical staff, you may request an appellate review within seven days after the meeting.

Sincerely,
Rosemary W. Cleaveland
Acting Administrator

"Carbon copies go to Mr. Highling and Mr. Monroe." She watched Peggy finish her shorthand.

"Next, 'Dear Dr. Harris. As evidenced by Dr. Karl Kreutzer's pathology journal and slides number one-five-four through two-five-seven, you have breached your medical ethics agreement with Riverside Hospital by aiding and abetting in the gross misdiagnosis of certain of your surgical patients, and thereby, endangering their lives.' Follow Kreutzer's letter, Peggy; just substitute chief of surgery. Next, set up an executive meeting for Thursday."

"If I were you," Peggy said, "I'd grab the next rocket to the farthest black hole and not return. They must have done something very bad."

"They did. Make two extra copies for my file, and bring in the originals when you finish." Rosemary dictated a memo to the supervisors. "Okay, sport, send Steve in."

Remembering that he often monopolized time to such a degree that even a yawn couldn't discourage his endless chatter, she added, "Have Jayne stop by in five minutes."

Steve entered and, with a broad smile asked, "Are you free tonight?"

"No, I'm not."

"I just installed a totally absorbing, brute force cybernetic stereo system in my apartment. You'd love it."

"Sounds stimulating but high frequencies make my megahertz. Have a seat."

Steve laughed, placed his papers on the desk, and sat opposite Rosemary, his long legs crossed. Handsome in an impeccably tailored navy blazer and gray slacks, he looked as if he spent his entire salary on his appearance, and yet she noticed that his shoulders drooped, that he seemed tired.

"What did you do to your finger?" he asked.

Rosemary had her left hand raised in the air, unconsciously trying to keep down the swelling, although the stitches no longer bothered her. "I caught my finger in an electric can opener."

"Is it okay?"

"Feels terrific."

"How's the investigation going? They must be wrapping it up by now."

"I hope so. What can I do for you?"

Now that Steve was ensconced in the chair and had her attention, he apparently did not want to be rushed. "My stomach's been bothering me. It's that damned survey and everyone ordering everyone else around. They need more notebooks for their policy manuals. They need page dividers, typewriter ribbons, reams of erasable onionskin. They need Ajax, Windex, and floor wax. And they need it all yesterday."

Steve rarely complained. Apparently the department heads and personnel were more unnerved than she had suspected. "I hope your stomach mends soon. What have you got there?"

"These have been piling up. Will you sign them?" He handed her an assortment of purchase orders.

"I've put a freeze on spending," she warned.

"I know, but these are for small, everyday items."

She took them and started signing her name to the bottom of each.

"Machines seem to be falling apart as soon as they're installed. Do you think the changeover in electrical outlets has something to do with it? Maybe the wattage is too strong."

"I never thought about it. You could be right. I'll ask one of the computer engineers."

"Do you have that list of syringes I wanted?"

"My secretary is typing the list now."

Rosemary held up the next purchase order. "Another autoclave?"

"For the O.R."

"Where's the purchase evaluation sheet?"

"I didn't get one. The autoclave is part of the O.R.'s capital equipment budget for this year."

"Will the electrical components fit with the MOM III

computer system?"

"I guess so. Speaking of that, have you spoken with Mr. Monroe about Compuletrics?"

"Yes. He recalls discussing both systems but he can't remember approving the change. We'll review the matter when he returns."

"Do you still intend to cancel the order?"

"Yes."

"You'll be sorry."

"Why?"

"Because I could have saved the hospital over a hundred thousand dollars."

"I'm tired of talking about it, Steve. Thanks for stopping by."

Steve got out of the chair and came around the desk.

"How about a drink before your date."

"No, thank you."

He bent down, pushed a lock of curly hair away from Rosemary's ear, and whispered, "Tomorrow night, then. It's Saturday and we could catch a movie, some dinner, do things that would make you happy, you know."

She brushed him away. "No. I have work to do and I'm sure you do too."

The intercom on Rosemary's desk buzzed. She pressed a button. "Yes, Peggy?"

"Mrs. McCarthy is here to see you."

"Send her in."

Steve picked up the purchase orders. "One of these days, you'll find out what you're missing. Keep me in mind if you get lonely over the weekend." Steve winked at Jayne as they passed by each other.

"Sit down, Jayne," Rosemary said. "Would you like some coffee?"

"No."

"I would, wait right here."

Rosemary went into Peggy's office and asked her to bring two large cups of coffee. Picking up the telephone on Peggy's desk, she called the number for the pharmacy.

"Kelley here."

"Hi, it's Mrs. Cleaveland. Has Jayne been down to see you today?"

"No, not today."

"What about Lieutenant Tanner?"

"He sure did, thank goodness. He gave us a few super pointers on catching a thief."

"What's the plan?"

He outlined what he, Ilse, and Pete were scheming for Fran's capture. "Will you be around?" he asked.

"I'll be back here at ten o'clock tonight."

"See you then."

"Good luck, John, and please be careful."

"We will, thank you."

Rosemary went back in to her office and saw that Jayne was standing over by the window, looking at the panorama of Boston. She turned and, with eyes averted, went over to a chair and sat. "You wanted to see me?"

"Just to talk. Do you feel the nursing units are prepared for the inspection?"

"Yes."

"What do you intend to do about Fran Porter?"

"Who? Oh, her, fire her I suppose."

"What's John Kelley's plan?"

"He and Ilse are setting her up tonight."

"I know that, what's their plan?"

Jayne hesitated. "Do *you* know what it is?"

"I'm asking you."

"I'm not sure." Jayne rose from her chair. "Can I use the telephone? I'll find out."

"No, you may not use my telephone. I want to know the plan, and if you don't know, then I want you to tell me why not."

"I've been busy."

"Doing what?"

"Loose ends, tying up the loose ends before next Monday." She sat down.

"What loose ends?"

"You know, medical staff crap, and nursing policies, staffing, things like that."

"What are you doing tonight?"

Jayne's face darkened. "That's none of your business."

"No? Well, I have news for you. At ten tonight you'll be right here at Riverside with John Kelley, Ilse Jensen, Lieutenant Tanner, and myself. You'll assist John and Ilse with their plans, so I suggest you find out what they are before you leave today."

"Why don't you tell me?"

"It's your job to find out."

"My job, my job, to hell with my job. You can take my job and shove it up the Auxiliary's mink-tufted assholes. If I were the administrator around this sordid joint, I'd run things a lot differently."

"You're not the administrator."

"Thank the sweet Lord."

Rosemary leaned forward, her voice low and serious. "Before you leave today, I want you to find out what John and Ilse have planned for tonight, and I want you to be here. I want you to find that grand master key. I want you . . ."

Jayne started crying.

Rosemary pulled open her desk drawer and withdrew a tissue. She handed it to Jayne. "I want you to tell me if the central supply and O.R. autoclaves are working now, and what the problem was."

Jayne bent her head and let the tears flow.

Rosemary watched her for a moment, then went into Peggy's office and returned with the coffee.

Jayne blew her nose and dabbed her red eyes. "You expect too much from me."

Rosemary placed the cups on her desk, sat, and waited patiently for Jayne to continue, offering neither sympathy nor encouragement for she felt that Jayne was on the verge of revelation and any interruption would spoil the moment.

"Nothing makes sense anymore," Jayne said. "I don't know, maybe it's my fault." Her attitude was changing as she slipped inside herself, leaving behind an appearance of dejected self-pity, for her head bent low again and she began picking at the folds in her uniform. A heavy sigh escaped from her lips. "I have other things on my mind."

"Can you tell me?"

"You wouldn't understand."

Rosemary chose her words carefully. "In my own way," she started, "as imperfect as it may be, I try hard to keep Riverside and all our employees on an even keel and it bothers me when someone I respect succumbs to pressures. I believe in your abilities because your past work has been excellent; your nurses believe in you too. Riverside is going through some difficult times right now and, unfortunately, we're the ones who must try to keep the boat above the rip. If we submerge, we pull their morale and our credibility down with us. I'm not asking to be your mentor although I would like to help you. But, please, don't keep this thing locked tight inside. I can see what it's doing to you."

With head still bent, Jayne whispered, "I know you want to help. You see, I've been dating someone and, well, we broke up recently."

Rosemary hid her astonishment. Jayne had never mentioned dissatisfaction with her husband, her marriage, her family, nor had she revealed any inclination toward needing another man's bed. "I'm sorry to hear that."

"Don't be. It's over and there's nothing you can do about it." She blew her nose and stood up. "Is that all?"

"Please don't go."

"It's late and you've given me tons of work."

"Right now, your problem is more important. Can you tell me about this fellow?"

Jayne cocked her head and said incredulously, "Fellow? What fellow?"

Feeling as if their entire conversation had passed overhead, Rosemary said, "The man you were dating."

"It makes no difference if you know, because it's over, but the last time I removed Betty McCloud's panties, she was no man." Jayne opened the door and left.

24

FRIDAY AFTERNOON
January 21

Stunned at the news, Rosemary fell back in her chair. Betty and Jayne having an affair? She mentally reviewed her last few meetings with both women but they had hidden their inclinations and their affair well. At least it was over. Jayne would continue to ache while her heart mended, but in the meantime she might begin to concentrate on her job again, and with so many other problems at the hospital, Rosemary didn't want to rally her through the sorrows of a carnal misfortune.

She opened the door to Peggy's office and saw two letters on the desk. "Are these ready for my signature?"

"Yes, here." Peggy handed her a pen. "I'm about to make copies of the executive committee notice."

"Do it quickly; they must go out today. Then call Dr. Harris's office and ask where I can find him."

"Excuse me ladies, may I bother you?"

They looked up and saw J. B. Harris. His sudden appearance bordered on telepathy. The doctor hesitated when he saw the two women staring at him. "It's me, J.B. You look as if you're seeing a ghost."

"Please come in," Rosemary said, "I have something to ask you, too."

As J.B. entered, he smiled at Peggy and, tilting his head sideways, tried to read her typed sheets. She leaned forward and covered the papers with her elbow.

He glanced around furtively, then followed Rosemary into her office.

"Sit there, J.B. What can I do for you?"

Instead of sitting, the doctor leaned against a bookshelf. "Oh, nothing, really." His eyes darted over her desk, around the room, and across the floor.

"You look as if you're about to have a seizure."

"Ah, no, I'm all right; I'm always all right. By the way, do you have the medical staff bylaws? I think I need to read them again."

"I have a copy right here." As she thumbed through papers, J.B. strode over, shuffled through an adjacent pile, and read each heading.

Rosemary reached over and placed her hand on the stack. "I have a suspicion that the bylaws are furthest from your mind."

"What?"

Rosemary found the document and handed it to J. B. "I would suggest you read article nine on corrective action."

"Why?"

"As of Monday morning, you and Dr. Kreutzer are summarily suspended from Riverside, although your surgical privileges are revoked as of this minute. The weekend will give you time to find another surgeon for your inpatients."

J.B. smiled broadly. "That's a good one, Rosemary. I'll have to use it on several of my surgical dissenters; it'll bring them right into line again."

"I'm not joking."

The doctor's grin vanished. "Oh, yes you are. Let me remind you, young lady, that it is the sole responsibility of the president of the medical staff to impose any measure

198

of corrective action on peers; the authority rests on my shoulders, not yours. Secondly, I would like to know the reason behind your derogatory implications. You are walking on dangerous ground."

"Let me remind *you*, Doctor, that summary suspensions may be imposed by the chief executive officer or by the executive committee of either the medical staff or the governing body, as well as yourself. However, since you are indeed implicated, you have forfeited your authority, and since I am acting for Mr. Monroe, I am now responsible for stopping you and Kreutzer. You know the reason perfectly well, but to joggle your memory, you have been surgically removing benign tissues. Under your aegis, Dr. Kreutzer has falsified medical records and tampered with pathological findings."

"Whose records?" he yelled.

"Emma Stormer, Mary Cote, . . ."

"Mrs. Stormer had intraductile carcinoma!"

"Her tissues were benign."

"Wait *just* a minute," he said, his voice low and serious. "Don't accuse me of something about which you have no medical knowledge and no surgical expertise. That woman had a breast malignancy that would have killed her if I hadn't removed it."

"Come on, J.B., you know perfectly well that Kreutzer's frozen section was benign . . ."

"I have no such knowledge."

". . . that he used slides from a patient named Levine for Stormer's permanent findings . . ."

J.B. slammed his fist on the desk. "No! None of that is true, not one bit. I don't understand you, Rosemary; only a madman would dream up such hideous lies."

"Dr. Kreutzer's journal, slides, and copies of your medical records have been analyzed by a State forensic pathologist, who concurs that your practices fall grossly short of what the medical profession defines as ethical."

"What State pathologist?"

"At this time, I'm not at liberty to reveal his name."

"Then you are lying. You saw no such person." J.B.'s face reddened and his nostrils flared. "Those tissues were malignant and I don't care who says differently. Kreutzer is tops in his field; he would never consciously misdiagnose a case, never."

Rosemary sank back into her chair and glared at him. "And *you* would never think of misdiagnosing a case."

"I don't do the frozen diagnosis. In any event, and in any case, you know I would never, in a million years, take a woman to surgery if I thought she was benign." He began pacing the room. "This is absurd. What am I doing trying to justify my actions to you?" He turned sharply and pointed a finger in her face. "Prove what you say is true; show me the journal and slides, show me where I tampered with the records."

"I would but they're not in the hospital," she lied.

His hand dropped. "You left everything with a State pathologist?"

"No." She buzzed Peggy. "Bring me those letters, will you?"

J.B. was pacing again. "You will be very sorry. Medical records belong to Riverside Hospital and cannot be removed except by subpoena or court order."

"That's right."

Peggy came in and handed Rosemary the letters. "Can I go home now?"

"Sure. Have a nice weekend and I'll see you Monday." She waited until Peggy left, then pulled out a letter. "Read this, J.B., and find your replacement over the weekend."

He snatched the paper, scanned its contents, and tore it

up. "We'll see who is suspended on Monday." The doctor stormed out, muttering obscenities under his breath.

Rosemary caught herself shivering, a reaction caused by a mixture of anger, boldness, and surprise at J.B.'s sudden visit. She had needed time to absorb Dr. McArdle's statements, time to prepare her case logically, time to reflect on her own judgments. Instead, J.B. had caught her off guard and ill prepared. What the hell, she thought, whether the facts were presented on a cushion of marshmallows or in a jar of bees, both men had to be stopped. She guessed that J.B., like a provoked child anxious to tattle, was now in search of Kreutzer.

She swiveled around in her chair, expecting to see Boston's twinkling skylight, but the black evening had absorbed the view and changed the window into a mirror which reflected her office, and herself, looking lonely and vulnerable. She studied her reflection for a moment, then bowed her head and listened to the hushed silence. No typewriters clacked, no voices chattered down the hall, no telephones rang. The silence billowed up around her, and she felt the same stifled eeriness of the night before.

She shook her head and picked up the letter of suspension to Kreutzer. She considered leaving it on his desk but that solution offered no guarantee that he would read it. She couldn't wait until morning, when more people would be around, because she was required to give him a seven-day notice before the board meeting. She considered asking Pete to escort her upstairs, or one of the supervisors; surely Ilse Jensen would go with her.

Why worry about his reading it, she rationalized. Kreutzer would be on his way to Amsterdam on Sunday night. Suddenly, her thoughts were disturbed by the sound of metal turning against metal and, with quickened pulse, she looked up and reached for her letter opener.

Again, the same sound, but this time she realized the doorknob was twisting in its metal housing. Her free hand moved toward the telephone.

"Mrs. Cleaveland, if you're in there, open up; it's Mike Dow."

Still carrying her letter opener, she headed for the door, although a certain pinch of caution kept her from opening it. "Are you alone?" she asked, hoping Pete was with him.

"Yeah. I want you to look over some papers; the ones from your office."

The moment she twisted the knob, he brushed by and went to her desk. She watched him tuck his hat under an arm and spread the sheets out. "I'm glad you're here," she said.

Dow glanced up briefly. "You thought the intruder had returned. I don't blame you, I guess. It took a while to tape these papers back together, but they're readable. This here's a computer run that lists employees alphabetically. This one lists them by department. Look familiar?"

Rosemary nodded.

Dow moved to another stack. "Let me know if these are complete."

Rosemary looked through the original copy of the medical staff bylaws. "Yes, it's all here."

They went through several other documents before Dow asked, "Is anything missing, anything at all?"

Rosemary leafed through the papers again while trying to recall what had been on her desk: manila folders with the daily mail, medical records of outpatients with suspected gonorrhea. "Some lab requisitions are missing, and purchase orders." She explained the pregnancy tests for old ladies, and then thought about the purchase orders. "One was for computer components, one for an electron microscope, several for annual equipment replacements."

"All from the same companies you've used in the past?"

"I think so. Actually, I didn't pay attention. Why?"

Dow straightened up. "In my conversations with Fielding, he mentioned that several recent purchases were from companies you've never used in the past."

"That's not unusual."

"It is when the new company charges more for the product, and you buy it."

Ted Fielding had never expressed these suspicions to her before. Why would he tell Dow and not her, she wondered.

"In my book," Dow continued, "inflated pricing means collusion."

"Kickbacks?" Rosemary asked with an edge of irritation in her voice.

"That's another word for the same thing. I understand that only you and Mr. Monroe approve large orders."

Rosemary knew that, in the past, Felix had authorized capital purchases without consulting her or Ted Fielding. She didn't agree with the practice for it meant vendor favoritism. On the other hand, she thought, Felix's intentions had been to speed up the purchasing process, not to form collusive networks or kickback schemes.

Dow continued. "Did you know that Mr. Monroe purchased a new chemistry machine last week? The one you've got didn't break down until this week. Now why would he do a thing like that? In fact, Tony Carasino and Dr. Kreutzer were expecting another leased one, and Steve Hammond and Ted Fielding say they never saw an approved purchase order for the new one."

"It *is* curious, Sergeant Dow, but I can't see how Mr. Monroe or a chemistry machine relate to Maria's murder."

"Collusion could. That lab slip in her pocket was an order for distilled water. It's not an expensive item, but the amounts purchased over a year add up. Four months ago, this hospital switched intravenous fluid companies to one that costs more, not less . . ."

"Sergant Dow, don't you understand that with items as important as I.V. fluids, it's not the cost, but the quality."

" . . . Nursing service wanted plastic bottles, not glass. I asked Frank Grinnell, who says he orders anything nursing wants."

"Now that everyone seems to be on the line, how about Ted Fielding? Once department heads establish their budgets for the upcoming year, Ted's the one who spreads the cost of equipment over the fiscal year. He then oversees the entire purchasing procedure, from pre order to post receipt. And what about Steve Hammond? If department heads don't request specific vendors, then Steve is responsible for evaluating the market and prices. He and Ted work together on all purchase orders. Mr. Monroe may not consult with Ted, or Steve, but Ted doesn't have to consult with anyone once the budget has administrative approval."

Dow had picked up a pencil and was studying the eraser. "Makes me wonder why he mentioned it."

"We're all getting paranoid." She shrugged. "For all I know, Kreutzer broke in here to get his log, saw his electron microscope purchase order on my desk . . . it already had an official P.O. number . . . forged my signature, or Mr. Monroe's, and sent it to the company. Who'd be the wiser, until maybe next year when someone asked me about it? By the way, where's Pete?"

"Setting up for a drug raid."

"Will it be tonight?"

Dow looked at her. "Why do you want to know?"

Rosemary swallowed a fresh wave of irritation. With Dow in her office, she felt insulated against another intrusion and she decided to use his presence advantageously.

204

"Because I'm hoping he'll be here when we catch Fran Porter."

"He'll be here." Dow put the pencil on the desk. "I've got to be going."

"Wait a minute." Rosemary picked up a letter. "Will you do me a favor and take this to Dr. Kreutzer?"

"What's it for?"

"It suspends his medical privileges. I'm sure Pete's told you about him."

"I'm not a courier, lady."

"It will take just a few minutes, and you even agreed that I was vulnerable. Please?"

Dow took the envelope. "I'm not doing this as a favor to you. Tanner asked me to keep an eye on you and I'm just following orders."

After Dow left, Rosemary grabbed the log, slides, and records, and fled down the hall to Felix's office. Without lights on, she bumped her shin on Miss Truslow's desk and let out a mild oath. She pushed open the mahogany door and waited a moment while her eyes adapted to the thin light coming from the skyline of Kenmore Square. The library of books lining the walls of Felix's office offered many hiding places. She chose a row of administrative policy manuals and slipped the log and slides behind them.

As she stepped back into the corridor, she saw a beam of light spread slowly across the blue carpeting as the door leading from the stairway down the hall opened. Rosemary drew back into the shadows of Miss Truslow's office and watched, half expecting Dow to emerge. A large figure, dressed in jeans and a work shirt, walked swiftly to Rosemary's office door.

She held a hand over her mouth to keep from breathing.

He knelt down, looked under her door, then retraced his steps to the stairwell.

For a few minutes, Rosemary panted as her heart pounded in her body and ears like a jackhammer. She couldn't return to her office, couldn't risk going to the lab in search of Dow, couldn't use the elevator or stairway anyway, so she remained for a long time in the shadows, her back pressed against the door, eyes riveted down the empty hall.

25

FRIDAY NIGHT
January 21

"Let's wind it up, kids," Fran Porter called to her evening staff. She asked everyone for a brief report on their patients, then doled out a few last-minute assignments. When the staff had left the nursing station, she ducked under the counter and withdrew her purse from a cabinet. Glancing up quickly, satisfied that no one was nearby, she pulled four ampuls of morphine, one of Demerol, and several packages of Valium from her pocket and stuffed them into her purse. She stood up quickly and carried her purse into the utility room, kicking the door closed behind her.

Once closed, she didn't see Ilse Jensen sneak by the door.

Ordinarily, Fran got her urine specimens to the lab earlier, but the Gold Coast had been unusually busy. Workng fast, knowing that any staff member might walk in, she pulled out seven bottles of urine from her purse and lined them up on the counter.

She had already imprinted the lab requisitions and gummed labels, and she attached a label to each bottle. Pulling a small notebook from her purse, she marked which patient's name she had used for each of her friends and associates. She charged them ten dollars for a pregnancy test and the requests were beginning to exceed the number of discharged patients.

She picked up all the bottles and placed them into a wire basket marked. LAB SPECS ONLY. She opened the door and stepped out just as one of the the other nurses came around the corner.

"Stealing toilet paper again, huh, Fran?"

The nurse laughed and Fran laughed with her. "No, this week the hospital is giving away those tiny bars of soap." The nurse passed by and went into a patient's room.

Fran was almost at the nurses' station when an aide called out, "Miss Porter? Mr. Mongenetti needs something for pain."

"Okay." Fran grabbed his medical record and went into the medication room. Placing her purse on the counter, she scanned through the chart, noting that an hour ago he had refused a pain shot but she had recorded one given and had stolen the ampul of morphine. Now she was in a dilemma. If she took out another ampul, the count would be off, but she needed that stolen ampul for her boyfriend. She stood and thought for a moment. She wasn't due back on duty until Monday so if her boyfriend had to ration his drugs over the weekend, he'd be furious. She opened the record. Mr. Mongenetti's doctor had ordered morphine for pain every three hours as needed. Quickly, she changed the time she had previously recorded from ten to eight o'clock. That would have to do. She unlocked the narcotic box and withdrew the box of morphine which contained two ampuls. Pulling one out, she placed it on the counter, then opened the narcotic book, wrote the patient's name, room number, drug, amount given, her name, her initials, and subtracting one ampul from the total count, she wrote three. Wait a minute, she thought, the count says three and yet only one is left.

She looked at the box, then at the narcotic sheet and a quickening sense of panic raised small beads of perspiration on her brow. Something was wrong. Had she miscounted sometime during the evening? She couldn't remember and forced her mind to work. Of all nights, of all times, why now? She tried to think back through the night but she couldn't concentrate. She wanted to get home and didn't need the aggravation of calling the supervisor, recounting, making out an incident report, the whole time-consuming, shitty procedure. She snapped open her purse and quickly took out two ampuls of morphine, placed them in the box, then locked the cabinet.

One of the night nurses rapped on the door, and Fran's edgy nerves made her jump from surprise. "Hey, Fran, come on out and start report; we're all waiting."

"Keep your socks on, I'll be right there." She opened a needle and syringe and drew up the morphine. Grabbing her purse and a betadine sponge, she raced out the door. "I'll be right there; let me give this injection," she said over her shoulder.

"Hurry up, will you?" one of the nurses said.

Within minutes, Fran was back, giving her report. She was halfway through when, out of the corner of her eye, she noticed Ilse Jensen walk into the unit, stop at the medication room door, insert a key, and go inside. What the hell was Ilse doing in the medication room? Ordinarily, Fran could maintain her composure under difficult circumstances, but a slow feeling of dread crept over her.

"Come on, Fran," a nurse said. "You're not making any sense. Mr. Lothers did not have an appendectomy; he had his left toe amputated."

Fran apologized and continued, keeping the medication door in her peripheral vision. The door opened and she looked over. Ilse was carrying a narcotic box and the narcotic logbook; she pulled the door closed, did not look at the station, but walked directly off the unit.

Unable to quickly fabricate a sensible excuse for her multiple narcotic count errors, Fran became desperate to flee the hospital, and finished her report by skimming over the last few patient names, mentioning only their vital signs and any condition changes.

"You must have a hot date tonight, Fran. That was the worst report I've ever received."

"Sorry. Listen, will you count narcotics alone? That hot date is waiting and I'd hate to stand him up." She unpinned the keys from her pocket and handed them to the night nurse.

"Ah, spring love in the middle of winter. Does my heart good," the nurse said.

"See ya." With her pocketbook held tightly under her arm, Fran ran out of the station.

Several other evening nurses were waiting by the elevator when she arrived. She boarded with them and rode down. One of them asked Fran if she wanted to have a beer with them, but she declined.

When the elevator door opened, Ilse and John were standing, looking in, searching the faces. They stepped aside to let the nurses pass. Fran followed closely behind the others with her head bent.

"Wait a minute, Miss Porter," Ilse demanded.

Sheer panic almost collapsed Fran's knees.

"Come with me."

The other nurses glanced at Ilse and saw she was looking at Fran.

"I'm off duty now," Fran said, and started forward, but

the others had stopped walking and were watching.

"Open your purse, Miss Porter," John ordered.

"I'm off duty and my purse is none of your business." She noticed the assistant administrator was standing close by with the director of nursing and a man in a three-piece suit. They were looking at her. She had to get out of there fast. She laughed nervously and said, "Come on girls, let's go get that beer. These people think they can invade my privacy." She stepped forward again but the others didn't move.

"Ladies," John said to the nurses, "I believe Miss Porter has stolen some narcotics from the Gold Coast and I'd like her to open her purse and show you that I'm wrong."

The nurses glanced from John to Fran and back again. One of them said, "Come on, Fran, do as he says, and let's get out of here."

"No."

The nurse spoke again. "If you took the drugs, then heaven help you."

Another nurse added, "Open your purse, dear; show the nice man you only carry lipstick and a hankie." They laughed and the first nurse said, "Yeah, maybe a few girlie items too." She gave the second nurse a nudge.

Ilse interjected, "I would advise you to come with us and save yourself the embarrassment of opening your purse in front of your friends." She gently took Fran's elbow. Fran winced but gave in and let Ilse lead her down the corridor, followed by John, Jayne, Pete, and Rosemary.

26

FRIDAY NIGHT
January 21

Rosemary kicked off her lamb's wool slippers, turned off her bedside light, and snuggled down between the sheets that were warmed by an electric blanket. With Skittles wrapped in a ball beside her, she listened to the soft purr and reviewed Fran's capture.

After a shouting battle between Fran and Jayne, John carefully explained how he and Ilse Jensen had laid the trap by altering the morphine count. In the end, Fran confessed to stealing drugs and running a pregnancy testing business for her friends. She was fired from her position at Riverside and taken to police headquarters.

Rosemary felt relief mixed with remorse for the young nurse who would have difficulty practicing her profession in another hospital, or at least in an institution that required a recommendation. She guessed that Fran might find work in a small nursing home; they were usually desperate for registered professional nurses.

She rolled over and enjoyed the comfort of her bed. It had been a long day. The telephone rang and she listened to the rings, not wanting to move her body, but it was insistent and she reached over and picked up the receiver. "Hello?"

Silence.

"Hello, who is this?"

The voice was low and scratchy, the same voice she'd heard in the storeroom. "You're a dead woman."

A cold fear swept over her and she couldn't speak.

"You'll be dead by tomorrow afternoon." The phone clicked.

She held the receiver tightly and forced her mind to think. Who was he? Why did he want to kill her? She threw the receiver down and jumped out of bed.

At her apartment door, she checked the dead bolt, the chain, and then propped the back of a wooden chair under the knob. Not satisfied, she found several empty bottles and put them around the door. If it opened, the bottles would fall on one another and wake her up.

A drawer in the kitchen contained all her sharp cutlery. She found a butcher knife, then began checking the windows to make certain each was locked. Without slippers or bathrobe, she felt goose bumps rise on her skin from the chill in the apartment.

Skittles watched from the warm bed as Rosemary felt the locks on the windows. She then climbed into bed, placed the knife on her bedside table, and dialed Pete's number. He wasn't home. She dialed the police station and waited while someone went off to look for him.

"He's not here, lady, can I help you?"

"Yes. My name is Rosemary Cleaveland; he knows me. Please have him return my call the minute he checks in."

"Will do."

"Repeat the message, please."

"What?"

"Repeat the message."

"Listen, lady, I'm not illiterate."

"Did you write it down?"

"Yes."

"Well then, repeat it."

"Call Cleveland."

Rosemary chewed her bottom lip as her temper began rising. "Call Cleveland? Do you know how many people live in Cleveland, Ohio? Hundreds of thousands of people live in Cleveland, Ohio. I am not Cleveland, Ohio, I am Rosemary Cleaveland, spelled C-L-E-A-V-E-L-A-N-D. If you would be so kind as to write down my name correctly and add the time and date of my call, maybe, just perhaps, Lieutenant Tanner will get the message, if of course, you bother to give it to him, which you haven't bothered doing in the past. My life has been threatened and if my body is removed from my apartment by a medical examiner tomorrow morning, you can rest assured that I'll visit you from the grave and haunt you the rest of your life. Got it?" She slammed down the phone, more angry now than frightened.

Just as she was climbing back under the covers, the phone rang again and she jerked it up to her ear. "Pete?"

"You've got twelve hours to live."

27

SATURDAY MORNING
January 22

Since the first death threat, Rosemary's assailant had telephoned every hour. "You have eleven hours to live," he wheezed through the receiver at four in the morning. At five, she blurted out, "Who *is* this? What have I *done* to you?" But she heard only his evil reminder, "You have ten hours to live."

Rosemary moved to the living room couch carrying the telephone, a glass of brandy, the butcher knife, and a down comforter. The lights were on and the couch gave her a straight view of the apartment door. With Skittles on her lap, she waited, wide-eyed, until six when the phone rang again, and again, and again. She didn't answer it at first, but the persistent ring chewed at her brain. She lifted the receiver and held it away from her ear. After a few seconds, she replaced it in the cradle.

She was too tired to be afraid, too tired to think what she should do. The stillness in her apartment, broken softly by the cat's soft purring, lulled her to sleep.

Before long, the ringing awakened her and she strained to read the clock on the mantel. Six twenty-eight; too early for his call, she thought, and picked up the receiver.

"Rosemary? It's Pete. I just got your message, are you all right?"

"My nerves are shot," she answered while rubbing her eyes to brush away the heaviness of exhaustion.

"What's going on?"

As Rosemary explained the telephone calls, Pete cursed under his breath. "I'm sending a detective over to stay with you and trace your calls. Continue to answer as you've been doing, and do not, repeat, do *not* leave your apartment today."

"Don't worry, I won't. Will you come over? I'd rather spend the day with you."

"Ditto, but I can't right now. I'll check in now and then, on the half hour. Anyway, Sergeant Bosche plays a mean game of Scrabble. How's your finger?"

"Throbbing. How's Fran Porter?"

"I let her go."

"What?"

"She and I talked for quite some time. She lives at two-nine-three Third Street and, she's familiar with the drug ring. Her boyfriend often entertains shooters and cocainuts. She's willing to feed me information."

The address sparked a memory. "Jake Mason lived there," Rosemary said.

"Right. Is everything okay at Riverside?"

"Are you kidding? I suspended Harris and Kreutzer yesterday." Rosemary explained her confrontation with Dr. Harris, the letters, and Dow's suspicions about collusion. Pete listened without interruption and she couldn't guess what he was thinking.

"Are Kreutzer's slides and log hidden securely?"

"Yes."

"Good. When Bosche arrives, the password will be shish kebab. Open your door for no one else. I'll check with you later. Sleep tight."

"I will." Rosemary stayed awake until seven when the phone rang again. She lifted the receiver and listened.

"You've got only eight hours to live."

Unable to control herself, she yelled *"bastard"* into the receiver and then slammed it down, relieved that Bosche, whoever he was, would be with her soon.

The shut-off valves for the water and steam pipes that fed the Main building were in a mechanical room in the basement. Hank Downey from maintenance unlocked the door, entered, checked his watch to be certain the time was exactly ten o'clock, then turned both the hot and cold water off. He had fifteen minutes to change the flushing mechanism in the ladies room toilet on the second floor. If he took too long, the Gold Coast patients on the fifth floor would begin complaining, but worse, dietary on the first floor would have trouble getting lunch ready.

With his box of tools and equipment, he went to the second floor, placed a MAN WORKING sign on the bathroom door, and went inside to replace the worn mechanism. The job was tedious and, as he worked in the confined space, sweat began pouring down his brow. He glanced at his watch; only seven minutes left. He worked faster and was soon finished. On his way downstairs, he reached for the Tridione pills he carried for infrequent epilepsy attacks and popped one in his mouth. He felt lightheaded from too much tension and sweat.

In the mechanical room, he headed over to the shut-off valves. He turned the hot water on and, just as he raised his hand to the cold valve, his eyes glazed over. For a few seconds, he stood, like a man frozen in time, hand raised but motionless, eyes glassy; the only movement was the slight rhythmic twitching of his eyebrows.

As the seizure passed, Hank shuddered and clutched his nauseous stomach. He left, unaware that the cold water was still off, unaware that, just above him, pressure in the dietary sprayer hose was building and beginning to force hot water against a faulty cold-water check valve.

During their second game of Scrabble, Rosemary and Sergeant Bosche heard the telephone ring, both realizing that it wasn't the right time for the assailant's call. She picked up the receiver. "Hello?"

"Hello, dear," her mother said.

"Mom? How are you, how's Dad?"

"We're fine, but Rosemary, you haven't called us in ages and we're worried about you."

"I've been busy," Rosemary apologized.

"We'd like to have you come down for dinner and stay the night if you can."

"I'd love to come, Mom, but . . . " She glanced at Bosche, "I can't get there until this evening."

"Good, dear, we'll look forward to seeing you."

Rosemary hung up, genuinely pleased that her mother had called. She missed her parents and would enjoy not only seeing them, but getting away from Cambridge and her apartment. After she told Sergeant Bosche her plans, he phoned headquarters and left a message for Pete to call.

Dr. Bailey stopped by the nurses' station on the Gold Coast, pulled Rip Easterbrook's medical record from the rack and wrote a discharge order. He spoke briefly with the head nurse and left. The nurse went into Rip's room to tell him that he could go home today.

A lascivious blonde with a purple blouse and tight black skirt was sitting on the rumpled bed, smoking a cigarette.

She recrossed her legs and took a short drag from the cigarette which, the nurse, thought, smelled like hemp.

"Thanks, dearie," the blonde said, "but we already know."

Rip threw his bathrobe into a suitcase. "We already know," he repeated, then went into the bathroom and shut the door to work on his daily constitutional.

What Rip didn't know was that the nurses considered him an obnoxious, supercilious pain in the ass. He knew the food was lousy, the surgery had set him back two weeks on his filming, and the pneumonia was entirely Riverside's fault, but he didn't know that the nurses would cheer when he left.

After·he yanked on the toilet tissue, he reached around and pushed the handle. The toilet gurgled, sputtered, then exploded into a geyser of boiling water, scorching his rear, and shooting him off the toilet seat.

"YEEEOOOW!" he screeched at the top of his lungs.

Penny Abbott was not scheduled to work on weekends, but she was a competent, experienced, and conscientious girl, in spite of what everyone thought. She wasn't dedicated to Riverside as Tony was, but she was dedicated to her work. And a bacteriologist with a bad reputation cannot easily find another job. She had to find the reason for those no-growth cultures and she chose to work today, without pay.

For several hours, she had been running quality control checks. She appraised the tools, glassware, permanent and disposable equipment, and was now in the small lab storeroom checking the media, reactants, and standards when she heard Dr. Kreutzer bellowing at some poor technician. Penny grimaced, hoping the Kraut would choke to death on his own tongue.

She looked down at the carton in front of her. The culture broth inside was dated to expire in three days. She wondered if perhaps it had expired already. A day or two could get lost, although it hadn't happened yet. She found a paper and pencil, jotted down several numbers and dates, and returned to the bacti lab. She dialed information for the telephone number of the manufacturer, got it, and called. Introducing herself, she asked the man for information on her supplies.

"What's the lot number?" he asked.

"BLX-898-7002-R," she responded.

The phone was silent for a few minutes. "Hello?"

"Yes, I'm here."

"Don't have a very big lab there, do you?"

"I beg your pardon?"

"I said, you don't run many cultures. You an independent?"

"We run thousands of cultures a month, and no, this is a large, acute care hospital."

"Well, toots, you dragged that stuff up from the basement 'cause it's last year's media. This year starts with Q and ends with S."

Icicles hung from her voice. "Why would you send us outdated supplies?"

"We didn't. We ship to local distributors who handle the orders. I'd suggest you chat with your distributor."

Penny hung up. She had to call Tony immediately, but she was too shocked to move.

28

SATURDAY AFTERNOON
January 22

A brief snowstorm had covered the ground and whitened the dirty snowbanks along Garden Street. Rosemary had fed Skittles, left several lights glowing in her apartment, and packed a small suitcase that sat beside her in the car. As she drove to Bosche's cruiser in front of her building, she heard the radio announcer say, "Chance of more snow this evening with accumulations of two to five inches expected. Lows in the twenties." She intended to check the syringe lists at Riverside before heading down to Westport, and hoped the snow would hold off. Pete had instructed Bosche to keep an eye on her until she left Cambridge.

Despite his incessant desire to play Scrabble while maintaining a constant monologue, he was a comfortable man. Not once had he complained about staying with her. At three o'clock, he had smiled and patted her on the shoulder as if to reassure them both that the danger had passed.

On Memorial Drive, she passed the Hyatt Regency, an enormous broad-bottomed structure with lights twinkling from the windows. The dark sky was tinted pink from neon lights dotted here and there along the horizon. Trees were mantled with fresh snow. Past the MIT dorms for married students, nestled among the institute buildings, was Riverside Hospital, appearing like a majestic lady wearing a snowy cloak, sparkling against the rose-colored sky.

The loading dock area was vacant and she pulled her car into a parking space. Bosche followed her up into the hospital and to the second floor, chatting all the way.

Peggy had left Frank and Steve's syringe reports on the desk. With her coat on, Rosemary sat and compared them. Disregarding the insulin, tuberculin, subcutaneous, and large syringes used for additives and irrigations, she concentrated on the intramuscular syringes with preattached twenty-one-gauge, one-and-half-inch needles. Frank was ordering two cartons from purchasing every Tuesday, two on Thursdays, and three on Saturdays. Steve, on the other hand, was receiving a shipment of thirteen cartons every Monday. Going back over the reports, she noted that Steve issued three cartons to various departments each week while Frank issued seven. Either Steve or Frank kept three extra cartons on hand and Rosemary wanted to know if all those new syringes existed inside those cartons.

She handed the lists to Bosche. "Come on, Sergeant, we have to take a walk downstairs."

The door into central supply contained a wire-mesh glass window. Rosemary noticed an aide pulling supplies out of an autoclave. They approached the woman.

"Excuse me. I just want to check your sterile supply room," she said. Near the autoclaves, she found two paper gowns and handed one to Bosche.

"What's this?" he asked.

"Put it over your clothes, like this."

"I'm not putting on a dress."

"You are if you're coming with me."

He grunted and slipped it on.

Finding the light switch, she located the syringes on shelving near the dutch door. Rosemary read labels and found the three cartons Frank should normally have to issue. At the end of the shelving were the three sealed on-hand cartons. Satisfied, she walked back up the aisle, counting, and glancing inside the open ones. She began wondering why she was risking her life being here rather than safely on her way to Westport.

She patted a carton. "Well, Sergeant, we can go now. Everything seems in order."

"Were you looking for anything in particular?"

"Syringes are being sold to a drug ring, and Pete Tanner thinks they're coming from Riverside."

"Yeah, I heard about that."

They pulled off the paper gowns.

"The supplier's name is Smoke," Bosche said, "and the department can't get a handle on him. One minute he's there and the next, poof, he disappears. I think they ought to take a closer look."

"What do you mean?"

"He wears a disguise, right? And when he takes it off, he looks like any old person on the street. Things ain't often what they seem."

Rosemary stood still and, while she stared at Bosche, his words sank in. "Come on, Sergeant, we're going back inside."

"Aw, shit," he muttered, taking a gown from her outstretched hand.

Something about those three sealed cartons was not right. She went to the end of the aisle and looked at them.

They were closed, not with the manufacturer's sealant, but with strips of clear cellophane tape. She ripped one open: empty! She ripped open the other two: also empty. "Bosche, when you get back to the station, get hold of Pete and tell him that this is the place the drug traffickers get their syringes."

29

SATURDAY EVENING
January 22

Bosche followed Rosemary across the bridge and onto Storrow Drive. Glancing into the rear-view mirror, she saw his headlights blink twice before he turned the cruiser back, and she was saddened as if losing a close friend. She was on her own now and the realization made her feel uneasy and lonely. But she was not alone. There was a stream of headlights behind her, including a dark car following her.

Swinging onto the busy Southeast Expressway, her thoughts turned to Riverside and Frank Grinnell. She wondered if behind his facade of concern was a man capable of killing Maria Silva to conceal his syringe trafficking scheme. The trash trucks sat in the corridor outside central supply, offering easy access to the used syringes inside the trash bags. It was possible that early Tuesday morning Maria had caught him stealing syringes from the truck and selling them to someone in the loading dock area. She took several syringes as evidence and ran. Frank met her getting off the elevator and lured her into the chute room. Rosemary envisioned Maria refusing a bribe and not giving the syringes to Frank. His emotions went haywire and, in a fury, he grabbed the gown tie and strangled her.

Although outwardly friendly with his staff, he was, in fact, incompatible with most and was the only department head who denied annual pay raises in an ignorant attempt to make his cost center appear more efficient. Fortunately, the staff didn't know, for Rosemary granted the raises anyway.

He was responsible for autoclaves in his department as well as in the operating room and he could be damaging their operation. Dow had mentioned kickbacks. Frank could be in collusion with distributors, switching vendors for his own gain, pocketing the difference.

He could be doing a lot of things, like stealing the grand master key during a visit to the supervisor's office; like breaking into her office and planting a surgical glove to throw suspicion on Kreutzer; like . . . Rosemary's pulse quickened. The man who lured her into the dietary storeroom had been about Frank's size. But why would Frank want to kill her? She hadn't provoked him, unless he felt she was getting too close to his involvement with the syringes.

As soon as Rosemary had passed Fall River and, swung onto Route 83, she accelerated. She should be in Westport within ten minutes. Then in her rear-view mirror, she noticed two headlights approaching quickly. Not relishing a speeding ticket, she coasted down to fifty-five miles an hour and waited for the car to pass.

It didn't. The car slowed and stayed directly behind her. She strained to see the car in her mirror, to see if it had the police cruiser bar of lights across the top, to see if the amber fog lights shone underneath the headlights as cruiser lights often do. She saw only the glaring head-lights, close behind, and her skin prickled with fear.

Was it Frank Grinnell? But neither he nor anyone at the hospital could know about her trip. She glanced back again. Maybe it's a little old lady who needs company. Just as Rosemary was deciding that the driver was harmless, her forehead smashed violently against the steering wheel as the car behind smacked into her rear bumper. Dazed, she touched her brow and felt a hard lump. The car had pulled back, but as she continued to watch, it gained momentum and came charging toward her again.

You bastard! She swerved into the left lane but the car caught her taillight and she spun into the sand along the road and skidded sideways back across the highway. She held the wheel and tried to maintain a straight path. As her car slowed, she looked in the mirror.

The headlights were approaching with lightning speed. Fearing for her life, she accelerated, hoping to avoid another impact. The car came up on her left, and the driver jerked the steering wheel toward her and hit her door. Shaken and scared, Rosemary mashed the brake, slipped her car in behind his, then pushed her accelerator pedal to the floor. Bumpers collided and his car bounced forward, taillights brightening as he braked in front of her. She smashed into him again and with her car pushing his, streams of smoke poured from his brake pads.

"Come on, baby," she said to her car, "don't give up on me. Don't quit now." She stayed on his bumper, praying that he would turn to the right so she could push him off the road.

His brake lights went off; he was accelerating too, and soon his car pulled away. She took her foot off the pedal and, as he sped ahead, Rosemary strained unsuccessfully to see the number on the license plate, as the car disappeared over the next rise.

Shaken and upset, she slowed to a crawl. He could be

waiting in ambush and she considered making a U-turn. At the top of the rise, she slowed further and looked into the darkness ahead. Nothing. No lights of any kind. She drifted to a stop.

He was up there, in the darkness, waiting. Rosemary switched off her headlights and looked out again. No stirring of any kind. But he must be out there waiting for her; she felt his presence in the black void ahead. He might, in fact, be out of his car running up the incline toward her. . . .

She turned her wheels to the left and inched toward the median strip in an effort to turn around, but suddenly her front tire pitched into the soft, sandy shoulder. She threw her gearshift into reverse. Spinning the rear wheels, the pungent smell of rubber filling her nostrils, she accelerated until the car lurched backward, freeing the front tire. She quickly geared into drive.

She was traveling down the wrong way and had only gone a short distance when a set of headlights loomed before her. Without hesitation, she pulled off the road and let the truck pass. Perspiration beaded on her skin as she tried to decide her next move. The nearest exit was miles away; she'd never make it, driving against whatever traffic might approach.

She rocked the car out of the shoulder by gearing into reverse, drive, reverse, drive, inching slowly out, maneuvering the car around until she was once again southbound.

Cautiously, she started forward without headlights, up the rise, down the rise, gaining momentum. Was the road ahead straight, or did it bend to the right? She couldn't remember. Which way did it go! Panicked, she pulled the knob for the headlights and then pressed her foot hard on the accelerator. The lights caught his car sitting dark and motionless in the brush beside the road. When she passed, he pulled out.

She kept her foot on the pedal, praying that her car would outrace his, praying that she could beat him to the turnoff, less than a mile away. Forcing herself to concentrate on speed, she leaned forward like a jockey trying to outdistance the next horse.

The impact came, suddenly, and with such velocity that she pitched sideways, pulling the wheel with her. Swerving, tires squealing, her car glanced against a mile marker, ricocheted back across the road, then bounced back again and plunged deep into the reedy border of a large marsh.

Shaking violently, Rosemary pushed off the headlights and fell headlong out of the car. Marsh plants scraped her face as her hands and knees cracked through the thin veneer of ice and touched, a few inches below, the cold, mucky bottom.

She grabbed a clump of tall cattails and pulled herself up. From the direction of the road, she saw a glow of headlights quickly doused, followed by the slamming of a car door. She charged forward, her feet breaking through the ice, sucking in and out of the mud.

A small flicker of light danced across the tops of the spartina grasses and she realized that the man had a flashlight. God save me, she prayed. The man would see the holes her feet were making through the frozen surface, and she tried to step only on the clumps of grass plants above the surface.

Calm down, Rosemary, you know this area, she thought as she pulled ahead, hidden by the reeds and cattails. Her parents lived only a few miles away, across the marsh, across . . . what else? She couldn't remember. Fields? Yes, as a child she played in the fields and around the upland areas of the treacherous marsh. She was familiar with the area, with the soft-shell crabs, fiddler crabs, mud snails, with the curlews and herons, the marsh elders, waxy bayberry bushes, and salt marsh asters. Her parents had warned her about going too close to the marsh for the bottoms of certain trapped pools offered little support, the dense mud acting very much like quicksand.

The flashlight darted close by. Rosemary held her breath. Icy water had seeped into her boots and she could no longer feel her feet. Quickly, she plunged ahead, trying to stay hidden in the spartina, trying to keep her feet from breaking through the ice, trying to hear beyond the roar of her heart in her ears. A dreadful coldness crept through her stomach as she realized that the man had probably followed her all the way from Cambridge.

She glanced back. The flashlight bounced briefly over the tops of the fuzzy cattails, then disappeared toward the ground. The dense reeds thickened and scraped against her face and hands as she plunged ahead, hoping the dry fields were close by. A burr bush caught her coat. Its prickly fruits pulled her back and she fought to get loose. Stepping forward, her foot hit a hard mound and she toppled into the frozen thicket. Grabbing a dense clump of spartina grasses, she bunched them around herself and tried to hide, feeling pathetically vulnerable.

Not daring to move or breathe, numbed from the knees down, she watched the tops of the reeds for signs of the flashlight. There, off about twenty yards, it danced through the cattails, then stopped, its beam piercing through the brush. The light bounced along again, then stopped, played across the ground, searching left, right, darting through the reeds, then pointed straight in her direction. Eyes wide, Rosemary watched the light bounce again as the man approached.

30

"Get away from me. Oh, God, get him away from me!"

"Rosemary!" her father called, shaking her shoulders and trying to awaken her. Her eyes opened and she looked straight at him. He was a big man with soft hair that puffed from his head like a white dandelion. His blue eyes shone through a face wrinkled from years of sunshine and laughing. "Hey, it's me, your old dad; you're okay now." He gently held her close to his chest and rocked her back and forth. "You're all right now; no one is after you, baby."

She looked down at the scratches on her arms, then reached up and touched the raised welts on her face. "I got away, Dad . . ." she began, blinking back the tears.

"Yes, baby, he couldn't follow your tracks once you reached firm ground."

Rosemary relaxed into her father's arms. She remembered running through the marsh, over several fields, falling, running wildly, away from the man, his flashlight, pounding on her parents' door until they opened it.

"My car!"

"Your car is fine. Zeke Bruno at the service station

towed it here last night and, aside from looking as if it belongs in a dump, the engine runs smoothly." He held up an old pair of bell-bottomed slacks. "Your mother found these in your closet, and here's one of her sweaters. Get dressed now, and join us." He turned at the door and smiled.

She loved him. Truly, he was the greatest dad in the world. Pulling back the sheet, she saw deep scratches and bruises over her legs. The mirror in the bathroom reflected a few raised scrapes on her cheeks and a large maroon bump on her forehead. She showered and dressed quickly and followed the delicious aromas of fried bacon and coffee into the kitchen. "Hi, Mom."

Mrs. Winston, an attractive woman who had maintained her trim figure and youthful face, and who had passed along her hazel eyes and curly auburn hair to Rosemary, went over to her. "Oh, my baby, you had a bad dream; how do you feel?"

"I feel fine." She kissed her mother on the cheek.

"I want you to stay here for a few days to relax and forget about last night."

"I must get back right after breakfast."

"No you don't," her father said, "you're staying with us. Nobody is chasing my daughter and getting away with it."

"I'll call Pete Tanner. He can meet me halfway."

"You're not going anywhere until Chiego calls."

"Who's he?"

"Chief of police."

Rosemary's heart fell. She didn't want to discuss Riverside's problems with a total stranger. "Was he here last night?"

"Yes, but you were in bed. We telephoned him as soon as you came."

Over breakfast, they talked about the incident and

Rosemary assured her parents that the man who chased her was an unknown, probably a sex pervert, a person who prowled the roadways by night and slept by day. She'd have nothing to fear on her drive back.

Her father listened in silence. He would make her wait for Chiego, but he couldn't detain her if the man was a local deviant.

They reviewed the incident again, both parents now prodding for more information. Rosemary de-emphasized the chase by reminiscing about the marsh; their first house built on a knoll and open to the breezes from all sides. She recalled families of curlews who flew in each spring, the fiddler crabs and soft-shelled clams now hibernating below the frost line of the thick mud, and the sea pinks and lavenders picked for winter bouquets.

They heard the wheels of a car crunch along the snowy driveway. "That's Chiego," her mother said, and got up to let him in. She returned with a man who looked like a quarterback for the New England Patriots. He was a huge mass of muscles and sinews. After nodding hello to Rosemary, he put his coat into Mrs. Winston's outstretched hand and sat at the table.

"You okay?" Chiego asked Rosemary.

"Yes, thanks for all your help."

"No trouble. Any idea who the man was?"

Rosemary shook her head.

He turned to Mr. Winston. "We tracked the prints out of the marsh."

"Find anything along the road?"

"Nothing, except the tire marks where she went off." Chiego accepted a mug of coffee and, as he stirred in a teaspoonful of sugar, he continued. "Couple of kids from Fall River have been touring our roads at night. So far, they've just been joyriding and doin' some tailgating. You remember the license plate?" he asked Rosemary.

"No. I'm sure it was just some man from around here looking for excitement."

"You got a job?"

Rosemary explained her position at Riverside and denied any malicious trouble related to her job. Chiego seemed satisfied. "You goin' back up today?"

"Right away."

"I can follow you to Fall River if you'd like."

Mr. Winston answered. "I'm planning on following her to Cambridge, thanks anyway."

"We've got a noon luncheon today, dear, and I was hoping Rosemary would join us," Mrs. Winston said.

"Wish I could, Mom. Lieutenant Chiego's idea is excellent. You two go ahead with your plans."

Her father won the debate and soon she was pulling her car behind Chiego's cruiser, followed by her father's station wagon.

Standing outside her apartment building, her father declined an offer for coffee before the long drive back to Westport. He pulled her into his arms, gave her a warm hug and a kiss on the cheek. "Don't forget to call me tonight."

"I won't." She watched him climb back in and while she waved until the station wagon was out of sight, a deep loneliness swept over her.

"Skittles, I'm home," Rosemary called as she walked into her apartment. "Where . . ." Her words trailed off when she saw her living room furniture, broken and lying in heaps, her paintings smashed over the upturned legs of the chairs, ashes from the fireplace strewn across the room. She carefully took a step forward and listened, fearing the intruder might still be there. Step by step, she walked through the dining room and saw the mahogany table scratched with a large X. Stuffing had been pulled from the upholstered chairs and her new Scott painting hung from the frame in ribbons.

In the kitchen, all the butcher knives were deeply imbedded into the counter. She pulled the longest knife free and continued, carefully, ready to attack. The shower curtain in the bathroom had been yanked from the overhead bar. Cautiously, she continued to the bedroom. Sheets and blankets were ripped off the bed, slashed brutally, the contents of the mattress spilled out like the entrails of a gutted animal. On the floor near her dresser, tiny prisms danced on the walls and over the carpet, remnants of her collection of crystal boxes. She went over and was about to look for her jewelry case when she heard a soft whimper.

"Skittles? Where are you?"

Frantically, she started out of the bedroom but, passing the closet, she heard the whimper again. Flinging open the closet door, she saw Skittles lying broken on the floor, fur sticky with blood, pathetically shivering as she fought off death.

Rosemary screamed and fell to her knees. Blood was oozing out of both of Skittles' eyes. Rosemary grabbed a blouse from above her head and laid it on the floor next to the cat. Tears welled up as she talked to Skittles, comforting her, telling her that everything would be all right. As she gently lifted the cat, her pet's head fell backwards and pivoted around. Neck broken, spinal cord severed, and eyes punched out, Skittles moaned, shivered, then lay still in Rosemary's arms.

For a long time, Rosemary sat on the floor and rocked Skittles back and forth, crying and apologizing. When her tears ran out, she slowly stood and went into the kitchen,

235

carrying the dead body, her sweater soaked with the cat's blood. She set a stool upright, sat, and placed the cat gently on her lap. With trembling hands, she lifted the receiver of her telephone and dialed Pete's number.

"Hello?" he answered.

"Pete," she uttered in a voice totally drained of emotion.

"Rosemary? I've been calling you all morning."

"My apartment, Pete . . . it's been ransacked . . . and . . ." Tears flowed from her eyes. ". . . and . . ."

"Are you all right?" he asked with mounting concern.

"Yes, but . . . "

"What?" he demanded.

"Skittles. Someone stabbed her eyes, broke her neck . . . She's . . ."

"I'll be right there; don't touch anything."

While waiting for Pete, Rosemary sat in the kitchen, numb and uncaring. She could replace the damaged furniture, paintings, crystal, but not the dead friend in her lap. Very slowly, her emotions changed from sorrow to rage.

The door buzzer sounded and she hurried into the living room to push the lobby door release button. The mirror near the door reflected her angry face and moist eyes. Her sweater and hands were smeared from the blood-soaked blouse around Skittles. She heard a knock on the door and flung it open.

Pete gasped when he saw the blood. "Rosemary are you, have you . . . "

"I'm fine, Tanner," she screamed, "but my apartment's destroyed and my cat Skittles is dead, and I want to know what you're doing, pussyfooting around with this murder investigation."

The defiant look on her face took him by surprise. "We're doing all we can, Rose . . ."

236

"That isn't enough."

He stepped forward and tried to hold her but she jerked away. "Listen to me."

"I am not listening to you anymore; you haven't done a damn thing." Slowly, she lowered her head and began crying again.

He put an arm around her shoulder.

"Last night, on my way to Westport, a man tried to kill me. And this morning I find that he gave up on me and killed my cat instead. It's Frank Grinnell, or Dr. Kreutzer, or Smoke. I don't know yet, but I'll tell you this, I'll find out and I'll kill him myself."

Pete set the living room couch back on its legs. "Sit, Rosemary, and tell me what happened." While she talked, he slowly went through the apartment, listening and noting the severe damage.

"Lieutenant Tanner?" she said, raising herself from the couch.

"Yes?" he answered from the dining room.

"I understand that you're in orbit with your space cadets, but I can no longer wait until you break the drug ring before you help me." Her voice softened. "I'll even pay you to stick around."

Pete had walked into the living room and was watching her as she spoke. "Mrs. Cleaveland, I am not in orbit. I'm close to breaking that ring, you're right on that score, and I have made the connection. During our raid last night, we picked up new syringes. Your used supply dried up on Wednesday; new ones hit the streets on Thursday; we're certain they're coming from Riverside."

"Is Frank Grinnell the Smoke person?"

"I'll know later, when we bag him in Revere. Fran Porter told me the pusher in her building is expecting a generous supply of drugs from Smoke today. He'll go to a Revere warehouse first, to pick it up."

"How do you know he'll go to Revere?"

"We know quite a few things about the Mafia and its people."

Rosemary massaged her temples. Too much information to absorb all at once.

Pete continued. "Last evening, your secretary, Peggy, identified Rubio Grasso, the phony telephone man."

"What?"

"Yeah, from mug shots."

Rosemary groaned. Poor Peggy would be in a state all weekend.

A silence hung over the room. "He's a hit man for the Mafia," she whispered. "He's the one who has been after me."

"Let me take your cat to the vet for you," Pete offered.

"No, thanks." Rosemary stood up. "I'll go change my clothes."

"Try not to touch too much."

The front door buzzer rang and Pete pushed the release button. "That's my fingerprint expert."

"Grasso killed my cat," she said forlornly as she headed toward her bedroom. She showered and put on a pale pink sweater and pink tweed skirt. Although her eyes were slightly puffy, her anger with Pete had dissipated. She found him in the kitchen, looking at the knives imbedded in the counter.

"I'm going now," she said.

"I'll be here when you get back."

"Pete, after the vet, I'm going to the hospital."

"You most assuredly are *not* going there today."

"I am, too."

Pete placed his hands on her shoulders. "For what reason? That inspection? It'll wait, baby; you've got all this week. Please stay here today. I've got Bosche coming over . . . "

"Send him to my office."

Pete apparently knew better than to detain her. As she closed her apartment door, she heard him say, "Damn! Why do women *look* for trouble?"

Dr. Newbury hung his coat in the emergency department locker room and went down the hall to find the doctors scheduled to go off duty at three o'clock. The head nurse found the physicians in the coffee room and doled out all the laboratory slips that had collected since the evening shift doctors had last been on duty. She reminded Dr. Newbury that he was on the CPR team today, and then told the doctors that the lab had recalled all culture kits. "New supplies will not be in until tomorrow, and by the way, take a look at those slips."

They did. Dr. Newbury had cultured sixteen people for gonorrhea and all sixteen were negative. He then noticed that all the bloods, sputums, throats, wounds were negative too. One of his colleagues whistled softly. "This is bad. We'll have to find these patients and get 'em back here."

Newbury yawned. "Not today. It's Sunday; let's take it easy."

Rosemary saw lights in the supervisor's office and went in. Ilse Jensen was trying to put a key on a large ring. They exchanged greetings and Rosemary watched her struggle to open the ring. "Is that a new key?"

"No, it's the grand master. I found it lying on the floor when I came in. We've been in and out of here hundreds of times and you'd think someone would have noticed it."

Still working with the ring, Ilse said, "Did you hear

about our infamous TV star, Rip Easterbrook?"

"Yes, a man from maintenance just told me."

"I hate to laugh, but he got what he deserved. He gave the nurses a hard time and he always had some voluptuous broad vibrating under the sheets with him."

"Well, he's out of your hair now."

"But not out of *yours*."

"Why?"

Ilse looked up. "He wants to drop his drawers and show you his polychromatic fanny. Then he wants to tell you a thing or two about Riverside in general and about paying his bill specifically."

"Thanks, I'll be sure he isn't sent a bill." Rosemary heard her name over the paging system. "Mrs. Cleaveland, call ten eighty-nine please." She used the supervisor's phone to dial the lab's number.

"Mrs. Cleaveland? It's Tony. I have terrific news; maybe not for you, but certainly good for me."

"What is it?"

"Yesterday, Penny Abbott discovered that our media and broth lots are outdated, all of them. But we knew they weren't the whole answer to our problem because certain specimens aren't put on those special culture plates. I have Penny up here today, and as a matter of fact, if it's okay with you, I'm going to pay her overtime for the weekend."

"She deserves it. Go on, Tony."

He continued proudly. "After checking all our supplies, like media, petri dishes, test tubes, we then put our equipment through some control checks. You know that new autoclave we have up here? Damn thing is on the fritz."

"How?"

"Overheating. Take chocolate agar. After we make up a batch, it has to be autoclaved at one hundred and twenty-one degrees centigrade for fifteen minutes. We never

240

thought about actually testing the temperature gauge because it always went up to one-twenty-one degrees. Anyway, Penny put a high-low temperature gauge inside the autoclave along with test packs, sterility indicators, spore suspensions, and other control items. Everything checked out except the gauge, which read over five hundred degrees, meaning that the autoclave has been killing the organisms and the nutrients in the media! Penny and I think the O.R. flash autoclave has a similar problem, only the temperature won't get high enough to kill organisms so we're going to the O.R. now with this high-low gauge. I'll let you know what we find."

"Wait, Tony. If it's broken too, notify the nursing supervisor immediately."

"Okay."

Ilse was looking at Rosemary with fascination. "What's going on?"

Rosemary explained the situation. "If he calls, I want you to get in the entire O. R. and central supply staffs and have them re-autoclave every sterile pack in the hospital. The nursing units will have to be notified, and the physicians."

"It'll take a while for Tony to get set up and know the results. Think I'll meet him in the O.R., I can call everyone from there. By the way, I thought Dr. Harris was suspended for incomplete medical records."

"He is," Rosemary replied. "Why?"

"He's doing a case."

As soon as Ilse left, Rosemary dialed Jayne's home telephone number and asked her to come in.

"I can't."

"Why not?"

"Betty's here and we're making up."

"I want you in here, Jayne; bring Betty if you have to."

Rosemary dialed J.B.' s office, then the surgical suite,

and finally found him in the recovery room.

"Rosemary," he whispered, "where have you been? I've searched this whole hospital for you."

"You're suspended, Dr. Harris. Why are you here?"

"Wait." He gave someone an order for medication, then whispered into the phone, "You were right! Kreutzer's flying out tonight, to the Netherlands, with *our* papers. Do you know what the slimy wedge of sauerkraut has done?"

"What?"

"I went to see him earlier, on the pretense of getting my copy of the papers. He had left the hospital, so I got a key from the lab people and went into his office. A manila envelope was on the desk with my name on it, so I opened it up. The copy was inside, with both our names listed as the primary researchers. I was going to leave, but I noticed his briefcase under the desk and opened it. A KLM airline ticket was inside, plus a log, slides, and the original papers with only *his* name. And Rosemary, he had a gun in there."

"What slides are you talking about?" she demanded. "I have his log and slides."

"Then yours are duplicates. It's all there, I tell you. He's leaving soon. What should we do?"

Rosemary was thoughtful. She didn't want Kreutzer taking Riverside's log and slide files out of the hospital, much less out of the country.

"I know what you're thinking," J.B. said, "and I agree that Kreutzer could have misdiagnosed a few frozen sections, but I had nothing to do with it. He acted entirely on his own. But we have to stop him."

Not certain about the extent of J.B.'s motives, Rosemary decided to deal with his staff privileges later. Right now, she had to prevent Kreutzer from leaving. "We'll take his briefcase. Meet me in your office in five minutes."

"I have a patient to check, but it will take only a few minutes."

Rosemary raced back to her office to get Bosche. He wasn't there. As she was leaving, the phone rang. "Hello?"

"Charlie Donovan here . . . "

"Charlie? I didn't know you were in."

"Sure. That Compulectrics order has arrived. Where do you want me to put it?"

"I'm not accepting it."

"Really?"

"Yes. I'll be down as soon as I can." She turned to leave, but the telephone rang again.

"Rosemary? It's Steve. I knew something was wrong when you asked about our syringe orders so I checked around. Frank's supposed to be keeping three extra cartons. He's not doing it because all three cartons are empty, here in Central. I put the squeeze on Frank and he's confessed to selling them outside the hospital!"

"He *has?*"

"Yes. I can't get hold of Lieutenant Tanner; what should I do?"

"Sit tight and keep Frank there. I'll be down as soon as I can."

The light for extension ten fifty-one flashed before the telephone started ringing. Tempted not to answer, she headed for the door, then went back. "Hello!" she shouted.

"Sergeant Mike Dow here."

"Where have you been? Where is Lieutenant Tanner?"

"We're at Two ninety-three Third Street."

"Will you get here this instant!"

"Fran Porter's been murdered."

Shocked, Rosemary could find no words.

Dow went on. "Her boyfriend too. They were tied up and the medical examiner thinks they were injected with some kind of heavy metal solution." After a moment, Dow said, "Can you find out what solutions Kreutzer uses?"

"Yes. How long ago were they killed?"

"About two hours."

She remembered what J.B. had told her. "Kreutzer was out of the hospital earlier today," she said. "Dow, tell Pete that Frank Grinnell has confessed to stealing our syringes. Steve Hammond is holding him in central supply, and if you two could wrap up that drug case, I'll meet you down there."

Before Dow could speak, Rosemary hung up and raced to the third floor, wishing she had Bosche by her side. Bursting into J.B.'s offices, she called his name. The doctor wasn't there. "Oh, God, he's gone alone." Fearing for him, she took the stairs up but stopped on the fourth-floor landing. Opening the door a crack, she peered down the corridor and saw that Kreutzer's door was open. She tiptoed down and looked in. No one was inside. On the desk the briefcase stood open. All I have to do is grab it.

She raced in and, with trembling hands, slammed the briefcase shut.

"Is this what you're looking for?"

She swung around and saw Kreutzer holding a gray metal specimen box. He flung it at her. "Look inside. It's something to add to your suspension charge. Look!"

Rosemary set the box on his desk and unclasped the metal fasteners. She lifted the lid only a couple of inches. "Oh . . . oh . . . " The lid fell closed. Rosemary shrank away, terrified. Floating in a yellowish liquid was a breast.

"It's people like you who impede scientific progress, Mrs. Cleaveland." Kreutzer took a gun from his pocket and held the barrel tip between her eyes. Rosemary tried to step backward, but he grabbed her arm and shoved her ahead of him. "Open the door and walk toward the chemistry lab. I have a glass of dimethyl mercury waiting for you."

She tried to get her brain working. Don't go to pieces now, she told herself; you can get away from him. Just as she put her hand on the knob, the door burst open, knocking her sideways. She heard J.B. shout, "Run!" before he leaped on Kreutzer. She jumped up, sped through the door, and was running for the stairway when she heard a shot. "J.B.?" she looked back and saw Kreutzer race through the door after her, with J.B. limping behind him. Rounding the second-floor landing, she heard a door above open and close and the sound of footsteps moving quickly down the stairs. She bounded down, praying that Pete was in central supply.

On the first floor, she ran through the Main building, yanked open the Concord door, and flew into central supply, just as she heard the Concord door reopen.

"Pete, Steve, Frank, are you here? Help me!"

The front door to central opened. Glancing over her shoulder, she saw Kreutzer, gun in hand, his face a livid red. She darted into the dark supply room and ran over to the dutch door leading to Main One. Frantically, she tugged on the locked door.

A crushing blow struck her from behind, followed by another on her neck. Rosemary blacked out, and her body slowly slid to the floor.

31

For a few moments, Rosemary stared up at the pitch-black darkness, a void so encompassing, so soundless, so still, that she imagined herself buried alive in a crypt. Lying perfectly still, arms at her sides, she touched the hard surface beneath her; warm, smooth, like metal sheeting. With her fingers, she followed the metal under her, then up the sides, higher, higher. Where am I? What is this? Raising herself slowly as she felt the walls, her hand stopped, then started across a ceiling. She quickly touched the walls, floor, ceiling around her; then on hands and knees, she started crawling forward until her hand touched another wall. She was entrapped in a large metal box! A tomb, a . . . The feeling of pure dread washed over her, prickling her skin, her hair, as she realized that her tomb was a large gas autoclave in central supply.

"Oh, my lord! Let me out, please!"

Negative pressure would soon build and turn her body inside out. Her vital juices would be compressed and sucked slowly through her skin; her eyes would cave in. Quickly, she felt her eyes.

"Someone, help me!"

She began frantically searching the interior of the autoclave, following the outline of the door, back to the rear, sides, ceiling, hoping for an opening, a handle, something, anything that would free her.

A vibration shook her, followed by a low hum. *It's on!* Perspiration poured through her skin and she licked her arm, expecting blood. Working quickly, she felt the rear of the autoclave again, and her fingers found a hole. She plugged it with a finger and continued her search. Another hole! She removed her slip and tried to tear the nylon. Chewing, ripping violently, she tore off several pieces and began filling the holes, one at a time, with hands shaking, and her heart thumping in her chest, in her ears.

Breathing grew difficult. She knew the oxygen was being replaced by ethylene oxide, a poisonous gas. She lay down and began weeping. Please someone help me, please, Pete, Mom, Dad. I'm here. She heard a thud, felt another vibration, and as the black space compressed her senses, she shuddered in an effort to gasp one last breath.

"Rosemary! Talk to me, say something, come on, please!"

Pete's voice bubbled through Rosemary's unconsciousness. Her eyes fluttered open and she stared up at him.

"Thank God that autoclave is broken," he said.

Sitting up, enclosed in his arms, she looked at Lulu's opened autoclave door, at the policemen, photographer, Bosche, Sergeant Dow, and she began to cry. "Where was Bosche? I couldn't find him anywhere."

"And he couldn't find you. I got your message," Pete said. "After Fran's apartment, we were sure he'd come back here to find you. Through the window in central's door, we saw him turning on the autoclave. I rushed in with the officers while Dow went around to the dutch door. He held us off with a gun until Dow could get the door unlocked, sneak in, and shoot the bastard."

Bosche and Dow were standing over a bloody white sheet that covered a form on the floor. She shook her head, relieved that Kreutzer had been stopped. "Why did it take you so long to nail him?"

"I wanted to be absolutely certain. He left the hospital earlier with syringes containing a metal solution. He picked up the drugs in Revere just before we got there, and wearing his Smoke clothes, he went to Two ninety-three Third Street where he sold the pusher only a couple bags of heroin. He told them the rest was going to New York; apparently he had a contact there who would pay off bigger than Cambridge. By the time we got there, he was gone. He had tied up Fran and Harry and injected them with the poison."

"Why would he kill them?"

"He probably found out that she was helping us; he knew someone had tipped us off about the supply from Revere. The coroner will know what the poison was."

"Dimethyl mercury," Rosemary said. "Did Fran know who Smoke really was?"

"No, but he didn't know that. We picked up a pair of surgeon's gloves in her apartment. One thumb was torn and we found several full thumbprints. They'll clinch our case in court."

Rosemary was thoughtful. "How did he ever have time for drugs?" she murmured.

"A desperate man finds the time. We'll no doubt never learn the whole story, but I suspect he was in deep financial trouble. Through old connections with the Mafia, he was given the Cambridge ring, and when that didn't ease his situation, he started selling syringes and double-dealing with vendors. I believe he intended to fence the bulk of the heroin in New York tonight, where he was going to pick up his kickback, and then skip the country."

"What about Rubio Grasso?"

"Vanished. Smoke hired him to get those syringes away from you, which he did, and to retrieve the purchase order from your office, which he also did. What he couldn't do was scare you off, no matter how violent his attacks were. But now that we've got Smoke you needn't worry about Grasso any longer."

"Help me up, Pete," she said, the nightmare in the autoclave beginning to vanish.

"Lieutenant," said Dow, "we're finished here. I'm letting them move the body 'cause his brains are seeping out all over the floor."

"Yeah, go ahead."

Rosemary's stomach churned. The white sheet was sopped with a pinkish-yellow liquid. "Kreutzer must have been shot badly."

"No, Kreutzer's head was bludgeoned with a pair of orthopedic scissors; went in one temple and out the other." He helped Rosemary to a chair. "Kreutzer was the scapegoat," he explained. "Those surgical gloves in your office, and in Porter's room, and the heavy metal solution that killed her, were planted to throw suspicion on Kreutzer."

Rosemary knew how easy it was for Frank to obtain those items. Exhausted, and still feeling confused, she asked, "Why would Frank want me dead?"

Puzzled, Pete's frown turned into a smile that spread across his face. "Remember your interpretation of Maria's words, 'See supervisor, see him and tell'? Try this instead, 'See supervisor, Steve Hammond sell.' "

The breath caught in Rosemary's throat. "That's impossible. He was with Ted Fielding."

"Good alibi, convenient too. Steve got off the elevator with you, and the moment you went into your office, he raced upstairs, killed Maria, and came back down to have breakfast with Ted. Business as usual."

"*He* was stealing syringes . . . " Stunned, Rosemary could hardly digest Pete's words. "I wasn't in my office that long before Charlie Donovan called."

"Twenty-five minutes. Charlie called you at seven-thirty."

"Didn't Ted remember the time?"

"It varied each morning. We had to break Steve's alibi, so yesterday Dow again pressured Ted. When Steve arrived Tuesday morning, they went directly down and ate breakfast, which usually takes them half an hour. Ted recalled he and Steve had joked about goofing off for forty minutes before the department head meeting, so they didn't get to the cafeteria until after seven-thirty."

"Why did Steve want to kill me?"

"You had canceled his Compulectrics order. The hundred thousand wasn't meant for Riverside. It was going into his pocket, in New York, after delivery. He had to have it delivered. The bum's been colluding with equipment manufacturers and supply distributors."

"What about Frank?"

"He's been home all day. Steve merely accused Frank to lure you down here. He waited for you in the supply room and I'm sure he didn't expect Kreutzer too. He knocked you out, bludgeoned Kreutzer, and put you in an autoclave."

"Where's Steve now?"

"On his way to jail. Come on, Rosemary, let's get you out of here." Pete put an arm around her shoulders and led her upstairs for her coat.

With Kreutzer and Hammond out of the way, she could handle the rest now. She felt Pete's warmth and wondered how she ever doubted him. Stealing a glimpse at his face, she asked, "Why didn't you tell me your suspicions?"

"Kreutzer kept you busy enough, didn't he?"

She nodded.

A silence fell between them as he held the elevator door for her. Alone with him inside the metal cab, she wrapped her arms around his waist. "How about that shish kebab?"